AN EYE FOR AN EYE...

The decision that had been left in the hands of the prime minister was a difficult one for her to make and, as she faced the two men, she had to justify it in her own mind. She spoke at length about the tragic fate of the Jews and their suffering down through the centuries. She spoke of the Holocaust and of the new threat to Jewish lives in Europe. Then she gave the command. "Send forth your boys," she said.

THE HIT TEAM

The unprecedented inside story of a top-secret Israeli anti-terrorist squad by DAVID B. TINNIN—European correspondent for *Time* magazine—with DAG CHRISTENSEN—one of Norway's outstanding journalists. A triumph of investigative reporting!

THE
HIT
TEAM

DAVID B. TINNIN
with Dag Christensen

A DELL BOOK

To Those Who Trusted

Published by
DELL PUBLISHING CO., INC.
1 Dag Hammarskjold Plaza
New York, N.Y. 10017

Parts of the postscript first appeared in *Playboy* magazine.

Dell ® TM 681510, Dell Publishing Co., Inc.

ISBN: 0-440-13644-X

Reprinted by arrangement with
Little, Brown and Company

Printed in the United States of America
First Dell printing—November 1977

SELECTED CAST OF CHARACTERS

(In order of appearance)

Mike———	Leader of the hit team
Zwi Zamir	Director of Israeli Intelligence
Ali Hassan Salameh	Black September planning chief
Moshe Weinberg	The first casualty in Olympic Village
Tamar	Israeli agent and Mike's mistress
Wael Zwaiter	Palestinian living in Rome
Dr. Mahmoud Ham-shari	Representative of the Palestinian Liberation Organization in Paris
Mohammed Boudia	The twelfth target
Kemal Benamane	A mysterious Algerian
Gustav Pistauer	Fake identity of a veteran Mossad agent
Zwi Steinberg	Veteran Mossad operative
Abraham Gehmer	Mike's deputy
Sylvia Rafael	Israeli agent
Dan Aerbel	Reserve agent of Danish background
Marianne Gladnikoff	New Mossad recruit of Swedish origin
Jonathan Ingleby	Fake identity of an Israeli killer
Danny	Israeli agent
Ahmed Bouchiki	Arab waiter in the Norwegian town of Lillehammer
Torill Bouchiki	Ahmed's pregnant Norwegian wife
Hōkon Wiker	Norwegian State Prosecutor
Leif A. Lier	Norwegian interrogator

FOREWORD

This book is true. It recounts the secret and until now untold story of the war of reprisal that Israeli intelligence waged against the leaders of Arab terrorism in the wake of the murder of eleven members of the Israeli Olympic team in Munich. As the reader will see, the outcome and consequences of that conflict helped to shape the course of events in the Middle East—and the world.

The story is quite fantastic, full of incredible coincidences, dramatic human failings, tragic miscalculations, and huge doses of audacity, cruelty, and surprises. To the best of my abilities as reporter and writer, I have recited the events the way they really unfolded. I have not fabricated one single fact or scene and the story adheres as closely to the actual events as possible under the circumstances.

In an afterword, I tell as much as I can about how I gathered the material and give credit to those who helped and can be named, though many obviously cannot. It is very likely that this book will provoke denunciations and denials. That is predictable; as a matter of routine, official organizations—whether governments or liberation fronts—deny their complicity in illegal operations. The facts of the book will, I am fully confident, withstand those attacks.

From the outset, the reader should know that the author has never been in the employ of any intelligence agency. I am a journalist, and have spent the past two decades as a correspondent, writer, and editor of *Time*, specializing in international politics and economics.

My aim in writing this book was, above all, to tell a dramatic and compelling story that discloses at least a little bit about how the world really behaves. I wanted to show the underlying, often totally hidden events and considerations that almost always are the actual moving forces in the interlacing and interacting chain of events that weaves the fabric of national and international politics.

DAVID B. TINNIN
Paris, Oslo, Tel Aviv
1973–1976

ONE

Dawn was just breaking over Tel Aviv on the morning of July 18, 1973, as a tan Volkswagen microbus began weaving its way through the still sleeping city. The vehicle belonged to the Mossad, the Israeli intelligence agency, and it was performing a very special chore. As it twisted and turned through the maze of Tel Aviv's one-way streets, it stopped to pick up agents. Then it sped north along the Mediterranean coastal highway to the suburb of Herzliyya, where a purposeful young man was waiting in front of a new high-rise apartment building. Next, turning inland, the bus raced through flat orange groves until it reached Ben-Gurion International Airport. At the main entrance of the terminal building someone was waiting to escort the agents around the security and passport checkpoints to the VIP room in the departure area.

On that particular morning, the VIP room was not serving its usual function of accommodating visiting dignitaries; the customary glasses of orange juice had not been placed on the sideboard. Instead, the room was off-limits to all outsiders, because it was being used for the briefing of an Israeli hit team. The man doing the talking was known as Mike. He was the chief of the Mossad's special operations and in charge of a secret campaign of assassination against the leaders of Arab terrorism. It was a shadowy war of kill and counterkill fought in the stairwells and streets of Europe. Neither side conceded its existence, and the public knew nothing of its scope or intensity. Yet, during the past ten months, Mike's teams had eliminated twelve of their enemies. Now he was leading the hunt for the thirteenth target. The wanted man was a handsome young Palestinian named Ali Hassan Salameh.

But Mike did not give any details. "The Office has been on the look out for a certain Arab for a long time," he merely told the agents. "We have indications that he is moving north. We have pictures of him and you will learn his name later."

Soon the public-address system announced the departures of El Al flights for Europe, and the team, splitting into two groups, boarded separate blue and white Boeings.

The operation called "The Chase for the Red Prince" was underway. It was to be the climactic retaliation in the secret war, which had begun on another dawn many months earlier. Ali Hassan Salameh was the man whom the Israelis held responsible for the massacre of the Olympic team in Munich.

Munich, 4:30 A.M., September 5, 1972

"Is this the Israeli team?"

The words, spoken in clumsy German, sent a sudden alarm through Moshe Weinberg, the burly and gregarious coach of the Israeli wrestling team. He had been out partying until an hour earlier and must have been sleeping heavily. Roused by an insistent rapping, Weinberg had shuffled to the door of the apartment he shared with other Israeli athletes in the Olympic Village and opened it a crack.

Who would want the Israeli team at that hour in the morning? Instantly, Weinberg, sensing the danger, threw his hefty frame against the door and strained to force it closed.

"Boys, get out!" he screamed in Hebrew. "Get out!"

Shocked from sleep, Gad Zavarj, a wrestler who was Weinberg's roommate, bolted from his bed, smashed the windowpane with his elbow, and prepared to spring out.

The attackers, small thin men, were unable to budge the powerful Weinberg, who weighed more than two hundred pounds. But they had other means—and they were very impatient. One of them aimed his Soviet-made AK-47 attack rifle at the wooden door and fired.

The slugs were a military type, with brass core and jacket. They ripped effortlessly through the flimsy door and slammed into Weinberg's thick chest and neck. As he poised to jump from the window, Zavarj threw a quick glance at Weinberg. He saw that his friend's T-shirt was already turning red from blood.

As Weinberg collapsed, the attackers managed to shove open the door and storm into the room. Some lunged to the broken window and shot at the fleeing Zavarj (they missed). The rest of them rushed from Weinberg's bedroom into the two connecting apartments where Israelis were also sleeping. In the first one they encountered Joe Romano, the Israeli weight lifting champion, whose injured knee had just led to his elimination from the Olympic competition. When Romano put up a fight, they shot him at point-blank range, splattering his blood and flesh across the flat's sparse furnishings.

The shouts and shooting roused the other members of the Israeli team, who scrambled wildly to pull on clothes and flee. In the third apartment Joseph Gutfreund, a weight lifting referee, locked his large hands around the handle of the connecting door and held it closed long enough to enable his roommates to escape. Sacrificing himself, he was taken prisoner. In the flat across the hall Tuvia Sokolsky, a weight lifting coach, had also been awakened by the knocking on Weinberg's door. He peeped out to see armed men in disguises shoving against the door. Sokolsky managed to get away; so, too, did ten other Israelis.

Few on Weinberg's side of the hall were so fortunate. The attackers quickly rounded up nine Israelis. Using rope precut to the correct lengths, the raiders bound their captives in a manner that rendered them helpless: arms fastened in a painful position behind the back, and ankles tied together. Then the prisoners were forced to hobble to a third-floor bedroom just vacated by their fleeing teammates. While two armed terrorists stood guard, the captives were ordered to sit on two cots. Romano's riddled body was dragged into the room, a reminder of the threat that hung over them.

The men who held the guns were members of Black September, and they had carefully prepared for this moment. Five of them had started their trip in Tripoli and traveled to Scandinavia first, to approach Munich from the north. The other three had been in the city for some time. One had worked as an architect in Olympic Village and knew the layout of the dwellings; he refreshed his memory by a visit to the Saudi Arabian team. Two had taken jobs as kitchen helpers in the Village, and had scouted the Israeli quarters.

A Uruguayan athlete who lived in the same building remembered meeting an Arab in the stairway the day before the attack. "I asked him what he wanted," recalled the Uruguayan. " 'Some fruit,' he answered, so I gave him an apple."

In small separate groups, the raiders had collected their weapons from the checkroom of the Munich rail station, where they had been placed by an accomplice. They all met for the first time at the fence surrounding Olympic Village and were surprised at how many they were. As camouflage they wore colorful sweat togs that made them look like regular members of an Olympic team. The Arabs easily scaled the six-foot wire mesh fence and handed over airline flight bags. Two German telephone repairmen, on their way home from an emergency call, saw them climbing the fence and laughed, supposing they were tired lovers returning from a night on the town. Inside the Village some cleaning women and a guard also noticed them, but they too paid no special attention. It was not an unusual sight for athletes to be coming home at late hours.

The men who knew the way through the maze of tall and squat buildings in the Village guided the others toward a small and relatively inaccessible apartment house located at Connollystrasse 31, named for the American hop-skip-and-jump gold medalist from the 1896 Olympics. En route, the eight paused. While some smeared charcoal powder on their faces as disguise, others pulled stockings or ski masks over their heads. Unzipping their flight bags, they took out disassembled AK-47s, snapped barrels into stocks, and eased heavy banana-shaped magazines into the breeches. They also hefted hand grenades and pistols, tucking them into belts and pockets.

Black September knew the Israelis were quartered at Connollystrasse 31, but they also knew that other teams lived there too, and they were uncertain which apartments were occupied by the Israelis. Hence, as they crept down the hallway, they sought to locate their targets by rapping on doors. "Is this the Israeli team?" they asked.

Black September's code name for the operation was "Iqrit and Kafr Birim," two villages of Maronite Christians in northern Palestine who had been forced to resettle in a less exposed part of Israel. Along with their weapons, the raiders carried an apology to the Olympic athletes, composed the night before. "It would do no harm to the youth of the world to learn of our plight for only a few hours," they wrote. "We are asking them to know that there is a people with a 24-year-old cause. We are not against any nation, but why should our place here be taken by the flag of the occupier? Why should the whole world be having fun and entertainment, while we suffer with all ears deaf to us?"

The world was deaf and blind no longer. By the summer of 1972, terrorist groups in one country after another were already ripping at the fabic of society and causing effects and repercussions far out of proportion to their limited numbers. But nothing had ever approached Munich—Ali Hassan Salameh had chosen the setting well.

A number of factors combined to turn Munich into the first truly global drama. Television crews from all over the world had gathered in the city to broadcast the Olympic games. Now they would focus their cameras on a competition of a very different nature. The actors were playing out roles thrust upon them by a cruel and ironic fate. The terrorists were the sons, real or spiritual, of the families who had been driven away from their homeland by the fathers of the men whom they now held under their guns. The hostages were the survivors of a race that only three decades earlier had been subjected to the most widespread genocide in history, and in desperation they had reclaimed their historic homeland as a sanctary.

In the wake of World War II, during which six million Jews died in the Nazi extermination camps, the world felt pity for those who had escaped death. Torn from their homes and native countries, the survivors were huddled in miserable displaced person camps in central Europe. The climate of international public opinion, reacting to a sense of guilt, encouraged the Jews to establish a state in Palestine, where their influx uprooted some of the Palestinians and shoved them into new camps, as miserable and desolate as those just abandoned by the Jews.

The scene of the Munich attack greatly heightened its poignancy. Olympic Village was the most incongruous place for young people to be killing others. As a legacy from the ancient Greeks, the Olympics are supposed to be a time of truce. As early as the eighth century B.C., the Greek rulers of the constantly warring city-states pledged to refrain from attack on the site of the games and to grant safe conduct to the participants. The Olympic truce read in part:

> Olympia is a sacred place.
> Anyone who dares to enter it
>   by force of arms commits an
>   offense against the Gods.
> Equally guilty is he who has
>   it in his power to avenge a
>   misdeed and fails to do so.

In modern times, Olympic Village has been romantically idealized as the perfect community of international amity and cooperation.

The West Germans called the XX Olympiad the "Games of Peace and Joy," and they were doing their very best to make them that way. The last Olympics held in Germany—the 1936 Berlin games—had been used by Adolf Hitler as a showcase for the Nazis and had unintentionally served as a harbinger of the coming war. By contrast, the 1972 Olympics, held in the very city where Hitler got his political start, were to be the ultimate demonstration of German regeneration and atonement. From the ashes of Hitler's Third Reich, West Germany had developed into a peaceful and responsible nation, which was playing an increasingly crucial role in bringing about reconciliation and closer cooperation among the nations of Western and Eastern Europe. The participation of the Israeli team in the Munich games was an important symbolic gesture of forgiveness for crimes no Jew can ever forget.

To give the Olympics a pleasant and pacific atmosphere, the Germans decorated stadiums and buildings in light pastels, friendly red-dressed hostesses were everywhere, and security measures were kept to an absolute minimum. There should be no police dogs, no gun-toting guards, no barbed wire in Munich—nothing that could be a reminder of the Nazi era or the fact that Dachau, one of the most infamous concentration camps, was located only a short distance from the city. It was the lack of security precautions that made it so easy for Black September to take the Israelis prisoner.

Connollystrasse, 7:00 A.M. After the fleeing Israelis raised the alarm, more than five hundred policemen were quickly rushed into the Village to cordon off the building in which the hostages were being held. The first official to reach the scene was Munich Police Chief Manfred Schreiber. As he approached the apartment building, the terrorist leader stepped out, his face obscured by large sunglasses and the turned-down brim of a tennis hat. He was called Tony by the other team members, but his real name was Mohammed Masalhad. A Libyan, he was the architect, and spoke several languages.

As they stood talking in German, Schreiber suddenly thought to himself, "Maybe I can take him." But Mohammed immediately sensed the threat. "Do you want to take me?" he asked, uncurling his fist to reveal a hand grenade.

"I thought better of it," confessed Schreiber later.

Bonn, 7:15 A.M. The telephone rang on the bedside table of Chancellor Willy Brandt, waking him up to a nightmare. The duty officer in the Chancellery was calling. On hearing the news, Brandt put the gears of his government into motion. Interior Minister Hans-Dietrich Genscher should fly at once to Munich to coordinate activities with the Bavarian officials, who under West Germany's federal system had the legal responsibility for decision-making in Munich. Brandt was told that the Israeli ambassador, Eliashiv Ben-Horin, wanted to be flown to Munich, and the Chancellor ordered that he be given a plane. Then Brandt scheduled a cabinet meeting for noon. Meanwhile, Foreign Minister Walter Scheel assembled a small task force of his senior assistants to start canvassing Arab governments for possible help in negotiating with the terrorists.

Connollystrasse, 9:00 A.M. From a window fluttered two pieces of paper bearing the signature Black September. In return for the lives of the nine Israeli hostages, the terrorists demanded the release from Israeli jails of no less than two hundred Arab prisoners. The list included Kozo Okamoto, the sole survivor of the Japanese Red Army trio that, three months earlier, had carried out the wholesale slaughter at Lod airport. Black September also demanded the release of the two recently captured West German urban terrorists, Andreas Baader and Ulrike Meinhof, imprisoned in a Frankfurt jail.

The message carefully spelled out the procedure for the exchange. The Israeli government should fly the two hundred imprisoned terrorists to an Arab capital to be designated later. As soon as the Israelis had given their pledge of cooperation, the West Germans should provide three aircraft to fly the Black Septembrists and Israeli hostages to the same capital. The arrangement was to be trickproof. The second group would not depart from Munich until the first group had safely arrived at its destination, and the third group would not leave until the second had landed safely. Black September warned that any attempt to interfere with this procedure would mean immediate death for the hostages. The terrorists gave the Israelis and West Germans until noon to comply with the ultimatum. Otherwise, they vowed to "employ revolutionary and just violence to teach a very hard lesson to the warmongers of the Israeli military machinery and the arrogance of the Federal Republic [of Germany]."

Meanwhile in Jerusalem, head bowed and face drawn, Prime Minister Golda Meir walked into the Knesset, the starkly modernistic parliament set on a hill near the Valley of the Cross in Jerusalem, and immediately met with her chief ministers and advisers in the subterranean cabinet room. Moshe Dayan, who was the defense minister, proposed to lead a group of Israeli commandos to Munich. A few months earlier, he had achieved a great success by using commandos disguised as mechanics to overwhelm four Black September terrorists who had hijacked a Sabena jetliner at Lod airport. But Mrs. Meir turned down his plan. Instead, she decided to send at once the chief of the Mossad to Munich as her personal emissary. He was Zwi Zamir, a former army major-general with a matter-of-fact and deliberate manner. Accompanied by a colonel who spoke Arabic, he left for Munich in a Westwind twin-engine executive jet.

The West Germans had asked for guidance on Israeli thinking about the handling of the crisis, and Mrs. Meir discussed with her advisers what their response should be. In the past, whenever they had compromised with the terrorists, they had found themselves in a worse position than before. Hence, deciding to stand very tough, they formulated three guidelines:

1) There would be no deals whatsoever with Black September—an exchange of prisoners was completely ruled out.

2) Israel would hold West Germany entirely responsible for the rescue operation.

3) Israel would not object if the Germans offered the terrorists safe conduct to an Arab country in exchange for freeing the hostages, but the hostages must be released prior to the departure of the terrorists. Under no circumstances were the hostages to be allowed to leave Germany in Arab hands.

The Israeli position was transmitted to Ambassador

Ben-Horin, who had now reached Munich, for delivery to the West Germans.

Then Mrs. Meir gave a brief speech to the Knesset, explaining the government's action. As she spoke, she made a plea to the Olympic authorities to halt the games, now entering the tenth day. "One cannot imagine that the games will continue as though nothing happened," she said.

But the games did continue as though nothing had happened. At 9:00 A.M. the volleyball match between West Germany and Japan had started on an outdoor court not five hundred yards from Connollystrasse 31 where the terrorists occasionally came out on the balcony to look at the crowds gathered behind police lines. At 10:30, the equestrian dressage event began in the opulent setting of Schloss Nymphenburg, an old palace in Munich. The Uruguayan Olympic team, quartered on the first floor, went out for breakfast, and the terrorists let them pass. "They are very polite," reported a Uruguayan. "They are all young, all rather small, and all very nervous," added another.

Connollystrasse, 12 noon. As the deadline grew near, Schreiber, accompanied by a small delegation of German Olympic officials, went to Connollystrasse 31 where Mohammed again stepped from the doorway. They begged for a short extension. Negotiations with Israel were underway, and the West German government would soon have an important message for Black September. Mohammed agreed to a one-hour extension. As he strode back to the building, he held up two fingers. Some onlookers and TV reporters, watching from a distance, thought he was giving a signal of victory, or perhaps agreement, and hoped optimistically all might be well. In reality, the gesture meant that Black September would execute two hostages by one o'clock if their terms were not met.

In Jerusalem, as the sun blazed through the high windows of the Knesset, ministers and members of parliament waited tensely for the news bulletin about the noon deadline. (The time in Israel was one hour ahead of Munich.) One minister suspended his soupspoon in midair to listen to the announcement. When the newsmen said that the deadline had passed without the execution of hostages, he brought the spoon to his lips and went back to drinking his soup.

At the same time in Bonn, in the cabinet meeting, Chancellor Brandt and his ministers formulated a proposal they hoped would tempt the terrorists. In return for the release of the hostages, the Federal Republic would pay an unlimited ransom (the terrorists could name the amount) and guarantee safe conduct to any destination the terrorists might choose. As a gesture of sincerity, German officials would take the place of the Israeli hostages for the flight. Brandt fully agreed with Mrs. Meir's position that the Germans could not allow the hostages to be taken from the country. "An honorable government cannot allow the hostages to be sent off like an airmail packet to an uncertain fate," he told his ministers. "We are responsible for the lives of these people."

Connollystrasse, 12:40 P.M. Equipped with the West German offer, Interior Minister Genscher went to talk with Mohammed. But the Black September leader totally rejected the West German terms. Genscher asked for an extension of the new deadline, now set to expire in another twenty minutes. He told Mohammed that the Israelis were checking against their own files the names of the two hundred prisoners whom Black September had demanded should be freed. It would take time for the Israelis to verify that they actually had those prisoners in their jails. Mohammed was highly skeptical. He agreed to postpone the deadline until 3 P.M. but expressed his misgivings about the sincerity of the Israelis.

"We know the Israelis will never release those prisoners," he said. "Therefore the hostages are already dead."

In Jerusalem, one hour later, Mrs. Meir read the names of the dead and the hostages to the Knesset: Berger, Friedman, Gutfreund, Halfin, Romano, Shapira, Shorr, Slavin, Spitzer, Springer, Weinberg. The names epitomized the melting pot character of Israel. Romano had been born in Libya. David Berger was an American. Mark Slavin, eighteen, had emigrated from Russia only four months ago; he had demonstrated in front of the KGB headquarters in Minsk for the Jews' right to emigrate from the Soviet Union. The predominance of German names was a reminder that Israel is the home of the survivors of the Holocaust. Again, Mrs. Meir appealed for the games to be halted.

Meanwhile, in Beirut, Lebanese Prime Minister Saeb Salem summoned leading members of the Palestinian Liberation Organization to his office. Only moments before, he had taken a call from Willy Brandt, who had asked for help in finding someone able to reason with the Black September terrorists.

"How do I go about contacting someone in authority in Black September?" Salem inquired of the PLO leaders.

"We know nothing about this group," one of them replied. "None of us belongs to it."

At least one of Salem's guests was lying.

And in Connollystrasse the Black Septembrists were placing long distance telephone calls to Beirut and Tunisia. The West Germans traced them, hoping for leads to the terrorist headquarters. The Beirut number turned out to be a Palestinian refugee organization. The Tunisian ambassador to West Germany reported that the number in Tunis belonged to an "honorable personage" but refused to say who. In any event, no one was picking up the phone on either of the lines.

Connollystrasse 31, 2:26 P.M. In yet another meeting, Genscher gave Mohammed the impression that the Israelis had agreed to the exchange of prisoners, and that the only remaining problem was the double checking of Black September's list of names with the rolls of prisoners in Israeli jails. Genscher explained that the Israelis did not want to promise they could release someone whom they did not have in custody.

Mohammed consented to a third extension—this time to five o'clock. But he warned that it would be the last.

"Don't think you can play games with us," he declared. "We will not allow ourselves to be worn down. We did not sleep all night and we know our own limits. We will get this job done today. At the moment the new deadline expires, we will begin to execute the hostages."

Krisenstab Headquarters, 3:00 P.M. The ranking West German and Bavarian officials had established their *Krisenstab,* or crisis staff headquarters, in the administration building of the Olympic Village, only a few hundred yards from Connollystrasse 31. Following the last conversation with Mohammed, the "crisis managers" became fully convinced that the showdown could not be postponed after five o'clock. Brandt, who had flown to Munich, agreed with that assessment. Israeli Ambassador Ben-Horin strengthened the German conviction by reiterating his government's refusal to agree to an exchange of prisoners.

Connollystrasse 31, 3:30 P.M. At the request of the West German authorities, Tunisian Ambassador Mahmoud Mestiri tried to talk with the Black Septembrists. They rejected his approach and told him that the five o'clock deadline still held.

At Olympic Headquarters, fifteen minutes later, the Olympic International Committee decided that the games should be suspended for twenty-four hours. Events in progress, however, would be allowed to continue. Less than one hundred yards from Connollystrasse 31, the Soviet Union and Poland engaged in a spirited volleyball game until 5 P.M.

In the vicinity of Connollystrasse 31, 4:35 P.M. Fifteen police volunteers began creeping into positions for an assault on the building. They were dressed in sweat suits and some had pulled on warm-up jackets over bulky flack jackets. Since many of the police were overweight, the spectacle amused Olympic athletes, who were watching from a distance.

"Hey, fatso, you'll never make it," shouted one of them to a corpulent German sharpshooter whose rear stuck out from behind a concrete pillar.

Meanwhile, outside the Village fence, thousands of

people stood in silent vigil. By now, the television crews had been chased from the immediate area for fear their broadcasts would alert the terrorists to the coming assault. A group of young Jewish people sang "We Shall Overcome."

Connollystrasse 31, 4:50 P.M. Genscher, Schreiber, and Bavarian Interior Minister Bruno Merk returned to the besieged apartment building for what they thought would be the last visit. To their astonishment, Mohammed had a proposal of his own this time. He wanted a plane to fly his squad and the hostages to Cairo.

"If you refuse," he said, "we will shoot the Jews and take new hostages."

Genscher replied that before agreeing to the demand, he would have to speak with the hostages.

He was escorted alone to a room where the Israelis were sitting on cots.

"How do you feel?" he asked.

"All right," one of them replied.

"Are you willing to be flown with your captors to Cairo?" Genscher inquired.

"Yes," answered an Israeli, "as long as our government has agreed to swap the Arab prisoners for us at the destination."

Krisenstab Headquarters, 7:00 P.M. By the time Zwi Zamir finally arrived from Israel, the West German rescue plan was already worked out. Three sets of sharpshooters were to lie in ambush along the route from Connollystrasse to the air force base of Fürstenfeldbruck, near Munich. As Zamir examined the scheme, he had doubts.

"Do you really believe this plan will accomplish your goal?" he asked. "Will this free the hostages?"

The West Germans assured him that it would.

From Hotel Bayerischer Hof in Munich Willy Brandt telephoned Mrs. Meir to ask if there were any condition under which the Israeli government would consent to the hostages' being taken from Germany to an Arab country.

"I will consider the idea," she replied, "only if the Arab government in question gives ironclad guarantees that it will release the hostages as soon as they land."

Willy Brandt immediately placed a telephone call to President Anwar el-Sadat. The 1970 winner of the Nobel Peace Prize, Brandt had intended to use the Olympics, where so many world leaders were gathering, for secret diplomacy aimed at an interim agreement between Israel and Egypt. Instead, his entire efforts were now devoted to try and save the lives of nine Israeli athletes. Before the call came through, Brandt was summoned away on a different chore.

Between 8:00 and 8:35 P.M. a grim-faced Willy Brandt spoke to the nation from a Munich television studio. "These were the Games of Peace and Joy," he said. "This morning, Arab terrorists broke into the Olympic Village and destroyed the whole thing." After his short speech, Brandt moved to an office in the television building to wait for the connection to Cairo.

Finally, the Chancellor got Sadat's office on the line, but was told that the President would not be available to take the call for another hour and a half. After a few more minutes of being kept waiting, Brandt was put through to the Egyptian Prime Minister Aziz Sedki.

Brandt quickly explained the situation and asked for Egyptian cooperation.

Then, according to the Egyptian version of the conversation, Sedki inquired: "Has this proposal of yours been agreed to by the fedayeen?"

To which Brandt responded: "I don't know exactly what the fedayeen want."

But according to Brandt, Sedki replied: "This is not an Egyptian matter. I cannot understand how or why Egypt should become involved in what is happening in Munich."

In any event, the line to Cairo went dead.

Connollystrasse 31, 10:00 P.M. A gray German army bus pulled to a stop in the underground service road beneath the apartment building. The terrorists still in disguise and carrying their weapons, emerged warily from a door. For the first time, the Germans got an accurate count of the terrorists involved. It was three more than they had supposed. The Black Septembrists herded the Israelis, who were tied together in two groups between them, making an intertwined knot of captors and captives.

Five sharpshooters were waiting in the basement to get a shot at the terrorists, but they had no opportunity.

Edge of the Olympic Village, 10:10 P.M. The terrorists and hostages climbed into two Bell Huey helicopters belonging to the Border Guard. Zwi Zamir and the Israeli colonel entered a third machine with Genscher, Merk, and Schreiber. The three helicopters took off for Fürstenfeldbruck, fifteen miles to the north. Five sharpshooters who were hidden near the helicopters saw no clear targets and did not fire.

Fürstenfeldbruck, 10:30 P.M. The helicopter bearing Zamir and the others landed and its occupants rushed to the control tower. Five minutes later, the second and third machines put down side by side on the apron. Their plexiglass cockpits were facing the control tower only about forty yards away. They landed in the center of a brightly illuminated area.

Even before the machines came to a complete rest, Mohammed jumped out, and so did a companion from the second helicopter. Nervously gripping their AK-47s, they began to walk toward the Lufthansa 727 jetliner standing about one hundred and ten yards directly to their right. Two other terrorists sprang from each machine and motioned the pilots and copilots to get out. During the negotiations, Mohammed had promised not to take the crews hostage during the flight to Fürstenfeldbruck. So much for that. The Black Septembrists were holding the four under their guns.

10:38 P.M. Mohammed reached the 727 and stepped inside, closely followed by his companion. Meanwhile, watching their progress from the control tower, Manfred Schreiber, the man in charge of the operation, could easily imagine what was going through the minds of the two Arabs. The plane was cold. There was not even any pretense that it was prepared for

The Hit Team   25

flight. Lufthansa had failed to find a crew willing to act as decoy; police officers had then put on blue flight uniforms and had practiced an ambush in the plane, but had rejected it as a poor idea.

Schreiber had only five sharpshooters left to deal with the eight terrorists, but he had arranged them in a pattern that would catch the targets in crossfire. Three were stationed on the control tower roof and two lay on the airfield behind the helicopters.

The police chief passed the word to the lead sharpshooter on the roof: fire when the maximum number of targets are in sight.

10:44 P.M. Just as Mohammed and the other terrorist reached the midway point between the 727 and the helicopters, the sharp crack of a sniper's rifle broke the eerie silence. The lead marksman had aimed for Mohammed but missed. At once, the four remaining sharpshooters fired. The two Arabs standing guard over the helicopter crewmen fell dead. Mohammed's companion was hit in the first volley and killed in the second. But Mohammed darted beneath one of the helicopters and began to fire back. The four Black Septembrists in the helicopters also started shooting. The police were badly outgunned; they were firing bolt-action rifles capable only of a single shot at a time. Black September was replying with the world's most effective attack weapon, pouring long bursts of fire into the control tower. Their bullets knocked out the tower's radio. They also struck the electrical controls. Suddenly the field went dark. A Munich police sergeant stepped outside the tower to see what was happening and took a fatal bullet in the head.

For six minutes, the firefight raged, the long staccato bursts of the Black September weapons punctuated by the occasional single bark of a sniper's rifle. Then came a lull. The West Germans asked Zamir's aide to address the terrorists. In Arabic, German, and English, Colonel R. asked them to throw down their arms and surrender. AK-47 bursts answered his appeal.

At 11:00 P.M., Conrad Ahlers, the silver-haired and superbly self-assured spokesman of the Federal Republic, was seated at a desk in a Munich broadcast room. He was just about to be interviewed on the evening television news program "Tagesschau," or "the day in review." The telephone rang on his desk; it was Brandt calling. He had that moment received a message from a Bavarian police courier. The rescue operation at Fürstenfeldbruck had proceeded according to plan. This was precisely what the German press agency, DPA, had reported thirty minutes earlier. Ahlers, not a man to understate successes, reasoned that Brandt's information only confirmed the earlier bulletin. Hence, Ahlers repeated on television that the rescue operation had achieved its goal.

Whereupon in Israel, after hours of praying and weeping, the families of the hostages erupted in joy and thanksgiving. Neighbors rushed in to embrace them.

At her home in suburban Tel Aviv, where she had been keeping a vigil with several cabinet ministers, Golda Meir opened a bottle of cognac and placed it on the dining room table. It would be drunk for the traditional Jewish toast of *l'hayim* (to life). But Mrs. Meir first wanted to be absolutely certain that Ahlers's report was correct. She talked with Ambassador Ben-Horin on a hot line that had been kept open for them all day. He told her that he was in contact with the control tower but that no one there could verify the report of the West German spokesman. Most likely, the ambassador was speaking with Zwi Zamir.

"I can't find anyone who has seen a live hostage," said Ben-Horin.

The cognac remained untouched.

Fürstenfeldbruck, four minutes past midnight. Lunging from the second helicopter, a terrorist tossed a hand grenade back into the craft. Ripped by the explosion, it burst into flames. The Arab ran for the darkness. Still hiding under the unharmed helicopter, Mohammed made a break for the darkness, too. The light from the explosion illuminated their fleeing figures, and sniper bullets cut them down.

There were five Israeli hostages in the burning helicopter and, in an effort to rescue them, fire trucks pressed toward the blaze. They were supported by a phalanx of police armored cars, which had belatedly arrived from Munich. The terrorists in the other undamaged craft shot at the fire trucks but the police armored cars continued to advance. Realizing they were about to be overrun, the Black Septembrists leaped out and ran. Just at that moment, the fuel tanks in the burning helicopter exploded, turning it into a funeral pyre for the five Israelis.

Two of the surviving terrorists were hit by bullets and surrendered. The third, unhurt, threw himself on the tarmac and played dead. He was taken prisoner.

As the autopsies proved, four of the five Israelis in the burned helicopter had been dead for some time. They had been shot and killed by the terrorists before the explosion. The fifth, though he had been gravely wounded by two AK-47 slugs, succumbed to smoke inhalation. The four Israeli hostages in the other helicopter had also been shot dead by terrorist bullets. Evidently, Black September executed the Israelis at the moment the snipers opened fire.

The world, which had gone to sleep in the belief that the nine Israelis were rescued, awoke to the horror of their deaths. For the first time in history, the flags of the participants in an Olympics flew at half mast. As eighty thousand gathered in the main stadium for a memorial service, the Munich Symphony Orchestra played the majestic funeral march from Beethoven's "Eroica." In the section occupied by the Israeli team, eleven seats were left empty.

The mourning was not universal. Arab teams refused to participate, and even as the memorial service was underway, athletes from the Soviet Union and East Bloc indolently kicked soccer balls on nearby practice fields.

An embittered Zwi Zamir returned to Israel later that day. He was appalled at the inefficiency of the West Germans—the sharpshooters could not shoot straight, the crisis managers could not manage. To the Israeli general, Munich was by no means an isolated event. It was the climax in a long series of Arab outrages and European failures. As the Israelis repeatedly had experienced, the terrorist was more than a match for the European police. And European governments were afraid to take the necessary tough measures against terrorism because they did not want to offend the Arab countries on which they depended for oil.

Zamir must have reflected on the incredible irony of the situation. His country had succeeded in defeating the terrorists within its borders and even had managed to contain the resistance movement in the predominantly Arab West Bank territory seized during the Six Days' War in 1967. But now Israel was being completely outmaneuvered. By exporting the conflict to Europe, the Arabs had selected a battlefield where, for once, the Israelis were defenseless.

As the general's executive jet touched down at Lod, a helicopter was standing by. The chief of the Mossad was immediately flown to the helipad near the Red House, the prime minister's office located, for security reasons, within the heavily guarded grounds of the army general headquarters.

Outside the prime ministry stood the special armor-plated Dodges belonging to the prime minister and the defense minister. Zamir climbed the carpeted stairs to the antechamber next to the cabinet room. Asked to wait for a moment, he expressed his deep feeling to some friends.

"It was a desperate and desolate feeling to stand in the control tower at Fürstenfeldbruck and to have to face the realization that nothing has changed," he said. "Jews are dying again on German soil with their hands tied, and no one cares."

In a few moments, General Zamir was summoned to the cabinet room where the Ministers' Committee for Security and Foreign Affairs was in session. It is the highest council of the Israeli government and its deliberations are kept entirely secret. Even the committee's name is deleted from news reports by Israeli censors. The committee was deliberating a proposal that Zamir and other ranking intelligence officers had been advocating for months. It would be, in effect, the declaration of a clandestine war against Arab terrorism abroad. Zamir and his colleagues wanted to set up special killer teams that would hunt down and destroy the Arab terrorist leaders wherever they might be. Zamir's plan embodied the most unforgiving tenet of the ancient Hebraic code: an eye for an eye, a tooth for a tooth.

But Prime Minister Golda Meir, who had resisted the proposal, had always lectured the advocates of the plan that the risks to Israel's image in the world far outweighed the advantages of killing a few Arabs.

"You can't guarantee me that some day there won't be a mistake," she would say. "Someday, some of our people will get caught. Then, you tell me: what are we going to do?"

So far, she had given the go-ahead only on one occasion: after the Lod massacre, when three Japanese Red Army killers sprayed the arrivals hall with gunfire. Slipping ashore in Beirut, Israeli frogmen planted a radio-triggered bomb in the car belonging to Ghassan Kanafani. A Palestinian poet and novelist, he was the spokesman and ideologue for the Popular Front for the Liberation of Palestine (PFLP), a terrorist group specializing in skyjacking. It was the organization that the Mossad blamed for planning the Lod attack.

Tragically, as Kanafani entered his car on the morning of July 8, he was accompanied by his teenage niece, Lamees. For her birthday each year, he prepared a special book of poems, which he illustrated himself. The Mossad had not anticipated that she would be along that morning, but a frogman pressed the button nevertheless, transmitting the electric impulse that ignited the charge.

In his role as the PFLP spokesman, Kanafani liked to keep up to date on Israeli information programs abroad, and Arab embassies throughout Europe regularly sent him the latest batches of Israeli brochures. On that morning, he had been reading a packet of Israeli material that had been sent through Arab diplomatic channels from Denmark, and he carried the papers with him to the car. After the explosion, a small piece of paper wafted downward and settled on the carnage. It was the type of card that embassy employees routinely enclose with public relations handouts. "With the compliments of the Embassy of Israel in Copenhagen," it read.

Zamir briefed the special committee on the disaster at Munich and reiterated his recommendation to set up the liquidation teams. Again, the general was asked to wait in the anteroom. Then the committee voted to accept his proposal. An anonymous minute-taker recorded the moment in the cryptic language of top-secret Israeli proceedings: "The Ministers' Committee heard a report and decided to give the Prime Minister full authority to carry out the needed steps."

As the ministers departed in their cars, Mrs. Meir summoned General Aharon Yariv, the former chief of military intelligence. She asked him if he would accept an appointment as her special adviser for antiterrorist activities and he agreed. Then she addressed Zamir and Yariv together. The decision that had been left in the hands of the prime minister was a difficult one for her to make and, as she faced the two men, she had to justify it in her own mind. She spoke at length about the tragic fate of the Jews and their suffering down through the centuries. She spoke of the Holocaust and of the new threat to Jewish lives in Europe. Then she gave the command. "Send forth your boys," she said.

After a twenty-four-hour period of mourning, the Olympic games resumed in Munich. But the surviving members of the Israeli team withdrew from competition and accompanied the bodies of ten of their slain comrades aboard a special El Al 707 to Tel Aviv. The body of the eleventh victim—David Bergen, a weight lifter who was an American citizen—was flown by a U.S. Air Force C-141 to Cleveland for burial.

Hebrew tradition prescribes that bodies should be buried in prayer shawls. But the remains of Israel's athletes were placed in pinewood coffins. Some of the bodies, charred by fire and torn by the explosion, were too maimed to be contained in a shroud.

The 707 taxied to a remote corner of Lod airport, where the families of the victims were waiting. Each coffin, draped with the blue and white flag of Israel, was placed on the tailgate of an army command car.

Women wailed and men wept. Some people cried: "Death to the terrorists, death to the terrorists!" Grief-stricken relatives threw themselves on the coffins; their fingers, clenching in sorrow and anger, inadvertently tore the flowers from the funeral wreaths.

The chief rabbi of the Israeli Defense Forces led the mourners in the *Yizkor,* the traditional prayer for the dead. He intoned:

The Guardian of Israel neither slumbers nor sleeps.
The Lord is your guardian; the Lord is your shelter.
The sun shall never hurt you in the day, nor the moon by night.
The Lord shall keep you from all evil; He shall keep your soul.
The Lord will guard you as you come and go, now and ever.

The mourners responded:

The Lord is my shepherd; I am not in want.
He makes me to lie down in green pastures; He leads me beside refreshing streams.
He restores my life; He guides me by righteous paths for His own sake.
Even though I walk in the Valley of the Shadow of Death I will fear no evil. . . .

The words of the ancient prayers were often drowned out by the sobs of the mourners and the whine of jet fighter-bombers, which were landing at Lod after having escorted the 707 on the last leg of its flight. Meanwhile, from other airstrips in Israel, fighter-bombers were taking off for retaliatory strikes against Palestinian refugee camps in Lebanon and Syria.

In the absence of Mrs. Meir, who had gone to attend the burial of her sister, the speaker was Yigal Allon, the deputy premier.

"The elite of our sportsmen has died," he said, "and the Olympic spirit died with them."

The cortège of command cars drove slowly from the airport. They bore the bodies to various cemeteries where the families buried their dead. It was only two days before Rosh Hashanah, the Jewish New Year, a festival that celebrates the renewal of life.

A few days later, at the request of Libyan strongman Muamar Gaddafi, the bodies of the five slain Black Septembrists were released by West Germany and flown to Tripoli, where they were received as conquering heroes and accorded full military honors. A huge funeral procession bore the five dead terrorists to the mosque on Martyrs Square, where the *Ya Sin,* the Koran prayer for the dead, was recited:

> Who shall quicken the bones when they are decayed?
> Say: He shall quicken them, who originated them the first time; He knows all creation, who has made for you out of the green tree fire and lo, from it you kindle.
> Is not He, who created the heavens and earth, able to create the like of them? Yes indeed; He is the All-Creator, the All-knowing.
> His command, when He desires a thing, is to say to it "Be," and it is.
> So glory be to Him, in whose hand is the dominion of everything, and unto whom you shall be returned.

From mosques and minarets all over the Arab world, prayers of mourning echoed for the dead young men. They were called the "martyrs," conferring a special blessing and dignity upon their violent deaths. Along with the outpouring of sorrow went a tremendous surge of Arab pride in the bravery of the "Munich Martyrs." Arabs glorified the reckless courage of the dead men, and the name "Black September" suddenly became a rallying cry for Arabs who otherwise had had no connection with terrorism.

In the wake of the Munich massacre, many young Arabs liked to boast: "We are all Black September now."

TWO

Because you have stolen our land, killed our people, and come from all over the world to usurp our rights, we will harass you wherever you are.

—MESSAGE IN A BLACK SEPTEMBER
LETTERBOMB

Black September. It is a mysterious and ominous name, whose etymology tells a great deal about the nature of the Middle Eastern conflict. Black September does not take its name from the month of the Munich massacre. It comes from the month of another massacre two years earlier when the Palestinians were the ones being slaughtered. It was September 1970, a time of vicious fighting in Jordan, when King Hussein turned loose his fierce Bedouin troops on the Palestinian refugees. As they watched their families die in the camps under artillery barrages, young Palestinians cursed this as the darkest period yet in their people's tragic history. Black September was the month fellow Arabs sought to destroy the Palestinian nation.

The young men who took that name were dedicated to one ideal: revenge. They were consumed with a merciless fury, an urge to strike out against all forces and influences that had plunged their people into the total calamity of Black September. They were against non-caring Arabs, scheming Americans, indifferent Europeans, and the aloof world in general. Above all, they were dedicated to retaliation against the royalist Jordanians and the hated Israelis.

To try to enlist world sympathy, Black September frequently prepared eloquent apologies for its operations. "We are not bandits and murderers," the statements invariably would say, explaining that past wrongs done to Palestinians justified Black September's actions. Still, Black September became the number one international outlaw. Its methods were cruel and calculating.

Sometimes its targets were carefully selected—a Jordanian ambassador here, a Mossad agent there. But Black September also indiscriminately killed and maimed scores of innocent people. In fact, it seemed as if Black September operated on the principle that the more innocent the victims, the greater the shock value.

While the rest of the world was recoiling in horror at Black September, the Arabs, by and large, praised and cheered them. So, too, did radical and anarchist elements in the Western world. For the Arab masses, the terrorist was quickly adopted as the new hero. For centuries the Arabs, suffering from divisions and divisiveness, had tried and failed to channel the course of history toward their own goals. Now, a few armed men who were willing to die for a cause were able to influence events and terrify the world. Aware of the emotional chord they had touched among the Arab masses, Black September cultivated the image of selfless freedom fighters who would bring about a renaissance of Arab glory. By their acts of pure violence, they would purge Arab culture of lassitude and indolence. From the crucible of AK-47 fire would come a new sense of Arab unity and purpose. Their own deaths would be those of martyrs, and through their sacrifice would be born a new Palestine.

It was a poignant turnabout in Arab history that the new hero would step from the most miserable and downtrodden members of the race. It would be inaccurate and unfair to identify all Palestinians with Black September's cult of violence. But it is true that Black September grew from the misery and frustration of the Palestinian people.

Who are these people? They now number 2,700,000, of whom more than one-third live in Israel itself or the occupied West Bank area. The rest are scattered in a diaspora that stretches from the Persian Gulf states where many Palestinians hold important posts in government and industry, to Western Europe where they provide mainly low-cost labor. But some 900,000 remain registered as refugees and 500,000 of them are still living in squalid camps in Lebanon and Syria.

So much has been written and debated over the Palestinian Question (as it is called in the United Nations) that the human side of the issue has often been ignored. In order to grasp some understanding of the Palestinians, it is essential to comprehend how they regard themselves and their fate.

The Palestinians believe themselves to be a wronged and robbed people, and the tenacity of their convictions has kept them at the center of the Middle East tensions for three decades. Four wars have been fought either directly or indirectly because of them, and there will never be a lasting peaceful settlement in that area unless the Palestinians subscribe to it.

In the course of the 1948 war, after the combined Arab armies were defeated in their attempt to repulse the waves of Jewish immigrants, about 600,000 Palestinians fled from their homes into refugee camps in Jordan and Lebanon. At the time, many left at the behest of their leaders, who promised that the Arab armies would quickly restore them to their homes. But, as the Palestinians now see it, they were driven out of their homeland by violence—and hence, only by violence can they hope to regain it. As they huddled in the camps, sustained only by a dole from the UN refugee committee, the Palestinians were forgotten by the world. Their fellow Arabs, who made no attempt to find new homes for them, preferred to leave the refugees in their misery as living symbols of the Jewish usurpation.

Meanwhile, the Palestinians harbored an intense love of their lost land that is reminiscent of the Jews' enduring devotion to Israel. The plaint of the Jew during the Babylonian exile ("If I forget thee, O Jerusalem, withered be this my hand") is echoed some 2,500 years later in poetry of Nizar Qabbani, a Syrian advocate of the Palestinian cause:

> I wept until my tears were dry
> I prayed until the candles flickered
> I knelt until the floor creaked
> I asked about Mohammed and Christ
> Oh Jerusalem, the fragrance of the prophets!
> The shortest path between earth and sky!

The misery in the camps heightened the Palestinians'
longing for their homes, just as the persecution of the
Jews caused them to dream of a return to the Promised
Land. Of his feelings in a refugee camp, the Palestinian
poet Rashed Hussein wrote:

Tent #50, on the left, that is my present,
But it is too cramped to contain a future!
And "Forget!" they say, but how can I?
  Teach the night to forget to bring
  Dreams showing me my village
  And teach the wind to forget to carry to me
  The aroma of apricots in my fields!
  And teach the sky, too, to forget to rain.
Only then, I may forget my country.

After the 1948 debacle, the other Arabs counseled
the Palestinians to be patient. In time, the Arab nations
would solve their internal problems and regroup. Then,
in one glorious attack, they would vanquish the Israelis
and restore the Palestinians to their homeland. It was to
be the holy cause that would provide a rallying point for
the Arab world.

The Palestinians waited. In June 1967, Egyptian
President Gamal Nasser declared that the time was
right. The rest is well known. Thanks largely to their
superior intelligence information and airpower, the Israelis destroyed the combined Arab armies in only six
days. The consequence for the Palestinians: the Israelis
occupied the predominantly Arab West Bank area,
bringing thousands of Palestinians under their control,
while thousands of others abandoned their homes and
fled into the already crowded camps in Jordan and
Syria.

In the aftermath of the second debacle, two developments took place. The first was that the Palestinians
came to the realization that they could not rely on their
fellow Arabs for help; thus was born the era of the Palestinian guerrilla who was determined to reconquer his
homeland on his own. Secondly, the Palestinians, who
are generally more sophisticated than other Arabs, began an analysis of the reasons for the Arab defeat. "The

summation of our case is reduced to a sentence," concluded Qabbani. "We adopted the facade of civilization while our spirits remained antiquated."

> The flute and the lute
> Do not secure victory.
> We improvise courage
> While sitting in the mosque
> Idiotic—and lazy
> Composing verse—and reciting proverbs
> Supplicating victory over the enemy
> From Divine Providence.

The Palestinian soul-searching brought about a revulsion against the crippling heritage of Moslem religious teaching and a scorn for the older generation—"The generation of defeat," as the younger people called it. "Defeated father, Humbled mother, to hell with my inheritance of tribal teachings, my savage rites," wrote the Palestinian poet Sameeh Al-Qassem.

> I cut the stupid customs
> From the roots
> I spit my hate
> My shame
> Into the faces of the devout
> The holy ones
> I kick the garbage of my defeat and
> My humility
> Into the face of the dervishes—
> The barking half men—the office holders.
> From the depth of my Hell
> My voice prevails:
> I condemn you to death.

A new spirit had seized the young Palestinians, and Yasir Arafat, the leader of Al Fatah, the largest guerrilla group, sensed the change. By late 1967, there were ten quarreling and competing guerrilla outfits. But Arafat was molding an umbrella group, which became known as the Palestinian Liberation Organization, to provide a semblance of unity.

The guerrillas were Marxist in political orientation and they drew their inspiration from the independence movements throughout the Third World. According to their ideology, Israel was the outpost of corrupt Western imperialism, placed in the Middle East to cause confusion and disunity among the Arab people. While the Palestinians depended for weapons on the Russians and, to a lesser degree, on the Chinese, they looked for lessons in the conduct of revolutionary warfare mainly to the Cubans, whose less formalized and spontaneous approach appealed to them. "Ché" was a favorite nickname among Palestinian guerrillas.

Arafat and his colleagues called their campaign a "revolution," but it was one with a very special nature. Unlike the successful advocates of national liberation, the Palestinians were not trying to overthrow a corrupt and small upper class that was isolated from the masses; they were trying to frighten into surrender or to destroy an entire people who had conquered their country and were determined to hold on to it. The return of all Palestinians to their homeland certainly meant the destruction of the State of Israel. The bloodcurdling rhetoric of the Palestinian guerrillas, combined with their tactic of indiscriminate killing within Israel, only heightened the will of the Israelis to resist and made political compromise between Palestinian and Jew, which was a remote possibility anyhow, completely out of the question.

The basic weapon of the guerrillas was the Soviet-made AK-47 attack rifle, often called the Kalshnikov for the name of its inventor. The guerrillas, who shortened the word to Klashin, sang a song about the fast-firing weapon:

> Klashin makes the blood run out in torrents.
> Haifa and Jaffa are calling us.
> Commando go ahead and do not worry
> Open fire and break the silence of the night.

Following the 1967 war, as the Arab countries reeled in disarray, the Palestinian guerrillas decided that the moment had come for them to take the initiative. According to guerrilla doctrine, the Palestinians now had the perfect theater of operations—the West Bank, where thousands of Arabs had just come under Israeli occupation. But in a short time, the guerrillas had been dealt a disillusioning defeat. Their compatriots shunned them, refusing to provide support and hiding places. Arafat and company could not, to use Mao's dictum, swim among the masses of the West Bank. Equally bad, Israeli security forces proved to be exceptionally efficient. They rounded up terrorists and sealed the border to Jordan with an array of electronic devices, mines, ploughed strips, and "people sniffers." Israeli armor penetrations and air raids drove the guerrillas from their bases in the Jordan River valley, near the border, to remote hideaways in the hills from whence it was harder to stage forays into Israel.

Meanwhile, even as they suffered a beating from the Israelis, the Palestinians received no help from their fellow Arabs, who were still smarting from the last defeat. Each Arab government wanted to prevent the Palestinians from staging attacks from its area in order to avoid Israeli retaliatory raids. Thus, in trying to retain the freedom to launch attacks from Jordanian territory, the Palestinian guerrillas came into direct conflict with Hussein, who secretly wanted to come to terms with Israel.

By the summer of 1970, the Palestinian guerrillas had given up hope of bringing about a revolution inside Israel. Instead, they were using terrorism to frustrate any Middle East settlement that failed to give them back their Palestinian homeland. At that time, the so-called War of Attrition was in progress and Secretary of State William P. Rogers was negotiating a cease-fire between Israel and two of its antagonists, Jordan and Egypt. Fearful that the accord would lead to a suppression of the guerrilla movements, Dr. George Habash, the chief of the Popular Front for the Liberation of Palestine, vowed that he would "turn Middle East into a hell."

It became a hell for the Palestinians.
On Sunday, September 6, the PFLP staged a mass hijacking of jetliners. The attempt to seize an El Al

flight failed. But three other planes ultimately were skyjacked to a desert flat near Amman and a Pan American 747 was taken to Cairo airport, where it was blown up. The hijackings dramatized the vulnerability of the technologically oriented world to the threat of terrorism. The episode also underscored the impotence of King Hussein, who was unable to prevent his kingdom from being used as a landing strip for aerial bandits. For several months, the relations had been worsening between Hussein and the Palestinian refugees, who made up two-thirds of Jordan's population. In June, there had been widespread shooting between the Palestinians and Hussein's Bedouin troops. Hawklike men from the desert, the Bedouin despised the citified, posturing Palestinian. "Allah created the Bedouin and the camel," goes a desert Arab saying. "Then from the camel's dung he made the city Arab."

Hussein, a descendant of desert chieftains, depended upon the Bedouin for the survival of his throne. As the skyjacking drama unfolded in the desert, the king's elite troops, whom he had forbidden to intervene, became increasingly restive. At a review of an armored regiment, Hussein was outraged to see brassieres fluttering from the radio antennae of the officers' tanks. Rushing to the formation, he demanded an explanation.

"You have made women out of us," replied a tank commander. "You won't let us fight."

In his palace outside Amman, where Hussein kept a helicopter in the eventuality he would need to make a quick escape, his advisers warned that the patience of his troops was wearing thin.

Even before all of the hostages were freed from the hijacked planes, the king's troops—some of them with his picture taped to their tanks—began to hunt down the Palestinians. The guerrillas, who liked to swagger around Amman with their AK-47s, were not equal to the onslaught of trained and disciplined soldiers. In the street fighting, the Palestinians were badly beaten and withdrew to refugee camps. Using its vastly superior firepower, Hussein's army directed heavy artillery against the refugee camps, often firing phosphorous shells that burned the victims who had not already been killed in the initial blast.

"We tolerated a very great deal in the hope that we could avert such a disaster," explained King Hussein. "But then there was an explosion and the disaster could no longer be avoided."

After burying their dead, estimated as high as seven thousand, the Palestinian refugees began to make their way to camps in Lebanon. A small band of fanatical guerrillas remained in Jordan, however, and sought to hold a few hamlets near the Syrian border. The diehards were led by a craggy-faced, one-eyed fighter of great bravery and charisma who was idolized by many young Palestinians. He was Abu Ali Iyad, Al Fatah's field commander. During the summer of 1971, Hussein decided to allow his Bedouin troops to finish off the remnants of the Palestinian guerrillas. In a last stand near the northern Jordanian town of Jerash, Abu Ali Iyad was wounded and taken prisoner. Exactly what happened to him is unclear. There are reports that he was killed by the Bedouin and that his body was dragged behind a tank through surrounding villages.

But his followers believed a different account. According to their version, he was taken to one of Hussein's closest associates, Wasfi Tell, who had been appointed prime minister shortly after the September massacre. Tell allegedly tortured Abu Ali Iyad to death. It was another grave mark against Tell, who was an old antagonist of the Palestinians. They also held him responsible for inciting Hussein to unleash the Bedouin in the first place.

A group of Iyad's followers, his sister, and some other relatives swore oaths to avenge his death by taking the life of Wasfi Tell. The memory of Iyad provided an inspiration for other young Palestinians, who also were thirsting for revenge.

In the early afternoon of November 28, 1971, Black September made its debut. Prime Minister Tell, who had just attended a luncheon of Arab League chiefs of government in Cairo, was striding from his car toward the main entrance of the Sheraton Hotel. He acknowledged the salute of the doorman and stepped into the foyer. At that instant, he was hit by five pistol slugs, fired point-blank. He reeled backward and sought to draw his own gun. But he was already too weak. As he fell mortally wounded, a gunman knelt and lapped up his blood.

About three weeks later, Black September struck again. As the Jordanian ambassador to Britain was being chauffeured to his London embassy, a lone gunman, standing on a traffic isle, sprayed the car with submachine-gun fire. The ambassador escaped unhurt. So, too, did the would-be assassin, who was an Algerian named Frazeh Khelfa. The British legal authorities tracked him to France and asked for his extradition. But the French instead turned him over to the Algerians, who pretended that he was wanted for a crime committed in his home country.

In quick succession Black September bombs and gunfire shook Europe, which the terrorists found to be a far more favorable field of operation than the heavily patrolled borders of Israel. During February 1972 alone, Black September blew up two oil storage facilities (in Hamburg and Rotterdam), bombed a West German factory supplying electrical motors to Israel, undertook two hijackings (one succeeded and one failed), and executed five Jordanians in the basement of a house near Bonn, on the suspicion (probably correct) that they were agents of Hussein's intelligence service.

Even as it continued its campaign of terror in Europe, Black September sought to liberate the terrorists who had ended up in Israeli prisons as a consequence of the failure of earlier operations on the West Bank. On May 8, 1972, four Black Septembrists seized a Sabena jet on its flight from Vienna to Tel Aviv. After it landed at Lod, the guerrillas, two men and two young women, held the passengers hostage and demanded freedom for hundreds of imprisoned Arabs.

Moshe Dayan, taking personal command of the operation, lured the terrorists into a false sense of achievement by promising to meet their demands. Then Israeli commandos, disguised as mechanics in white overalls, stormed the plane, killing the two men and capturing the women, who had wired themselves to explosives like living bombs. Mercifully, the women had failed to touch the connections that would have blown plane and passengers into a million bits.

The Sabena failure was a disgrace for Black September. In order to restore its image in the Arab world, it would need a spectacular revenge. Later that month, it just so happened, the Popular Front for the Liberation of Palestine (PFLP, called "flop" by its detractors) held a conference of worldwide terrorist organizations at a refugee camp called Badawi, near the Lebanese city of Tripoli. The theme was how the terrorist groups could work together by pooling resources, by providing mutual assistance, and by coordinating operations. The guest list read like the Who's Who of Violence: representatives of the Baader-Meinhof gang of West Germany, the Irish Republican Army, the Japanese Red Army, and liberation fronts from Iran and Turkey. There were also at least three Black September participants.

Only a short time later, the fruits of the Tripoli conference became shockingly evident. Aided by PFLP's contacts, Black September engaged the services of three Japanese Red Army killers. They deplaned like ordinary tourists at Lod airport, but upon claiming their luggage, they pulled out Czech-made automatic rifles and sprayed the arrivals hall with bullets. The toll: twenty-seven dead and seventy-eight wounded. Many of the casualties were Puerto Rican Catholics on a pilgrimage to the Holy Land. A dazed survivor was quoted as saying: "What are Japanese doing killing Puerto Ricans in Israel?" The answer: It was international terrorism in action.

Black September, having more than fully repaid Israel for the Sabena failure, prepared for future spectaculars.

Black September cultivated an aura of mystery. If asked about it, Yasir Arafat would reply: "We know nothing of this organization and we are not involved in it, but we can understand the mentality of these young

men, who are willing to die for the life of Palestine."
His words were echoed by other ranking PLO leaders.
Many Palestinians disingenuously insisted that Black
September did not exist but was a figment of the Israeli
propaganda to justify the killings of innocent Arabs.

Outside investigations were not welcome. British
journalist Christopher Dobson, while engaged on the research for his excellent short book *Black September*, received threats against his life. *Newsweek* senior editor
Arnaud de Borchgrave was told by anonymous telephone callers to start saying his prayers after he named
Daoud Bakarat, a Geneva-based representative of the
Democratic Republic of Yemen, as a Black September
leader. No West European government has ever dared
to hold Black September prisoners for long; invariably
they have set them free, either on some pretext to avoid
future retaliation, or as the ransom in a new Black September operation. Double agents who infiltrated Black
September have met sudden and violent deaths. The
killers of Wasfi Tell were quickly set free by the Egyptian government and never brought to trial.

Black September had no office, no stationery, no
spokesman. To a degree, it was, as some Arabs insisted,
a state of mind. But it was also an organization. Despite
the disclaimers, it was a secret branch of Al Fatah.
Only one high-ranking Black September officer was
ever captured and interrogated. He was Abu Daoud,
seized in Amman while plotting an attack to kidnap
Jordanian leaders. In his confession, Daoud defined
Black September as "the special operations organ affili-
ated with [Al Fatah] intelligence." The special operations branch was known as Razd, and it was the smallest and most effective arm of Al Fatah intelligence. The
arrangement enabled the PLO clandestinely to conduct
terrorist operations while maintaining its innocence to
the outside world.

The chief of Black September was Mohammed Yusif
Najjar, known as Abu Youssef. An experienced intelligence operator, he was one of Arafat's two top aides in
the PLO, and his chief deputy for planning and operations was Ali Hassan Salameh. Black September embraced the theory that it made better publicity to kill

one Jew or Jewish supporter in Europe than to kill one hundred Jews in Israel. Therefore, Salameh's main area of operations was Europe, and he enjoyed virtually a free hand in the way he planned and executed his missions.

For help in setting up the operations, he could depend upon a net of contacts throughout Europe, the Middle East, and North Africa. Sometimes these were Arab diplomats and PLO representatives; at other times they were Razd agents.

The people who actually performed the missions were drawn from a pool of a hundred or so young Palestinian men and women. They had undergone some training in how to handle an AK-47 and hand grenades. But their main qualification was dedication. Their profiles were very similar: bright, educated, and highly motivated, most had been born and raised in the camps, but they came predominantly from families that later had been able to find jobs and establish homes on the outside. Nearly all of them had attended college, usually the American University in Beirut, and spoke at least one or two Western languages. A number had studied in European universities.

When they were selected for an operation, they were administered a special oath of silence and allegiance to Black September. Each operation had a code name of specific significance for Palestinians. Just as the code in the Munich operation was the name of two Arab villages in Israel, in the abortive Amman raid Daoud was planning it was "three no's," standing for no peaceful settlement, no United Arab Kingdom, no solution that involved the liquidation of the Palestinian people. The code name usually played a role in the formulation of the password for the operation. (Question: "How many no's are there, my brother?" Reply: "Three, my honored friend.")

For funds, Black September could count on the PLO, which exacted a tithe from Palestinians employed in Arab countries, notably the Gulf states. The terrorists also received direct subsidies from Arab regimes, including even the archconservative oil sheikhdoms along the Persian Gulf, which Black September had vowed to destroy. The organization's main sponsor was Libyan leader Muammar Gaddafi, who admired the terrorists' violent approach to political problems. As a reward for the Munich massacre, he awarded Black September a cool five million dollars.

Even more important than money were the diplomatic facilities that Gaddafi and other Arab leaders placed at the disposal of Black September. Due to the long-standing practices of diplomatic immunity, embassy personnel can move more easily than other persons from country to country and are almost never subjected to searches at airports and border crossings. Furthermore, the contents of a diplomatic pouch are inviolate; hence all manner of weaponry and explosives can be carried by diplomatic couriers. On several occasions, Arab couriers were seized at West European airports when the packets they were lugging were too blatantly suspicious, and sometimes Arab diplomats were found to be carrying letterbombs in their baggage for delivery to Black September. Often those "diplomats" were not authentic, but were actually Al Fatah or Black September operatives who had been issued credentials by an obliging embassy. In any event, Black September was able to move weapons at will throughout Europe and pre-position them in embassies for future use. The main ammunition dump was located in the basement of the Libyan embassy in Bonn. The British-made Sterling 9 mm. submachine gun used in the attempt on the life of the Jordanian ambassador in London and the Sterlings employed in the execution of the five Jordanian agents in West Germany were traced to a consignment sold to Libya. As one Israeli security officer put it, "If somebody would have dropped a match in the Libyan embassy, half of Bonn would have been wiped out in the explosion."

Equally important was the access to unlimited numbers of passports. The Arab diplomatic missions would issue new travel documents under assumed names to Black September operatives, enabling them to travel freely with little fear of being detected, even if they were wanted by police under another identity. For example, Daoud, while participating on the fringe of the preparations for the Munich attack, was using a new Iraqi passport under the name of Sa'd ad-Din Wadi.

The embassies served as sanctuaries where Black September operatives could coordinate activities and issue orders without fear of arrest or interference by West European police. They were also able to communicate by code, using the diplomatic cables and short-wave. On ultrasecret operations, however, they relied on couriers rather than on electronic means, which can be monitored. The central command post was believed to be the Algerian consulate in Geneva. Since the Swiss city is home of so many United Nations and other international agencies, the presence of a few more Arabs would attract no attention, and the Algerians, who have an extremely tough intelligence service, undoubtedly were excellent advisers for Black September. Ali Hassan Salameh did not spend much time in Geneva himself, but he sometimes coordinated operations through the Algerian consulate, and couriers shuttled between his various hideaways and the consulate.

The Black September planning chief probably began thinking about an attack on the Israeli Olympic team in late spring or early summer of 1972. One of Salameh's greatest strengths was his ability to keep secrets and to organize operations in such a way that only he had the overall picture, while the others knew as little as possible. The case officer Salameh assigned to the Munich attack was named Fakhri Al Umari, who was chief of Black September's killer section. He collected the weapons, evidently from an Arab diplomatic mission in West Germany, and packed them in airline flight bags, which he deposited in the checked luggage room of the Munich rail station. Fakhri Al Umari tried to enter Olympic Village to ferret out information on the Israeli team, but the police guards turned him back.

At that point, the Libyan architect Mohammed Masalhad was given the spying assignment, which he competently fulfilled. He was then tapped to command the assault squad. Meanwhile, two Black Septembrists had been told to get jobs in the Village. The Syrian embassy in Bonn vouched for the particulars they listed on

the employment questionnaires. These two men undoubtedly had no idea about what was being planned
until the very last minute. The five other squad members had undergone training in a Palestinian refugee
camp near the Syrian town of Deraa before leaving on
the circuitous journey that finally brought them to
Munich.

As devised by Ali Hassan Salameh, the final stage of
the operation called for taking the Israeli hostages by
plane to Tunis. That accounts for the phone calls placed
by the Black Septembrists from the Israeli quarters to
the "honorable personage" in the Tunisian capital. But
the personage—who must have been high-ranking in
the government—evidently became frightened and
backed out.

Perhaps because operation "Iqrit and Kafr Birim"
ended in a massacre, it achieved a shock value far sur-
passing other terrorist acts of the era. Without a doubt,
Ali Hassan Salameh, who watched the operation from
the safety of a Black September hideaway in East Berlin, won by proxy the gold medal for violence at the
Munich Olympics. But, to his own ultimate discomfort,
he provoked a reaction in Israel. The tough men around
Golda Meir now had a new reason to insist that terrorism was a game that two sides could play.

THREE

On that Saturday in September, as Prime Minister Golda Meir gave the go-ahead to Yariv and Zamir for the start of the hit team operation, there was little doubt about the number one target. It was Ali Hassan Salameh. He was far more than just another Palestinian terrorist. Ali Hassan Salameh became the embodiment of all that Israel feared in the Palestinians, and the desire to kill him developed into an absolute obsession for Israeli intelligence.

Among Israelis, Ali Hassan's name provoked a chilling fear that harked back to the dreadful days of the 1930s and 1940s when Jewish settlers frequently were terrorized by marauding bands of Palestinians. Ali Hassan's father was Sheikh Salameh, who led one of the largest and most brutal of these gangs. His home base was the town of Ramle, which sits astride the road linking Tel Aviv with Jerusalem. During the 1948 War of Independence, Sheikh Salameh commanded the lifeline over which the supplies passed from the seacoast to the besieged Jewish community in Jerusalem; the battle for control of this sector of the road, which rises from the plains after Ramle into craggy hills, has been memorialized even until today by the wrecks of jerry-built Jewish armored trucks, whose burned-out hulks have been placed on concrete bases along the Tel Aviv—Jerusalem highway as testimony to that desperate struggle. Undoubtedly many of them were destroyed by Sheikh Salameh's men.

During the height of the War of Independence, members of the Haganah, as the Jewish fighting force of that period was known, managed to secret a bomb in the Sheik's headquarters in Ramle. While he was conferring with his staff, the bomb exploded, killing everyone within the immediate area. After the death of Sheikh Salameh, the Israelis succeeded in opening the highway to Jerusalem.

The mother of Ali Hassan fled from Ramle with her small son, then only four or five. They traveled northward to the town of Nablus, in the West Bank territory then under Jordanian rule. Relatives gave them food and shelter. The area was crowded with refugees living in shantytowns of tents and lean-tos. Thus the son of the famed Palestinian warrior grew up among thousands of his fellow countrymen who had fled or been driven from their homes. Ali Hassan developed into a strikingly handsome young man whose good looks and elegant manners reflected his aristocratic forebears. Tall and athletic, with fine features and slender hands, he had a relaxed, easy way of conversing and a quick smile. He was also a good student, emerging from a school in Nablus with a secondary education that qualified him for admission to the American University in Beirut, which was a gathering place for the intelligent and frustrated Palestinian youth.

Ali began to study engineering, but his name and family connections marked him for a leading role in the Palestinians' struggle to regain their lost homeland. In addition to his father's legacy, Ali Hassan married into one of the Arab world's most prestigious families, noted for an implacable hatred of the Jews. His wife was a Husseini and a direct descendant of the Grand Mufti of Jerusalem who during the 1930s and 1940s had agitated against Jewish immigration to Palestine.

In the early 1960s, the young Salameh came to the attention of Yasir Arafat, who soon would take over the quarreling Palestinian refugee organizations and mold them into the PLO. Sensing Salameh's future value, Arafat sent him to Egypt. For one year, Ali Hassan studied the dark arts of intelligence work and evidently proved to be a quick learner. In the late 1960s, Arafat assigned Salameh to a newly organized, ultrasecret intelligence unit within Al Fatah. Its mission was to prepare for the start of terrorist operations. At that time, Al Fatah was being badly outmaneuvered by more radi-

cal Palestinian groups whose use of terrorism had won
enthusiastic support among young Arabs. Arafat, a
clever political tactician, evidently felt he could only
outwit his rivals if he had a clandestine terrorist wing
within his own organization. Hence, in mid-1971, as a
group of young Palestinians swore to avenge the death
of their beloved Abu Ali Iyad, Arafat already had prepared the framework for the organization that would
funnel their fury into terrorism. As a confluence of Arafat's foresight and the bitter events in Jordan, Black
September was born, and Ali Hassan Salameh, who for
months had been held in readiness, now went into action as the organization's chief planner. He quickly
posed as great a threat to Israeli lives and security as his
father had done two and a half decades earlier.

As they reflected upon their new assignment, Yariv
and Zamir, the two Israeli intelligence chiefs, were fully
aware of the difficulties they now faced. It had been
easy enough to brief the cabinet about the desirability
of a liquidation operation. It would be quite another
thing to set up and supervise a killing machine. Yariv
and Zamir knew that it would not suffice only to assas-
sinate Ali Hassan Salameh. Though he was the emotional target for Israeli vengeance, the killing of merely
one leader, even Salameh, would not bring terrorism to
a halt. Another leader would step forward to take his
place. If the operation were to stop terrorism, it must
eliminate not just one leader but the entire leadership.
The life of an Arab terrorist chief must become so perilous that finally no replacements would dare to volunteer.

In order to achieve this goal, Yariv and Zamir had to
devise a new form of counterterrorist warfare. "Killing," as one Israeli assassin once remarked, "requires a
certain art." When undertaken on a large scale, it also
requires a smoothly functioning organization. It would
not be practicable simply to send one or two killers to
Paris or Beirut or wherever Ali Hassan Salameh or one
of the other Black September leaders might be. The assassins would not know their way about in a strange
city. They would not be familiar with the habits of the

intended victim, the capabilities of the local police, the fastest escape route from the country. In fact, they would know hardly any of the dozens of crucial bits of knowledge that would be essential in killing a man and escaping without a trace. Consequently, they might fail to make the hit or, worse yet, they might bungle the killing and get caught.

Yariv and Zamir realized that the war against Black September would require the creation of a new combat unit within Israeli intelligence. There would have to be different squads that prepared the way for the killers, shadowed and identified the target, picked the optimum time and place for the assassination, established getaway routes, handled communications, provided transportation, arranged hotel accommodations and safe houses (espionage parlance for a hideaway where agents can live for brief periods without undue fear of being detected), and the like. The killing operation would take time. Therefore, the team would have to be self-contained and able to maintain itself in the field for weeks at a stretch with a minimum of outside assistance.

There was a further essential consideration: under no circumstances should the team be traceable to Israel. In striking back at Arab terrorism, Israel was, in one respect, operating at a great disadvantage. It was a state that subscribed to all decent and humane conventions of international behavior and could not therefore be caught conducting itself like a criminal. The terrorists, by contrast, were shadowy organizations that had no identifiable states behind them. The Israelis often tried to hold responsible the different Arab countries from whose territory the terrorists operated. But the Arab states simply shrugged off the charges. Hence, if the Israelis were going to fight terror with counterterror, they would have to be very careful not to get caught. The operations would have to be conducted in a manner that minimized the likelihood of discovery.

Among other things, that meant using only highly skilled veteran agents and taking precautions that no equipment or clothing could betray the Israeli involvement. It also meant that the team members should be cosmopolites who could easily pass for citizens of other countries. And, just in case there ever were a mistake and arrests were made, the agents would have to be equipped with very solid fake identities that would stand up even under investigation by foreign police or intelligence agencies.

The complexity of the operation indicated that the team would be large; otherwise, it could not contain the required talents. But the size also had disadvantages. A big team would be difficult to manage, and the greater the number of members, the more chance there was for error or capture. Those were risks the Israelis decided to accept. After a great deal of deliberation, the structure of a hit team was agreed upon. It would be composed of fifteen people, including a leader and his deputy, and would be divided by function into five squads:

—*Aleph* (for the initial letter in the Hebrew alphabet) would consist of two killers to be drawn either from the Mossad or the elite Israeli military units whose members are instructed in the ungentle art of silent assassination. Unlike combatants in modern warfare, who seldom see the victims of their weaponry, the Alephs would be killing with handguns at close range. Sometimes they would look directly into the face of the victim, hear his screams, and see their bullets tear away a life. Since close-up killing can be a shattering experience, the Alephs would have to be highly motivated or very callous—or preferably both.

—*Beth* (for the second letter) was to be made up of two guards and would operate as a unit with the Alephs. While the killers would be performing their mission, the Beth squad would protect the getaway route. If the Alephs ran into difficulties, the Beths would come to their rescue. Both Beths must be good shots and would carry automatics. At least one of them would be a skilled driver (the Mossad has a special course in high-speed and evasive auto-handling techniques). Both Aleph and Beth squads would be forbidden to mix with the other members of the team so that if the killers or guards were ever arrested, other team members could not identify them, should they, too, be apprehended.

—*Heth* (for the eighth letter) would set up the cover that would enable the rest of the team to operate without detection. It would be composed of two people, most often a man and a woman, since a couple attracts less suspicion than two men. The Heth squad would rent apartments, arrange hotel reservations, provide rental cars, and supply all the other necessary logistic support. Since the Heth members would be the front people for the operation, they would need to be especially cosmopolitan, and would require carefully devised covers betraying no trace of the Israeli connection.

—*Ayin* (for the sixteenth letter) would perform the central support role in the operation. Composed of six to eight persons, it would have two crucial functions: 1) tracking the victim to learn his habits and movements in order to determine the proper time and place for the hit, and 2) providing the protective corridor through which the Aleph and Beth squads could quickly withdraw and leave the country.

—*Qoph* (for the nineteenth letter) would handle the communications. Generally, there would be two men. One would keep in touch with the team from a secret post near the scene of operation. The second, stationed temporarily in an Israeli embassy, would act as the relay between the post and the Mossad central in Western Europe, which in turn would provide a direct link to the Tel Aviv headquarters.

In planning the campaign against Black September, the Israelis were not starting from scratch. At the time our story begins, in 1972, Israeli intelligence rightfully enjoyed the reputation of being the country's first and most reliable line of defense. It was famed for its deep, almost uncanny penetration of the Arab nations, which enabled the Israelis to learn enemy intentions far in advance and take measures to block them. It is axiomatic that only an intelligence agency's failures, never its successes, are made public. Yet, on the few occasions when the Israeli hand was exposed in the Middle East, even the failures were impressive. In Syria, the Israeli undercover agent, Elie Cohen, managed to insinuate his way into the top echelon of the country's leadership. For two

years, he radioed incredibly detailed reports on both
political and military affairs to Tel Aviv. But then he
was unmasked as a spy and hanged in the Damascus
Market Square while thousands of Syrians looked on.
The swift and decisive Israeli victory in the Six Days'
War was due, in large measure, to accurate intelligence
information that again testified to the high degree of the
Israeli infiltration into Arab governments and military
establishments.

Because of its extensive information-gathering network in the Middle East and North Africa, Israeli
intelligence possessed much valuable data that it could
swap with Western espionage agencies. The Israelis
traded information and cooperated closely with most
intelligence agencies of the NATO countries as well as
those of France and Switzerland. The chief of the Mossad attended the secret meetings of the heads of Western intelligence agencies, which take place every six
months.

Over the years, the Israelis developed a special relationship with the United States Central Intelligence
Agency, sometimes recruiting Arab agents, who would
have refused to cooperate with Israel, by telling them
that they would be working for the CIA. Sometimes information from those agents was shared with the Americans. Israeli intelligence and the CIA also participated
in a number of joint espionage ventures and scored one
of the major coups of the 1950s, when two Israeli
agents in Moscow managed to secure a copy of the
famed de-Stalinization speech, which had been delivered in secret by Nikita Khrushchev at the twentieth
Congress of the Soviet Communist Party. The CIA arranged for selective leaks of the speech, which contained revelations about Stalin's crimes against his own
people that shook Communist regimes, especially in
Eastern Europe.

From 1969 until mid-1972, Israeli intelligence maintained secret and incredibly sensitive relations with Jordanian intelligence. For long periods, the Israelis kept
resident agents in Amman who passed on to Jordanian
intelligence information on the Palestinian terrorist organizations and the capabilities of Arab armies on Jor-

dan's borders. During this time, King Hussein held a number of clandestine meetings with Israeli leaders (they would meet at night in cars that drove without lights to prearranged rendezvous spots in the desert south of Jerusalem or on an island in the Gulf of Eilat). Israeli security agents were directly involved in the protection of King Hussein's life against repeated assassination attempts by the Palestinian terrorists. That is one reason those attempts never succeeded.

The organization that is generally referred to as "Israeli intelligence" actually consists of three separate services. There is military intelligence, which Yariv headed for a decade until 1972; the Shin Beth (the Hebrew initials for security service), the equivalent of the American FBI, which is responsible for internal security and counterespionage; and the Mossad, the external intelligence agency which was directed by Zamir. The name is taken from the organization's long title—the Central Institute for Information and Espionage. The chief of the Mossad plays a considerably larger role in his country than do his counterparts in the United States and Britain. He is often invited to attend Israeli cabinet sessions and is called upon to brief the secret Ministers' Committee for Security and Foreign Affairs. He deals directly with the prime minister and his advice on security matters is almost invariably followed.

The chief of the Mossad presides over a complex organization that is more than just an intelligence agency. It is also truly the secret arm of the Israeli government abroad. One of its major branches is a clandestine foreign ministry, which deals with countries whose governments, because of political, religious, or geographical reasons, feel they cannot afford to have open diplomatic relations with Israel. In such cases, the Mossad dispatches its own envoy who works with a clandestine official contact; the contact is frequently also an intelligence officer himself. Among the nations maintaining relations on this secret basis with Israel are Turkey, Iran, and Morocco.

A second large division of the Mossad concentrates exclusively on furthering and coordinating Israeli intelligence activities with those of friendly foreign agencies.

Other intelligence services also have liaison operations, but the Israelis, because of their exposed position in the Middle East, make a greater effort to weave their activities into the Western intelligence community.

The three other branches of the Mossad perform more customary intelligence duties:

—An evaluation department analyzes the information supplied by Mossad agents and triangulates it, whenever possible, with data furnished by friendly foreign agencies and other information-gathering means, notably monitoring radio transmissions, interception of telephone conversations, and the like.

—An Arab affairs section specializes almost entirely in infiltrating deep-cover Israeli agents into Arab countries and enlisting Arabs to serve as informers for Israel. Sometimes this section comes under the direction of special operations for specific missions; at other times, it functions alone. For many years it was the most dreaded unit of the Mossad, and the Israelis worked at keeping it so. (Once, when asked why Israel had taken the risk of placing Cohen in such a perilous position in Syria, a high-ranking Mossad officer replied: "Because we wanted to increase the fear of Israeli intelligence.")

—A special operations branch runs the covert intelligence-gathering activities and organizes the occasional "dirty tricks," such as blackmail and recruitment of double agents. Or worse.

Within the special operations branch, the Mossad maintains a killer group that specializes in the liquidation of enemy agents. Earlier, this group was involved in hunting down and killing scores of Nazis, mainly in Europe and South America, who had escaped Allied and West German war crime tribunals. During 1963–1964, this section also provided the gunmen who killed or intimidated the German scientists whom Egyptian President Gamal Nasser had enlisted to build rockets that could have destroyed Israeli cities. By 1972, the killer group's activities were concentrated on the behind-the-scenes war that is ceaselessly being fought among hostile intelligence agencies, especially in the Middle East. Outsiders almost never learn about these killings, but spies are dying all the time. By a conservative estimate, the Israelis alone have lost at least forty agents in the war of the spooks. The deaths are often made to appear as consequences of an innocent auto accident, a self-inflicted wound, or a mysterious disease. In many instances, the person simply vanishes. Later, in a river or a garbage dump, a body is found with all identifiable features surgically removed.

The primary mission of the special operations branch, though, is the secret gathering of information. The special branch maintains a worldwide network of agents, double agents, and informers. Since 1969, when the Arabs started to export terrorism to Western Europe, the Mossad has built up a large covert counterterrorism operation as a defense against attacks on Israeli citizens and property in Europe, using the tested Mossad method of infiltrating the Arab organizations and learning their plans in advance. In this operation, however, rather than alerting Israeli security forces, the Mossad would pass the information to West European police and intelligence agencies. In the early 1970s, after the United States organized an antiterrorism bureau in the State Department to coordinate the activities of the CIA, FBI, and other Western intelligence agencies on a worldwide basis, the Mossad's European operation provided many invaluable preventive tips.

For larger operations, especially those of a paramilitary nature, the Mossad turns for expertise and manpower to a secret outfit of the Israeli army. It is identified only as a reconnaissance unit of the general headquarters. In reality, it is the fire brigade of the Israeli defense forces. Composed entirely of officers and senior sergeants selected mainly from paratroopers and frogmen, the GHQ unit is an elite organization that always has some members on combat alert. The men have to be accustomed to lonely and hazardous duty and capable of fighting in small groups against heavy odds. No trace of their service in the GHQ unit ever appears on their records. Fictitious entries of illnesses and leaves of absence for studying abroad mask their true activities during this period.

Even after an officer or sergeant has joined the unit, he must show selfless courage and great initiative before he is fully accepted. One of the rites of initiation used to be a voluntary trip by foot from the Israeli border across a stretch of the Jordanian desert to the abandoned city of Petra. The thirty-mile journey, which took four or five days, was especially dangerous because the trail passed through moist wadis where a hiker unavoidably left footprints, and he would then be pursued by a Bedouin battalion that guarded the sector. At least twelve men died on the journey to Petra. There was, to be sure, no official requirement to visit Petra, but at one point or another a senior officer in the unit would put the question to a newcomer: "By the way, have you been to Petra?" If the answer was no, the new member would not be considered for extremely perilous or solitary missions.

Unlike the rest of the Israeli army, the GHQ unit's busiest period is peacetime. It specializes in sabotage, reprisal raids, and secret missions far behind enemy lines. Among other things, the GHQ unit blew up the bridges near the Aswan dam in 1968, destroyed fourteen airliners at Beirut airport the next year, and later occupied an island off the shore of Yemen to assure Israeli ships passage through the straits leading to the Red Sea. It was members of the GHQ unit whom Dayan used in spring 1972 to overpower the four Black September terrorists who had hijacked a Sabena jetliner to Lod, and it was this unit that Dayan had wanted to take to Munich on that fateful Tuesday in September to try to free the Israeli hostages from Black September's grip.

In terms of manpower and equipment, Israeli intelligence has never approached the CIA or even the British, but those deficiencies were more than offset by the extremely high caliber of its agents. Of the men recruits, 95 percent came from the paratroopers, frogmen, and other elite branches, including the GHQ unit. Hence, the intelligence newcomers were already well screened for physical toughness and psychological endurance. The women recruits either came from the military services or were selected by veteran agents after they had already proved their aptitude in some aspect of intelligence work.

The basic training of an Israeli agent is extremely arduous, thorough, and hazardous. It lasts one year. During the first six months, the curriculum concentrates on the elementaries of espionage: the use of codes, the handling of weapons (chiefly automatics and submachine guns), and self-defense with judo and karate. There are grueling hours of physical training—"you never know when you are going to have to run," as one veteran agent puts it.

There are equally tiring hours of memory training. At some future time, there may be no possibility to photograph an important scene or person or document, and the agent's mind will be the only recording device available. Agents are told to watch an ordinary movie. Suddenly the film stops and the lights flash on in the classroom. "OK," says the instructor, "you have one minute in which to describe the scene in the last frame, repeat, only the last frame." Students are led to a table that is crowded with objects. They are just beginning to memorize them when a cloth is spread over the table. "What were the ten items in the upper right corner?" demands the instructor. Over and over again, the trainees are shown documents, maps, area photos, and pictures until they learn to recognize the important features and commit them to memory.

They are also introduced to basic espionage techniques that can only be mastered by experience. Shadowing is one of them. The trainees are taken out on the streets of Tel Aviv and someone is pointed out to them. "Follow him," they are told, "but don't let him know it." The person under surveillance is a trained agent who has developed a knack of sensing when someone is on his trail. A second veteran agent keeps the recruit under observation to watch for mistakes and make suggestions for improvements.

When shadowing, the trainee learns to assume a chameleonic role to blend into the local conditions. Rule one is never to do any of the things that spies and detectives do in bad movies and sometimes even in real life. For example, when watching someone in a café, one should never sit alone and read the proverbial newspaper or linger over a solitary cup of coffee, but should instead try to strike up a conversation with some girls, or joke with the waiter, or befriend a drunk. "Do anything to fit into the landscape," Israeli agents are told. "Don't stick out!" The trainees also learn not to telegraph their presence to the suspect by following him too closely. They are taught to put gaps in the surveillance and to hand a subject from one spotter to another, so that the person being trailed does not become suspicious by seeing the same face behind him once too often.

The next field exercise concerns the proper use of assumed identities. The learning process begins with harmless games. The agents are given fake passports with assumed identities and taken to the aircraft arrivals area at Lod where they are told to mix in with passengers debarking from airliners. The test is to see whether they can con their way past the unsuspecting passport control officers at Lod without betraying themselves by signs of nervousness. After that, the agents begin to study infiltration techniques. From the start, this is a potentially dangerous business. A military installation or air base is chosen as a target, and a trainee is told to study the layout and find a way to slip inside. The assignment is to leave, or perhaps collect, a message at a certain point within the restricted area and get back out again without being detected. Unbeknown to the student, the base commander has been alerted by Shin Beth that a terrorist group is planning a raid that evening. Hence, as he tries to carry out the exercise, the student faces the possibility of being captured or even shot at.

By the end of the first six-month period, 30 to 45 percent of the trainees have either dropped out on their own accord or been discouraged by their instructors from trying to continue. The survivors face a far rougher and more realistic second half. In the classroom work, they begin to concentrate on the countries in which they may be operating. Since sometimes they will be expected to pass themselves off as genuine citizens of those countries, they must learn the habits and idiosyncrasies of different social groups within those societies, so that their own actions do not betray them as outsiders.

Social customs and everyday practices are completely taken for granted by native members of a society. But for a stranger who is operating under tension, traveling in several different countries and pretending to be the native of one of them, local practices can pose major stumbling blocks. The various currency systems of ten or twelve European nations alone can cause confusion. How large is the tip you give to the taxi driver? How do you use the pay telephones? Do you deposit the money (and which coin, by the way, do you use?) and then dial, or must you push a button first? What is the procedure for checking into a hotel? Which forms do you sign and how thoroughly are you expected to complete the questions? Do you just sign your name and leave the rest to the reception clerk? What is the standard tip for the hotel porter who carries your bags? What are the general topics of conversation that the man standing next to you in the bar would expect to discuss with a countryman? What are the pressing political issues and how do the various parties divide up on them? Who are the major sports figures? Which two soccer teams have a rivalry going? The amount of detail that an agent must learn in order to operate unobtrusively in foreign countries is absolutely mind-boggling.

The trainee agents have something else drilled into them, too, and that is discipline—a tough, unforgiving, Prussian style discipline. Over and over again, the student is told, in essence: "Always obey orders. Obey the orders one hundred percent—not ninety-nine percent and not one hundred and one percent—but exactly one hundred percent. Do precisely what you are told to do and do it exactly when you are told to—not one minute sooner and not one minute later. If your orders are not completely clear to you, ask at once to have them explained again. Be very, very certain that you fully understand what you are being told to do—and do it. Mind your own business. Don't take an interest in what other agents around you may be doing. You have your job, and they have theirs. Just make certain you do yours.

"Think only when you are ordered to think. Remember: when you are out on an operation, you are just one single person and you cannot possibly know the overall situation. We have the big picture and we will do the thinking for you. We don't want your impressions or analyses of a situation. We want only the facts—the hard, cold, bare facts. We will put them together. You are a member of a team. You must trust your leader entirely, follow him with total confidence, and do whatever he says. This can save your life and it can save the organization."

The recruit is sent through endless exercises to instill a sense of obedience and precision. These drills are to the fledgling agent what close-order marching is to the infantryman—the training that makes response to commands become an automatic reflex. The intelligence trainee, for example, is given a highly complex itinerary that requires a tiring trip through part of Israel. He must make countless bus changes, switch to cabs for certain segments, and arrange to walk past certain points at exact times. Along the route, unseen Mossad officers monitor the student's progress. The trainees are also given assignments that strain both their endurance and patience. They are sent on completely bogus missions to stand on this or that street for hours and watch for a certain person who never comes by. After completing dozens of these exercises, the student begins to grasp the sobering reality that intelligence work is exactly the opposite of what spy novels and the popular imagination make it out to be. It is not romantic and thrilling. It is a business filled with dull routine, long periods of monotonous waiting, and huge amounts of frustration. The agent starts to realize that what his instructors have been telling him is true—he should not think. He must reconcile himself to a situation in which he may never know the pieces of the puzzle or even catch a glimpse of the entire chessboard.

Toward the end of the final six months, the agents are taken individually to Western Europe for a tryout under simulated operational conditions. At some point early on in the trip, after an experienced agent has explained a few of the ropes, the test begins.

"Here is your passport," says the veteran, handing the trainee a travel document. "You are Fritz Schmidt, born October 6, 1943, in Hamburg. Your father and your morther are dead [Israeli agents almost invariably are orphans, which is one of the giveaways of their assumed identities]. You are a salesman for Mercedes Benz. You work in Cologne. You earn fifty thousand deutsche marks a year and you are on your way to a meeting of salesmen in Stuttgart. Here are one hundred marks. Good luck!"

Imagine yourself in the position of such a trainee. Your escort officer has dropped you off in Düsseldorf and told you to meet him again at 2000 hours outside the main post office. You show up, but no one is there. You come back two hours later. No one. Fours hours later, still no one. Anxiety grips your belly. You have been ditched.

What do you do? You can go to the Israeli embassy in Bonn and ask for help, but then you are disgraced and finished. You can turn to the Jewish community and try to borrow some money. You may even be able to keep your behavior secret for a while, but as soon as the Mossad learns what you have done, you will be fired. In the first panicky moments, you have no clear idea of what you are supposed to do. But that is precisely the point of the exercise. Your superiors are eager to observe how you will react in an ill-defined and potentially perilous dilemma.

As you gather your thoughts, you assess the situation. You know you need money and you have two possibilities: you can steal it or you can earn it—though big sums in such circumstances come quickly only by unscrupulous methods. But you will not be judged by the methods, only by the results. If you want top marks, you know you should make your way back to Israel in a short time without having betrayed your cover or your mission.

You will also pass if you are clever enough to double back on the route you have just come along and locate the people who brought you to your present predicament. But reflect for a moment: can you find your way to the Israeli safe house in Frankfurt? Now you remember, you were driven there at night and the auto kept making turns. Was that all done purposely to confuse you? Will you be able to find the agent who shook you off? He was probably wearing a false mustache and a wig, and most certainly he was using a fake name concocted only for the occasion. Can you really hope to find him again? By now he may be on his way to Tel Aviv, laughing at the trick he played on you.

If you do succeed in returning to Israel with your cover intact, you will be treated to an even more exciting excursion. The next trip is either to Cairo or Beirut.

A supervisor gives you a passport and a small file. These papers represent the identity you are expected to assume for the next assignment. "You are a tourist from Europe," the supervisor says. "What can you find out for us in three weeks in Cairo?" So off you go. You travel from Israel on your own Israeli passport to Western Europe, where you will switch to your new identity. But you have to make a decision: do you carry the Israeli passport with you to Cairo or do you hide it somewhere in Western Europe? You may not have had time to make up your mind yet when you are paged under your Israeli name on the public-address system in the airport arrivals hall. You report to the information booth and two men are waiting.

"Will you please come with us?"

"But why?" you object.

"We have to ask you some routine questions. Purely routine. Please come this way."

You are led away, not knowing what is going to happen. What may take place in the next couple of days can be very unpleasant. You may be arrested, interrogated, and perhaps even abused, physically as well as mentally. You may be charged with having come to, say, France with an assignment to gather information for a foreign power. Or, more likely, you will be told that drugs were found in your baggage and that the police have evidence that you have been serving as a courier for a narcotics ring. What should you do? Should you ask to be allowed to appeal to the Israeli embassy for help? Should you tell the police that you are really a nice Jewish boy working on your first assignment and "Look, officer, I even have a fake passport and a fake identity." If you still have your wits about you, you simply keep quiet. After all the harassment you have suffered already, you should suspect that this ordeal is only another test. Your masters will never be satisfied until they have stripped away your defenses and observed how you behave under the most severe stress. After having been captive for a week or two in a faceless safe house in an equally faceless Parisian suburb, you will then be freed, with back slaps and laughs all around, to continue your trip to Cairo.

For three weeks, you experience the emotional roller coaster of being a spy in an enemy country. No amount of training or psychological testing can quite prepare a person for the sensation of being surrounded by an environment that at any moment can turn completely hostile. You are so afraid of being unmasked that you have a surge of teary-eyed gratitude every time someone, be it chambermaid, hotel clerk, or newspaper vendor, routinely accepts you for what you are supposed to be and does not evince any suspicion. You learn to wrestle down your emotions and not to be overly courteous and too effusive. You also learn to control your nervousness when you approach passport checks and when you see police on the street. Under the heightened danger of a hostile country, you begin to realize that your salvation rests in maintaining your assumed identity and making it seem perfectly natural. Increasingly, you become the innocent tourist and less the Israeli spy.

And how much information can you gather in those three weeks? You cannot expect, of course, to divine any really important military or political secrets. But you are not expected to. You can, however, still learn quite a lot that will be of use to the Mossad analysts, who try to keep up to date on goings-on in Cairo. You assess the mood of the city by striking up conversations with people in cafés. You can learn something about economic conditions by going to shops, studying store windows, and making a few purchases yourself. You can make some estimates, admittedly not precise, about foreign influence in Cairo by observing the guests in the major hotels and trying to figure out their nationalities.

After you return to Israel, your performance over the year's course will be evaluated. If you have passed with absolute top marks, you will be assigned to a more advanced course that will prepare you for a specific assignment as a Mossad undercover agent. If you have scored high, but not quite enough, you will be assigned to an intelligence job in Israel, possibly within the Mossad headquarters, or as an operative for the Shin Beth. But if your superiors have any doubts whatsoever about your capabilities, then you have simply lived through a most educational year—about which you are forbidden to speak—and you are told to look around for a job outside the intelligence community. You were weighed in the balance and found wanting. But you should not feel badly; only 15 percent of the candidates who begin the course manage to finish it.

In setting up the new operation, one crucial question was, who should direct the hit teams? The choice was obvious. Michael ————, the director of the Mossad's special operations, was regarded by the inner circles in Israel as nothing short of a genius in intelligence work. He belonged to the tightly knit group that runs the country. And whenever there was an especially brilliant intelligence coup, he would be invited to the small private dinner given by the prime minister. Eastern European by origin, he had fought in the War of Independence as a member of the Haganah's intelligence service and, by 1972, had accumulated a quarter of a century of experience in espionage. He had overseen the establishment of the antiterrorist squads in Western Europe and took a day-by-day interest in that operation.

Mike's first job was to recruit the people for the hit teams. The ideal candidates for Heth (cover) and Ayin (surveillance) squads were the agents already serving in the antiterrorist operation in Europe, because they possessed the essential covers, language skills, and the know-how to conduct themselves unobtrusively in foreign countries. About a dozen or so of these agents were quickly recalled to Israel and sent to a hastily organized training center in the old Roman port of Caesarea, forty-five miles north of Tel Aviv. There they were introduced to the techniques and ground rules of the hit team system.

The hits would be meticulously planned like military operations and the procedures for ingress and withdrawal would be much the same. The Heth squad would enter a country first, followed by the Ayin. The last squads to arrive would be the Aleph and Beth, and they would be the first ones to leave. The Aleph and Beth would have separate travel plans, devised by a special staff, and other team members would know nothing about these arrangements. The Ayin would depart next, and the Heth people would be the last ones out. The communications operators of the Qoph squad would be recruited from among specialists and would not mix with the rest of the team. Everything was to be kept neatly compartmentalized, so that if one squad met with disaster or was captured, the others would not be involved.

In addition, the team members were briefed on the two principles dictated by political considerations: no Jewish communities abroad were to be drawn into the operations; and Israeli embassies and diplomatic channels were to be used sparingly, and then only when there was no chance of Israel's being implicated in the killings.

During the training, the ears of the hit team members echoed with one important exhortation: don't get caught! An escape system was set up to give quick aid and advice to agents who became separated from the team or got into serious trouble. The agent in distress was to dial a certain number in Tel Aviv, which was manned around the clock by Mossad duty officers. He had a code word to identify himself and then was to explain his plight in veiled language.

"My friends ran off without me and I don't like the new people who want to help me," the agent might say.

Assuming the agent was calling from Paris, the duty officer would reply something like this: "OK, go to Le Drugstore on Avenue Matignon in exactly three hours from now and contact a man reading the *Neue Zürcher Zeitung*. He will have a packet of Players cigarettes on his table. Introduce yourself as Löwenbrau beer and he will help you."

The first rule of survival in espionage is: when things

go wrong, start moving. Therefore, the man in Le Drugstore would slip Löwenbrau money, a plane ticket, and perhaps a new forged passport under a different name.

"There will be a message waiting for you at the information counter at Rome airport."

In Rome, Löwenbrau would find a note that gave him an Italian telephone number. When he called that number, Löwenbrau would be given detailed instructions for bringing him speedily to safety. If he were in real trouble and wanted by police, he would be sent back immediately to Israel. If he only had become separated from the team and run out of funds, he would be directed to a Mossad safe house where he could rest and then rejoin his colleagues when the unit regrouped.

In the event of a severe emergency, an Israeli agent's best friend is El Al. Once on board an El Al plane, he is as safe as if he were in Israel. El Al captains are under orders never to surrender a Mossad agent to local police, and the guards aboard El Al aircraft, who are reserve Mossad agents themselves, would fight to defend him. He also has no fear of being hijacked to an Arab country, since El Al crews have orders to fight to the death rather than surrender to hijackers. An El Al captain is under instructions to take off and fly immediately to Israel without passengers if that action is required to protect the life of a Mossad agent. Similarly, a flight would be held at the boarding gate to enable a fleeing agent to catch it.

Mike, who had no problems finding Heth and Ayin people among his squads in Europe, had no trouble finding killers either. Perhaps to his surprise, he even found a volunteer, so to speak, in his own bed. She was Tamar, a woman of exceptional beauty and wit. As a university student in Jerusalem, she had become a favorite with foreign diplomats and United Nations military officers. Because of those contacts, she was recruited by the Mossad and went to work for Mike in the intelligence-gathering service. At some point, she and her boss had become lovers.

It was a classic bittersweet relationship between a young woman and an aging man, made more poignant by the hazards of the profession. Mike, now in his early fifties, was headed toward retirement. For especially dangerous duty, Israeli intelligence awards points that enable agents to collect their pension a few years earlier. Mike had won many of them. But the last thing he wanted to do was to quit. As long as he remained a high-ranking intelligence officer, he had the smell of danger about him. For Tamar, this was the ultimate aphrodisiac. He must have feared that he could keep his mistress only as long as he retained a position of power and prestige. She was not an easy woman to please. Playful and willful, she was self-assured to the point of impertinence, confident of her charms to the brink of provocation. When Mike was entrusted with the command of the liquidation operation, Tamar developed a new interest, and he must have discovered that he had a new hold on his beloved.

Mike established one first-string, or "A," hit team, which was brought up to full fifteen-member strength. Then he set up a second, or "B," team, which had only eight or nine members. Just as sports teams rotate players, the "B" team members would replace weary "A" team members until they were fit and rested. During their breaks, they would come back to Tel Aviv, where Mike would keep operational headquarters. The Mossad's European central, located in the Israeli embassy in The Hague, would serve as a communications relay point.

Though The Hague was the center, many of the Mossad undercover agents already operating in Europe preferred to live in Paris, not only because it is a more pleasant city, but also because they blended more readily into the landscape there. (Paris had, in fact, served as the Mossad's European central until the late 1960s, when Charles de Gaulle told the Israelis to take their espionage operation elsewhere.) Mike, who frequently visited Europe, had rented an apartment for nine hundred francs a month near Montparnasse in the 14th arrondissement. Jonathan Ingleby, who became the most effective killer, had a flat at 124, Avenue Wagram, a few blocks from the Arc de Triomphe. One of Israel's most beautiful and talented women agents kept a flat on the Seine at 3/5, Quai Louis-Blériot, in the chic 16th arrondissement. Her real name was Sylvia Rafael, and she was South African by birth. But she operated under the assumed identity of a Canadian named Patricia Roxburgh and her cover occupation was free-lance photographer.

The agents in Paris noted down one another's telephone numbers according to various schemes that changed the digits. For example, Abraham Gehmer, Mike's deputy, subtracted three numbers from the last digit so that Mike's Paris number, which was 520–8010, became 520–8007. According to her system, Sylvia deducted one number from each digit, so that 520–8010 was written as 419–7909.

Spare keys to the apartments were kept by a Mossad agent named Zwi Steinberg. Born in Rio de Janeiro, he had dual Brazilian-Israeli citizenship. From 1968 to 1971, he lived under his Brazilian identity in Paris as Henrique Waldemar Steinberg and worked supposedly as a chauffeur in the Israeli embassy. Since then, he had lived alternately in Tel Aviv and Paris. A mysterious benefactor deposited three thousand French francs each month to his account in the Crédit Commercial de France in Paris. Steinberg was far too clever to write the addresses on the keys. Instead, he coded them with the name of the cinema nearest to the apartment. Sylvia's key, for example, was labeled Eiffel for a nearby movie theater; Ingleby's key was Wepler; Mike's key was Bobino, and so on. In all, there were at least eight separate Mossad apartments in Paris.

While the hit team members were training in Caesarea, Mossad armaments specialists were searching for the weapon best suited for the job. They began with the premise that it should be a small, relatively silent automatic. They quickly settled on the .22-caliber. For a long time their choice confused police and other intelligence agencies who, on learning details about the assassination, refused to believe that a professionally run liquidation operation would employ such a "harmless" weapon. Yet, contrary to popular conceptions, the .22 is not just a boy's gun fit only for picking off squirrels. It fires a highly potent bullet, and the Israelis already had selected a short-barreled automatic of that caliber for the security guards aboard El Al jetliners. For safety reasons, the cartridge in the El Al weapon carried a very light powder loading so that the bullet had a limited kill range. Thus, if a slug missed a skyjacker, it was less likely to injure a passenger fatally or puncture the fuselage. On the one occasion when El Al guards opened fire in flight, the passengers heard only a pop, pop sound, similar to that of small firecrackers.

In choosing the Aleph weapon, the Mossad experts followed the El Al approach. Since the killing would be done at very close range, the bullets could also carry light powder loadings, this time to reduce noise and attract less attention. The maximum effective range of the modified bullets was only about fifty feet. After testing a large number of .22 pistols, the armaments specialists decided on a long-barreled, semiautomatic Beretta normally used for target practice. This Italian-made weapon proved to be the most reliable, and the least likely to jam during rapid fire.

Two crucial modifications turned the Beretta into a very soft-spoken murder weapon. One was an adjustment of the trigger to make its action easier, so that the weapon could be fired more quickly. The other involved the reloading mechanism. To explain, a semiautomatic pistol is a very efficient piece of machinery that reloads itself after each shot until its ammunition supply is exhausted. This is done through a system of exhaust gas and springs. When the bullet fires, the explosive force drives back the slide, which runs along the top of the weapon, ejecting the spent cartridge. At that instant, the spring in the magazine, located in the pistol grip, forces a fresh bullet into the space in front of the firing chamber. Another spring causes the slide to travel back almost instantly to the closed position; during its swift passage, the slide cocks the hammer and slams the new bullet into the chamber. Consequently, if the Aleph Berettas were to operate properly with bullets that had less explosive force than normal, the spring in the blowback mechanism would have to be fine-tuned commensurately.

For ammunition, the Mossad specialists selected a cartridge manufactured by a West German munitions maker, and they extracted a part of the powder before replacing the lead projectile. The selection of foreign-made equipment was deliberate, for the weapons and ammunition should bear no mark of their true owners.

Meanwhile, other Mossad experts were working to disguise the origins of the hit team members as well. They were devising the fake identities and forging the foreign passports that would enable the hit team members to pose as other people. Some of the team would continue to use the covers that they had already established during their recent service in Europe. Others would require entirely new identities and supporting documents.

The creation of false but nonetheless convincing identities is one of the most important capabilities of an intelligence agency. It is also one of the most sinister. The fake identities throw a cloak of impenetrability over an intelligence agency and enable it to undertake operations that political leaders would not otherwise countenance. By the same token, the use of fake identities often has significant psychological effects upon the agents themselves: they are not as accountable for their own actions as they would be under their true names; yet, the psychological and moral strain of being two people can cause an agent to begin wondering who he really is, and the acts committed under an assumed identity sometimes come back to haunt the real person.

Few people outside the intelligence business know how false identities are devised or how much effort goes into their creation. All major intelligence agencies have special sections dealing exclusively with the construction of fake biographies and the forgery of official documents. Because of their wide international contacts, the Israelis are probably more adept than most in the manufacture of persons who really do not exist.

The Mossad fabricates three different categories of fake identities:

1) Temporary, meant to last no longer than seventy-two hours. That is roughly the time it takes for police investigators in the average major country to check

through Interpol with police and registrars of vital facts in the country of which the holder of the fake identity supposedly is a citizen. To devise a temporary cover is a simple matter. A name is picked, generally a fairly common one, and a fake passport produced, as well as a driver's license and an international vaccination record. The name may belong to a real person, or it may be invented. The agent is given only a bare sketch of the assumed identity; usually he or she need learn no more than occupation, parents' names, address, marital status, birth date, and the reason for the trip. These covers, of course, are extremely flimsy. If the agent is apprehended, the identity will be rapidly peeled away, exposing the hand of Israeli intelligence.

2) Semipermanent, intended to endure for months and even years, and to withstand limited investigation by police authorities or rival agencies. For these covers, the Mossad agents often select a real person in a European or North American country, who remains totally unaware that his or her identity has been usurped. Patricia Roxburgh, for example, did not know that Sylvia Rafael was using her name. The person is chosen by a Mossad investigator because age group and general physical characteristics roughly correspond to those of an Israeli agent. In most countries, bureaus of vital statistics issue copies of birth certificates to any person who writes in claiming to be that person. Hence, it is relatively easy for the Israelis, or any intelligence agency for that matter, to collect the basic documentation needed to establish a life.

The Mossad investigators then learn as much as they can about the real person and send a report to headquarters in Tel Aviv. There, other experts write the biography on which the new identity will be based. Often it is a composite of the real person's life and that of the agent, since the fewer details the agent has to memorize the better. The great drawback with this type of cover is that there are two persons of the same name, birth date, and parentage running around the world. If the agent is caught and subjected to a thorough investigation, the police are likely to discover that there is a second person bearing the same name and background. Further research will reveal the fraudulent nature of the agent's identity.

To avoid such embarrassments, the Mossad often tries to use the identity of a person who has disappeared. The Israelis maintain a small operation in Europe that deals with precisely that variety of identities. Through contacts in European police departments, they find out the names of people who, for some reason or other, have simply dropped from sight. They check the missing person out, trying to determine the probability of a sudden reappearance. If the person seems likely to stay lost, the Mossad may model an identity on him. Mike, for example, used the cover of a Frenchman named Edouard Stanislas Laskier, who apparently had disappeared sometime in 1972.

The Israelis may take measures to protect assumed identities. The Mossad may pay a sum of money, perhaps $10,000 or so, for the use of an identity. Most often, the person is moving to a new continent, and an Israeli agent, in effect, says: "Tell me everything about your life—your parents, your schooling, your friends, your career. Don't be surprised if you hear of another person using your name and don't come back without letting us know in advance."

The Mossad also avails itself of identities of immigrants to Israel. Unbeknown to the new arrivals, Israeli intelligence sometimes lifts biographical facts from the official files and bases a cover on them. It is a very solid identity, since the real person is within the borders of Israel, often in a kibbutz, beyond the reach of foreign police forces or hostile intelligence agencies who might trace the assumed identity to the authentic person.

3) Foolproof, or nearly so, designed to last indefinitely. Years of effort and large amounts of money can go into the establishment of such a cover. The new person may be entirely fictitious or may be based upon a real person who has died, disappeared, or moved to Israel. In any event, a fabricated biography is drawn up in great detail. It is then checked out by an agent, who travels to the places where the person supposedly lived. Do the addresses really exist? Or did they at the time? Has the childhood home been torn down and replaced

by a high-rise building? Is the name of his school correct? Who were his schoolmates? And where are they now?

After the general biographical outline is deemed to be viable, several agents may be engaged in giving the new identity breath and life. One agent assumes the new identity. The others cover his cover. They are the classmates who have not forgotten him, the friends with whom he exchanges letters, the teachers who have retired and now live in Greece, but would be happy to write a testimonial about their former student.

For example, let us suppose that the Mossad decides to create a prosperous Belgian businessman of German ancestry named Ditmar Stern. Stern comes to life first in Italy where he buys a house and property. He tells people that he has come there as a representative of a Belgian firm and was originally from the Flemish part of Belgium. Meanwhile, the Mossad supplies him with a business front in Belgium; he might, for instance, import Belgian lace to Italy. He uses a Belgian passport, which is actually a forgery.

Israeli agents in Belgium work to buttress the veracity of the cover. In Stern's name, they purchase property near the German border where Flemish is spoken. After a year or so, Stern himself comes to Belgium and settles in his property. He pays his taxes, continues the lace trade, and appears to be a highly respectable citizen. He becomes acquainted with the local authorities and, over a few convivial glasses of wine, expresses a desire to become a Belgian citizen. In Belgium, so far, he has been using a fake West German passport, and he has a forged birth certificate from a small East German town whose files were burned in an air raid two years after Stern's supposed birth.

At the opportune moment he presents his birth certificate to the Belgian authorities and finally becomes what he had said he was in Italy: a Belgian citizen. He now is well established in two countries with his new identity. His next step may be to start trading in lace and other goods with Arab countries and to begin traveling to them. Maybe later he will even move to one of them, in order to run his export business more effectively.

Or, the identity could be taken over by an Aleph killer or a Beth guard. This sort of very solid cover was used by the killer Jonathan Ingleby, who posed as a British company director living in London's fashionable West End.

By early October 1972, the A hit team was prepared for action. Already Israeli agents in Europe were lining up a list of victims. Above all, they were searching for Ali Hassan Salameh.

FOUR

As the Israeli agents quickly learned, Ali Hassan Salameh was not an easy man to find. He darted unexpectedly from one hiding place to another; sometimes he
traveled alone and at other times he was accompanied
by one or two bodyguards. In order to elude possible
pursuers, Ali Hassan made frequent switches of identity. Of course, he never used his own name and passport. Instead, he traveled variously under at least six
assumed identities, each with a separate passport. He
even had a French passport that listed his place of birth
as Corsica to account for his dark skin.

After the Munich massacre, Ali Hassan Salameh apparently crossed over from East Berlin to West Berlin
and went to West Germany. But there a roundup of suspicious Arabs was in progress. Ali Hassan was not
touched, but he prudently left Germany quickly for Beirut, where it appears he may have stayed for several
weeks before returning to Western Europe. To the utter
frustration of his Israeli trackers, he now had dropped
completely from sight.

Since the Israelis could not locate Salameh, the hit
team began its operation against targets a bit further
down the list.

In early October, a beautiful blond woman suddenly
started paying visits to a block of apartments in Piazza
Annibaliano, which is located in a pleasant residential
section of northern Rome. She was interested in a certain Arab living in one of the buildings, and she quizzed
the concierge and neighbors about him. She wanted to
know his habits—when he went to work, when he came
home—and who his friends were. In the course of her

investigations, she learned that he used Entrance C and that he usually came home late.

The Arab in question was Wael Zwaiter, a lively, wispy Palestinian who had been in Rome for sixteen years. If any one man ever appeared to be different things to different people, it was Zwaiter. Among his many artist and left-wing political friends, he was known as a gentle intellectual whose two consuming interests in life were publicizing the Palestinian cause and translating Arab poetry. His major literary achievement so far had been translating *A Thousand and One Nights* from Arabic into Italian. He seemed to be an utterly harmless person, who seldom kept one job for very long, moved frequently from one modest apartment to another, and was generally broke.

The Rome police took a more skeptical view of Zwaiter. They had observed that he sometimes made contact with members of Al Fatah's intelligence service, Razd, and they suspected that he might have knowledge of Black September operations. After Black September blew up a pipeline in Trieste in early August 1972, they pulled him in for questioning. A brother of Zwaiter's was expelled from West Germany after the attack on the Israeli Olympic team in Munich.

The Israelis had an even darker impression of Zwaiter. They regarded him as the Black September chief in Italy, and had a damning bill of particulars against him. Among other things, they held him responsible for the first El Al hijacking, when a Rome–Tel Aviv flight was diverted to Algeria, and more recently for a bomb explosion aboard an El Al 707 in August 1972. In that incident on a Tel Aviv bound flight, two young Arabs had given a tape recorder as a going-away present to two English girls they had met in Rome. In reality, the tape recorder was a bomb, triggered to detonate when the plane's atmospheric pressure reached cruising altitude. Fortunately, the girls packed the gift in their luggage, and since the baggage compartments in El Al jets are lined with armor plating, the plane did not disintegrate in the air. The El Al captain, seeing the flash of a fire-warning light, pressed the SOS signal that alerted the Rome control tower. Then the captain, who also flew Skyhawks for the Isareli air force, dived the 707 as if it were a fighter plane. Meanwhile, Rome control frantically cleared airspace and a runway for an emergency landing. Within six minutes from the time of the explosion, the El Al jet touched down safely.

The Mossad wanted to teach Arab terrorists a lesson on the consequences of imperiling El Al by making an example of Wael Zwaiter. There was a further consideration that put him so high on the Mossad's list: he was, as it is called in the trade, a "soft target." Like Ghassan Kanafani, whom the frogmen had claimed as the first victim in Beirut, Zwaiter did not have a bodyguard, carried no weapon, and took no safety precautions. His only protection was his well-established cover.

On the evening of October 16, Zwaiter spent several hours at the home of an Italian woman friend, chatting about the Palestinian cause. Then, on the way back to his flat, he popped into the Trieste Bar next door to make a phone call. At the time, he was working as a translator in the Libyan embassy, and was trying to recruit Italian technicians to work in the Libyan oil fields.

At precisely 10:30, as he headed toward the stairwell of Entrance C, a neighbor couple happened to be walking behind him. Just as Zwaiter reached the entrance, the couple saw shadows swiftly moving in the vestibule and, taking fright, made a quick detour toward another entrance.

Evidently, Zwaiter either failed to notice the strange figures or sensed no danger. His retreating neighbors heard him utter a loud cry. The "shadows" were two Israeli gunmen who quickly pumped twelve .22 bullets into his head and body. One of the slugs struck the book *A Thousand and One Nights* that Zwaiter was carrying in his right coat pocket and lodged between the pages.

Waiting outside in the getaway car, the Beth squad was having difficulty remaining inconspicuous. They were too good-looking and behaving in an unusual manner. Mike, the driver, looked elegant in a natty grey suit and Tamar, his companion, was wearing her striking blond wig. They had pulled their green Fiat 125 to the curb directly in front of Entrance C, but remained seated in the car. Other people were also parking cars along the street, but they were climbing out to go to a nearby movie. Furthermore, when another auto took the space in front of them, they gestured emphatically to the driver to give them more room.

"Oh, why not," the driver thought to himself and pulled forward.

Customers leaving the Trieste Bar were becoming curious about the couple in the car. Uncomfortably aware of the attention, Mike and Tamar sought to give the appearance of being two lovers by embracing and kissing passionately. But the display of affection only provoked greater interest, and bystanders edged closer to the auto.

"Look at those two kissing!" someone exclaimed.

At that instant, the killers rushed from Entrance C. The two men approached at a half-run, and the bystanders noticed that they held their arms in strange positions as if to conceal something. One of them held his right hand inside his suit jacket on his left hip while with his free hand he kept his jacket closed. The other crossed his arms over his chest to hold his raincoat closed and his right hand was thrust inside the flap. Hiding their Berettas in that manner, the Alephs, both large, strong men, brushed past the onlookers gathered near the Fiat.

As the two killers dived into the back seat, the car took off "like a bat of hell," as one witness put it. General Zwi Zamir, who was sitting nearby in a second car, must have caught his breath. The operation nearly ended in an accident. Driving without lights, the Fiat almost collided with a minibus at the first intersection.

Later, the getaway car was found abandoned on Via Bressanone, the street leading out of Piazza Annibaliano, about three hundred yards from the site of the killing. There the Aleph-Beth squads had switched to another auto. Wiped clean of fingerprints, the Fiat yielded only one piece of evidence: an unfired .22 cartridge, manufactured by a West German firm, whose shell matched the spent ones found in the vicinity of Zwaiter's body.

The Aleph killers rushed to Rome airport where they

caught a midnight flight that whisked them out of the country. Their total time in Italy: less than five hours.

Not all the Israeli antiterrorist operations were meant to maim and kill. Some were intended solely to effect the quick retirement of Arabs who so far had played only a smaller part in terrorist activity. The Israelis would try to get them just after they had been recruited or given an assignment for a more serious mission.

The scene: It is evening. A Palestinian worker and his family are together in their apartment in the Paris suburb of Gif-sur-Yvette. The phone rings.

VOICE *(speaking in Arabic):* Is this Abdullah Sayed, who lives in apartment 17E rue de la Gare, has two children—Farid and Leila—and whose wife is Fatima? And your dog is called Médor? And you work at the Foche Ball Bearing factory?

ABDULLAH: Yes, yes. But why do I have this honor?

VOICE: We want to bring you greetings from your mother and father. They are with us in Nablus [a Palestinian village on the Israeli-held West Bank].

ABDULLAH: How do my parents fare?

VOICE: They are well, but unfortunately they will soon be mourning for you.

ABDULLAH: What do you mean?

VOICE: Look, my friend, we do not want you to get hurt and we know that you are associating with people who will land you in very serious trouble. You received a message two days ago for a mission. Don't carry it out!

ABDULLAH *(angrily):* You go to hell!

VOICE: We'll see who gets there first!

Abdullah slams down the receiver. At that instant, some people start to pound violently on the front door until it collapses in splinters. Then there is the sound of men running from the building, and they are seen jumping into a car that speeds away. Abdullah's wife and children are crying. Médor is barking. Abdullah is very frightened.

* * *

Other methods: A large package arrives in the post. The recipient, again an Arab worker in Europe who has been recruited by Black September, opens the box only to find another box inside, and within it another one, and another until he rips apart the final small box. In it is an envelope. In the envelope is a note. "This could have been a bomb," it reads.

In other cases, the Israelis sent air tickets or cash. The message, whether explicit or implied, was always the same: quit now—or else! In this manner, the Mossad sought to chip away at the support Black September could command among the thousands of Arab workers and students in Western Europe. There are, of course, no statistics to illustrate the effectiveness of the Israeli campaign, but obviously their arguments were persuasive.

Even as the intimidation campaign was getting underway, the Mossad began designing its hits to have the maximum psychological impact on the Arabs. "Look at what a long arm we have," the Israelis were saying. "See how clever we are. No one can escape us." If the deaths of Kanafani and Zwaiter had caused fear throughout the Arab ranks, the dispatch of the third victim was meant to absolutely terrify them.

The target was Dr. Mahmoud Hamshari, the representative of the Palestinian Liberation Organization in Paris. The Israelis put out the word privately that Hamshari was the Black September chief in France. It was a designation that buttressed the Mossad's contention—at that time not widely shared by knowledgeable journalists and other intelligence agencies—that Black September was, in reality, an integral part of the PLO. The Israelis claimed that Hamshari had been involved in the assassination attempt against Ben-Gurion in Copenhagen in 1969 and later in the midair bomb explosion of the Swissair jetliner that killed forty-seven persons.

A middle-aged man who lived with his wife and daughter in an apartment at 175, rue d'Alésia, Hamshari moved freely about in Paris and had only just begun to take precautions for his personal safety. It would still have been a simple matter to shoot him down in the street. The Mossad preferred something far more spectacular.

For two weeks or more, an Ayin squad shadowed not only Hamshari but also his wife and daughter to observe the family's daily routine. The spotters established that on week-day mornings Mrs. Hamshari walked her daughter to and from school, leaving her husband alone in the apartment. Meanwhile, several explosive experts were brought to Paris from Tel Aviv.

As the chief PLO representative in France, Hamshari was the equivalent of Palestinian ambassador and, as part of his job, he met with journalists for interviews and off-the-record background sessions. In early December, a Mossad agent telephoned Dr. Hamshari and introduced himself as an Italian journalist. He invited the Palestinian to have coffee the next morning at a café in the neighborhood. The appointment was set for the time Mrs. Hamshari would be out with her daughter.

While Dr. Hamshari was having coffee with the "Italian journalist," the squad of Mossad bomb experts entered his apartment. Four or more Beth guards stood watch outside the building and in the hallway. The technicians affixed a highly sophisticated explosive device, well hidden from view, to the underside of the telephone table. It would not do to use the old-fashioned-type bomb that went off the first time the phone rang—this one had to be very special.

Throughout the day and part of the next (December 8), the explosive remained undetected and harmlessly inactive, even though the telephone rang repeatedly. Shortly before noon, while Mrs. Hamshari and the daughter were out, the telephone buzzed once more.

As Dr. Hamshari picked up the receiver, the caller identified himself as "the Italian journalist" from the day before.

"Is this really Dr. Hamshari?" the voice inquired.

"Lui-même," he replied—"this is he."

The next sound the PLO representative heard in the receiver was a high-pitched whine. It was an electronic signal transmitted through the telephone and it triggered the bomb under the telephone table. Severely wounded by shrapnel, Dr. Hamshari lived only long enough to tell Paris police about his meeting with the Italian journalist and the telephone call.

The Israelis were undoubtedly delighted that their victim had used his dying breath to provide a few details of the diabolically ingenious plot that led to his demise.

During the autumn of 1972, while the hit team was being set up, Arab gunmen had been busy. Their two main targets: Mossad operatives who had contacts among Arabs in Europe, and double agents who had infiltrated Black September's organization.

On September 10, only five days after the Munich attack, an undercover Mossad officer named Zadok Ophir, operating out of the Israeli embassy in Brussels, took a call from one of his Palestinian contacts. The Arab demanded a meeting. That evening, as Ophir approached the rear booth of a Brussels restaurant at the appointed time, he was struck by pistol fire and gravely wounded. The gunman escaped.

Black September interspersed their precisely targeted killings with less selective methods of murder. For example, shortly after the Ophir shooting they mailed from Amsterdam a flurry of at least forty letterbombs to Israeli diplomats and U.S. officials throughout the world. In London, the Israeli agricultural attaché, Dr. Ami Schechori, was delighted to spot a thick envelope with a Dutch postmark among his morning mail. "Now this is really important!" he said jokingly to a colleague. Schechori, who was soon to return to Israel, had ordered Dutch flower seeds he wanted to plant back home.

As he tore open the yellow envelope, he unwittingly triggered a small spring-loaded detonator similar in design to a mousetrap. A plunger whacked into three ounces of *plastique,* causing a violent explosion that sent a shower of fatal splinters from the desk into Schechori's body.

On November 13, three Arab gunmen forced their way into the Paris apartment of a Syrian journalist named Khodr Kannon, who had been trying to gather information for an article about Black September. The publicity-shy organization suspected he was an Israeli agent. Leaving him fatally wounded, the gunmen escaped in a Peugeot 304.

The tempo of attack and counterattack accelerated. On December 28, Black September invaded the Israeli embassy in Bangkok, taking several diplomats and their wives hostage. But after thirty-six tense hours the terrorists lost their nerve. Though their compromise was regarded by other Black Septembrists as a severe loss of face for the organization, the Bangkok commandos accepted a safe-conduct flight to Cairo personally arranged by President Anwar el-Sadat, who had been unavailable three and a half months earlier during the Munich crisis.

The next move was Israel's. For several uneasy years, the Mossad had been aware that the KGB, the principal Soviet intelligence agency, was providing weapons and training to the Palestinian guerrillas. Each year a certain number of terrorists, estimated at an average of eighty to one hundred, traveled either to the Soviet Union or Cuba for schooling in insurgency warfare and sabotage. There was also a limited interchange of information between the terrorists and the KGB. For example, Black September may have supplied information on Libya to the Soviets, who otherwise were shut out of that country. In turn, the KGB may have given Black September some data on Western and Israeli intelligence agencies. By far the most important Soviet contribution to the terrorist cause was weaponry, notably the AK-47 attack rifle.

For years the Israelis had suspected that the contacts between the KGB and the terrorists were made in Beirut. But later the Mossad managed to break the Soviet code and were able to decipher the secret Russian radio transmissions between the KGB headquarters in Moscow and their stations in the Middle East. As a result, the Mossad learned that the KGB central for Middle East terrorism was actually located in Cyprus. A KGB general and a GRU (Soviet military intelligence) colonel were secretly stationed in the Soviet embassy in Nicosia.

The Israelis were eager to discourage Arab terrorists from doing business with the KGB. In late 1972, a Mossad surveillance team arrived on Cyprus. Then, in mid-January, Mike——— and Jonathan Ingleby checked into the Olympic Hotel in Nicosia.

On the evening of January 24, an Arab who went under the name of Hussein Abad Al Chir returned to his room in the Olympic. He came directly from a meeting with the KGB and carried in his pocket a five-thousand-dollar check from a Cypriot undercover KGB agent. As soon as the Arab went to bed and switched off his light, an explosion launched him and his mattress into the ceiling. Somewhere in the vicinity, a Mossad agent had been watching. When the window went dark, he pressed the button on a radio transmitter, sending the impulse that touched off the explosive. It was the midnight version of the Hamshari exit.

Only two days later, Black September exacted revenge. By this time, the Mossad had gone on to the offensive in Europe and was not only trying to intimidate Arabs from cooperating with Black September, but was actively attempting to recruit them as informers. In one European city after another, Mossad agents were seeking out Palestinians and making offers. (*Sample approach:* "You don't have to like us, but at least we could work together. Just tell me whom do you meet with? What do you discuss? Do you have visitors from Black September? Are you asked to provide information? Is anyone trying to recruit you?") If the Palestinian refused to cooperate, the Mossad agent might very well return with more compelling means of persuasion, including threats against the man's family in the Israeli-held West Bank or pleas from them that he should be "reasonable."

It was a tough and uncompromising business. One of the practitioners was a Mossad agent named Baruch Cohen, who traveled frequently to Madrid where he had managed to recruit several Palestinian students at the university. On January 26, he had an appointment to meet one of his contacts near the kiosk at a sidewalk café on Avenue Martin. As Cohen approached the kiosk, he sensed he was walking into a trap. He reached for his weapon, but before he could draw, he was shot down. His assassin sped to the airport and made a clean getaway.

Cohen's death reminded the hit team members of an unnerving reality. True, they were the hunters. But they had to accept that they were also the hunted. And they were being stalked by utterly ruthless killers who might strike at any moment. The danger of sudden death greatly heightened the strain in a situation already more charged with tension than a normal person could bear.

Taken in small doses for short periods of time, danger can be a powerful aphrodisiac. But over a longer period, danger turns into a corrosive cancer that fatigues the brain and warps the personality. After a few weeks of living in peril, most agents begin to suffer from anxiety neuroses that turn even the simplest and most ordinary workaday routines into fear-laden episodes. The doorbell rings unexpectedly and the agent breaks out in cold sweat. The telephone rings and the caller has dialed the wrong number; the agent suspects the opposition was making sure he was home before sending over an assassin.

Agents can have no real friends outside their circle of colleagues, for they are always fearful that other people might see through their cover. About the only member of the hit team who still tried to retain any semblance of a normal life was the beautiful and vivacious Sylvia Rafael. She had been living in Paris as an undercover Israeli information-gatherer for several years prior to her recruitment for the hit team. Her hobby was playing bridge, and she had a number of friends, mainly United States and British journalists, who prized her as a clever and talented partner. After the hits began, Sylvia puzzled her friends by frequently canceling out at the last moment. On several occasions, the stood-up bridge players questioned her later about the reason for her sudden change of plan. She would reply: "Oh, I have this wonderful boyfriend Wolfgang, but we are always having quarrels, and I have to dash off and patch things up."

Even Sylvia, who was an exceptionally strong and well-balanced person, showed in the lines around her eyes the strain of danger and living lies. Most agents fare much worse. Seeking to allay their anxieties, they survive on a diet of tranquilizers, sleeping pills, and alcohol. Actually, no one survives for very long. The useful life of an undercover agent is generally no more than five years. The Israeli undercover agents are well paid (usually about five thousand dollars a month, or five times their normal salary), because when they finally have to retire, it is unlikely that their crippled nerves and weakened constitutions will qualify them for a good job. During the war of kill and counterkill, several members of the hit team developed stress-caused sicknesses, mainly mental depression and heart disease. They also aged shockingly quickly; a man or woman of thirty often appeared to be at least ten years older. Explained an Israeli assassin: "Each life you take diminishes your own."

The hit team's mission was especially perilous and taxing. They were operating in a no-man's-land where their opponents, thanks to the influence of Arab oil and European timidity, enjoyed more than an even break, and they were living without protection in Paris apartments. Their only real defense was their well-devised fake identities, yet their mission required them to jeopardize these covers. They were engaged in surveillance of Arabs and infiltration of Arab organizations not only in France but throughout Western Europe. This meant they had to show their faces. Hence, they could never know whether at some time one of their opponents might become suspicious. He would have seen their faces just once too often and would begin to ask questions.

Aside from the continuous anxiety, the hit team was working incredibly long and harrowing hours. The operational plans for the various hits were organized as thoroughly as the shooting script for a movie. Generally at least two or three weeks of surveillance took place before a target was definitively selected. Then, after the special branch in Tel Aviv had devised the scenario for the kill, another week or so of shadowing was required before the Alephs went into action. Surveillance work is both extremely boring and extremely demanding. It calls for a discipline that is painfully contradictory—to wait patiently for hour upon hour and yet to be always alert at precisely the moment something finally does happen. In addition to the surveillance duties, many of the hit team members were still engaged in their previous information-gathering jobs and in the intimidation operations by which the Israelis were attempting to frighten off lower echelon Black Septembrists with threats rather than bullets. Now, after the Cohen death, the agents had to add the fear of sudden death to all their other concerns.

Black September was proving to be more deadly and more ruthless all the time. On the evening of March 1, 1973, seven Arab gunmen invaded the Saudi Arabian embassy in Khartoum during a farewell party in honor of a departing U.S. diplomat. Their goal was twofold: 1) to ransom Black Septembrists and other terrorists from jails throughout the world; and 2) to expunge the stain of the backdown in Bangkok from Black September's record. In the process, the Black September raiders inadvertently buttressed the Israeli assertion that the PLO was behind the terrorists.

Until then, the PLO had denied any knowledge of or association with Black September, but Khartoum undermined their protestations. As subsequent investigations clearly established, the attack was planned by the chief of the PLO office in Khartoum, who departed for Libya shortly before it began. The Black September squad was driven to the embassy in a PLO Land Rover. Each terrorist carried handwritten instructions on how to conduct the raid, which had been prepared by PLO officials. One of the terrorists, whose cover name was Tareq, was told, for example: "Issue instructions strictly and violently in a strong voice to all those in the hall." As the biggest giveaway of all, the Black September raiders carried a portable radio to communicate with the PLO headquarters in Beirut.

After they had captured the embassy, the terrorists

released all the prisoners except five diplomats: the Saudi ambassador, the Jordanian chargé d'affaires, a Belgian chargé, and two Americans—departing Ambassador George Curtis Moore, in whose honor the party had been given, and his successor, Cleo A. Noel, Jr.

Then the raiders made known their demands by telephone. Jordan should release a high-ranking Black September leader, Abu Daoud, and sixteen other Black Septembrists; West Germany should set free the imprisoned members of the Baader-Meinhof gang; the United States should hand over Sirhan Sirhan, Robert Kennedy's assassin; and Israel should release the two Black September women captured in the Sabena jet at Lod. Otherwise, the five diplomats would be shot.

None of the countries was willing to meet those demands. As the hours passed, Black September reduced their conditions to the release of only Sirhan Sirhan and Abu Daoud. Still, the United States and Jordan would not budge. President Richard Nixon stated in a televised press conference that Washington would not cave in to blackmailers.

For a day and a half the stalemate dragged on. Since the terrorists were not empowered to take any further action on their own, they conferred by radio with Beirut, asking for instructions. The conversations were monitored by Israeli intelligence, even though the Black Septembrists were using ultrahigh frequency shortwave, which is difficult to intercept. After several talks, Beirut sent a code word: "Remember the blood, Nahr el Badawi." It was a reference to a Palestinian refugee camp in Lebanon, which had been attacked a few days earlier by an Israeli raiding party. The code meant to carry out the execution.

The killers aimed their submachine guns at the Belgian, Guy Eid, and the two Americans, Moore and Noel, who had already been beaten and bound. They began firing at the feet and legs and emptied a full magazine of bullets into each of the victims.

A short time later, the Black Septembrists were given another order by radio from Beirut, this time to surrender. The leader of the squad proved to be Rizig Abu Gassan, the deputy PLO chief in Khartoum. In the

PLO office, Sudanese police discovered sketches and plans for the attack.

"We are proud of what we have done," boasted Gassan.

Black September maintained its offensive. In quick succession, Palestinian gunmen carried out three operations in Cyprus in which they killed an innocent Israeli businessman, attacked the home of the Israeli ambassador, and unsuccessfully attempted to hijack an Israeli plane. In Rome, Black Septembrists shot down an Italian guard who was employed at the El Al ticket office. All the while, they kept up their campaign of death in small packages by mailing dozens of letterbombs to Israeli and American officials from unwitting post offices in Israel and Netherlands.

In grim counterpoint to the Black September killings, the Israeli hit team fought back effectively, and the European press began carrying a number of short items about the unexplained deaths of mysterious Arabs. In the space of only three months, the Mossad dispatched victims number five through twelve.

Late in the evening of April 6, a well-dressed Arab was seen hurrying along the stately streets of Paris's 8th arrondissement near place de la Madeleine. As he walked, he continually threw anxious glances over his shoulder. To other pedestrians, it was obvious that he was trying to outdistance two very athletic young men, who were gaining on him.

The Arab was Dr. Basil Al Kubaissi, a forty-year-old Iraqi professor who had taught at the American University in Beirut. According to the Mossad's information, he was in charge of the arsenals of firearms and explosives that were kept in Arab diplomatic missions throughout Europe. He made certain that the proper weapons were ready in time for terrorist operations.

On that April evening, Al Kubaissi was returning to his Paris hotel. Near the Grecian pillars of the Église de la Madeleine, the two young men overtook him, and drew their long-barreled Berettas.

"Non! Non! Ne faites pas cela!" he cried—"No, no, don't do it!"

The Aleph men opened fire at point-blank range. After nine shots, they stopped. They saw their victim was dying.

Commenting on his death, the PFLP radio said that Al Kubaissi had been on an important mission in Europe.

Three nights later, the Israelis claimed victim number six. He was the Black September replacement for the contact man with the KGB who had been blown to bits three months earlier. The new man, who used the name Zaiad Muchasi, had arrived on Cyprus only two days previously to reestablish direct relations with the Soviets. Like his predecessor, he had just returned to his Nicosia hotel room from a clandestine meeting with the KGB. He turned out the light and—bang.

Only four nights passed before the Israelis staged their most audacious operation yet—a raid into the very heart of Beirut. For months, the Mossad had been wanting to strike at the headquarters of Black September. Then two events took place that made the operation seem feasible and worthwhile: the Khartoum killing incensed U.S. and West European opinion against Black September and created a favorable atmosphere for a severe Israeli countermeasure; and a number of the organization's top leadership happened to be in Beirut at the same time. A scale model of the target—a large apartment complex—had already been built in Caesarea, and a combined force of Mossad killers, Israeli army commandos, and paratroopers had practiced the assault.

During the first days of April, eight hit team members arrived undetected in Beirut. Posing as tourists, they used West European passports and fake identities. Some of them even had American credit cards under their assumed names. (Later they paid the bills they ran up on the cards in Beirut.) Aided by resident undercover Mossad agents, they lined up safe houses and rented six autos from local rent-a-car agencies.

At 1:30 on the morning of April 9, about thirty Mossad agents, commandos, and paratroopers slipped ashore in rubber dinghies from three Israeli missile boats. Everyone was dressed in civilian clothes, and the

Mossad killers wore sheer stockings pulled over their faces as disguise. Heavily armed frogmen also went ashore to secure the bridgehead. The raiding party found Buicks, Plymouths, and a Renault, with keys in the ignitions, waiting on the Beirut promenade. Armed with grenades, Berettas, and submachine guns, the Israelis piled into the cars and headed toward three different targets. The Mossad hit squad, riding in three cars, drove through the city's gaudy nightclub district to two large apartment blocks, located at the intersection of streets named Khaled Ben Al Walid and rue 68. Due to a still unexplained lapse, the customary PLO squad of guards was not on duty at the entrances of the buildings. There were only three sentries, whom the Israelis quickly killed. Then the raiders unerringly made their ways to the correct apartments, an indication that they were privy to secret information supplied by double agents.

Splitting into three groups, they launched simultaneous attacks that disposed of victims seven, eight, and nine. Their method was brutally direct: they shot the front doors off the hinges. In one apartment, they cornered Mohammed Yusif Najjar, known as Abu Youssef, who was the leader of Black September and the number three man in the PLO. In Israeli eyes, he bore personal responsibility for the Wasfi Tell murder as well as the Sabena and Bangkok operations. Abu Youssef died in a fusillade of submachine-gun and Beretta slugs. His wife was also fatally hit and her body fell on top of his. Their children saw the parents die.

Hearing the noise, an old woman in a neighboring apartment opened her door and looked out. She, too, was shot dead.

At the same moment, several men burst into the apartment of another Black September leader, Kemal Adwan. He was Youssef's deputy and in charge of Black September's operations within Israel. He was cut down in a hail of gunfire at the door to his bedroom. His wife watched his death.

In the third apartment, the Israelis surprised Kamal Nasser, a distinguished Palestinian poet who was the PLO's chief spokesman. A fatalist and a bachelor, Nasser never carried a weapon. He died as he sat at his desk writing a speech.

After killing the three Palestinian leaders, the Mossad agents ransacked their apartments, gathering up a large number of files.

Meanwhile, the two other groups of Israelis were reaching their targets. The nine commandos arrived at the headquarters of a Palestinian terrorist outfit called the Democratic Popular Front, situated near a refugee camp in Beirut's southern outskirts. At once, the commandos killed two guards sitting in a car. But the gunfire alerted Arabs in the headquarters building and they trained a withering fire on the Israelis from the upper floors. A bizarre close-quarter battle developed in the yard around the building. Arab fighters unwisely used the building's elevators to come to the ground level, and as the doors opened, the Israelis cut them down with submachine-gun bursts. Arab reinforcements arrived from the refugee camp, and the two sides, both confused as to who was friend and foe, shot at one another from distances of only four or five yards. In the confusion, an Arab tried to carry to safety a wounded Israeli, thinking he was a Palestinian. The Israeli wrestled himself free. After about thirty minutes, the Israelis succeeded in placing a large explosive in the headquarters building. Under the cover of bazooka fire, they withdrew a few yards and, after igniting the charge, fled in their autos. They carried with them their casualties: two dead and two severely wounded.

Meanwhile, a squad of paratroopers had sped north to a group of warehouses. These were the workshops where Black September manufactured letterbombs and booby-trapped autos. More fortunate than the commandos, the paratroopers encountered little resistance. They quickly blew up the workshops. While the Israeli forces were in action in Beirut, Israeli air force helicopters hovered over the city, ready to render assistance. One chopper landed in Beirut to pick up a wounded army officer. It also took aboard some of the files taken from the apartments of the three slain Arabs. As the Israelis raced toward the seashore again to escape, the helicopters dropped spikes on the streets behind them to puncture the tires of possible pursuing cars.

Within ninety minutes, it was all over. The Israelis neatly parked the rental cars on the promenade where they had found them, and left the keys in the ignitions. Only blood stains in the luggage compartment of one of the cars gave a clue to the night's work. Only the commandos took losses. The paratroopers went unscathed, and the only wound suffered by the Mossad agents was a crushed hand, caught in a slammed car door.

Until now, the Israelis had not conceded complicity in the series of secret killings. According to the initial planning, the Israeli government had also intended to deny any knowledge of the Beirut raid. It was executed under cover identities precisely to mask the Israeli hand. But because of the loss of Israeli lives and the success of the operation, the government decided to acknowledge responsibility.

After personally welcoming home the raiding party in Haifa the next morning, General David Elazar spoke with newsmen. "Israel will not play by the rules of limited warfare," he said. "You can't win a war by defense. If we cannot prevent war, we will bring about a quick and decisive victory, as in the past."

"It was very marvelous," Premier Golda Meir told the Knesset. "We killed the murderers who were planning to murder again."

In a tremendous outpouring of public sympathy for the victims, more than half a million people marched that day in the funeral procession in Beirut. In Cairo, there was a huge memorial service at the Omar Makram mosque. Two of the Wasfi Tell assassins, bearing pictures of the three murdered Palestinians, led the procession.

After the deaths of Abu Youssef and Kemal Adwan, Ali Hassan Salameh was now the highest-ranking Black September leader still alive. And yet he remained as elusive as ever.

While his fellow terrorist leaders were dying of mysterious explosions and Israeli lead poisoning, Ali Hassan Salameh went into hiding in West Germany. For months, at least six Israeli agents had been trying without success to corner the Black September planner. But they had managed to learn a bit about his whereabouts: he was living somewhere in the West German city of Ulm with a German girl friend. He made frequent trips to Stuttgart and Frankfurt, both of which had large Palestinian populations. While on the move in West Germany, he would use hiding places provided by members of and sympathizers with the Baader-Meinhof urban terrorists. In Frankfurt, Ali Hassan Salameh, who had a reputation as a womanizer, would disappear among the city's multitude of pimps, prostitutes, and drug pushers. He was moving in a milieu that was difficult—and dangerous—for the Israelis to penetrate.

Still unable to strike at Salameh, the Israelis followed up the Beirut success by putting out of action victims ten and eleven in Rome. They were two Black September operatives who used the names Abdel Hamid Shibi and Abdel Hadi Nakaa. They were driving one of Black September's specially prepared booby-trapped Mercedes, and were setting off on a mission, most likely against the transit camp for Russian Jewish emigrants in Austria. Mossad experts arranged to have the car explode prematurely, gravely injuring the two occupants.

Victim number twelve was a man whose exact role in Black September had puzzled the Mossad for many months. He was a debonair Palestinian named Mohammed Boudia, who used an Algerian passport and lived in Paris where he circulated mostly among artists and theater people.

The files taken during the Beirut raid proved to be invaluable. After being translated and, in some cases, decoded, they yielded an incredible amount of vital information. For example, they disclosed Black September's agent network in Europe, the names of contact men in Arab embassies, secret codes, and even the plans for future operations.

The documents also revealed Boudia's true role—he was Black September's foreign minister for terror. His assignment was to knit the various terrorist groups in Europe into a coherent organization. Eventually he hoped to create a global network in which the wide spectrum of terrorists—from Basque separatists to Italian fascists to the Japanese Red Army to Black September—could stage joint operations, exchange intelligence, provide weapons and logistic support for one another, and undertake attacks simultaneously in different parts of the world. Already he had made some progress. The IRA, for example, supplied limited amounts of weapons to Black September, and the West German urban guerrillas of the Baader-Meinhof group advised the Arabs on West German police capabilities and helped to arrange safe houses.

Boudia, who worked as manager of the avant-garde Théâtre de l'Ouest, performed another clandestine job as well. He enlisted young Europeans as agents for the organization. His sexual prowess made him especially skilled at recruiting young women for terrorist operations. As early as 1971, Boudia played a role in organizing the so-called Easter Commando, which was composed of an elderly French couple and three young women. They planned to commit acts of sabotage in Israel during the height of the spring tourist season. (The girls carried explosives concealed in brassieres, girdles, lipsticks, and Tampax.)

Upon arrival in Tel Aviv, the group was immediately arrested by Israeli security, which had been tipped off by double agents. One of the young women confessed that Boudia had been the brains behind the operation. During their interrogations, the girls conceded that Boudia's reputation as a lover was somewhat exaggerated. "He wasn't all that good," said one of them, "but he thought he was so wonderful that we hated to disappoint him by telling him the truth."

On the morning of June 28, 1973, after spending the night with a French girl friend, he climbed into his white Renault 16 sedan in the rue des Fossés-St-Bernard. Then, an explosive charge, placed directly behind the driver's seat, went off. Boudia was killed instantly.

Parked less than one hundred yards away was a Volkswagen Bug. Its rear windows were covered with black masking tape. Peering out through small slits were two very interested spectators: Mike and Zwi Zamir.

Boudia's mission, which posed a chilling threat to the safety of the free world, had enjoyed the enthusiastic support of the KGB. After his death, the Soviets sent a replacement to Paris. He was a Venezuelan-born agent called Carlos, but his real name was Ilich Ramírez Sánchez. (In the European press, Carlos has been dubbed "the Jackal.") Acting on a tip from Israeli intelligence, French security officers went to his apartment one evening in June 1975 while he was giving a party for fellow South Americans. In a brief shootout, Carlos killed the two French policemen and wounded the informer who had been brought to identify him. With KGB help, he was able to flee to Beirut and fly from there to East Germany, where he resumed his coordinating activities. In late December 1975, Carlos astonished the world by leading the terrorist squad that kidnapped several minister-delegates of the Organization of Petroleum Exporting Countries and took them to Algeria.

Two days after Boudia's death, the war of kill and counterkill reached a new continent and an unsuspecting victim—Colonel Yosef Alon, one of Israel's most famous pilots who was now an air attaché at the embassy in Washington. As he stepped from his auto in the garage of his suburban home, he was killed by a volley of pistol fire. The local police and the FBI failed to solve the murder. According to Israeli information, his death was the product of terrorist cooperation on an international scope. The Mossad believes that he was shot by Black Power gunmen on a twenty-thousand-dollar contract placed by a Black September representative in the United States.

Declared *Al Moharrer,* the Beirut newspaper that advocated the terrorist line: "The fact that the arm of Palestinians has reached the American stronghold in Washington is another piece of evidence that nothing—absolutely nothing—will stop the Palestinian people from expanding the scope of the war against its enemies."

* * *

100 David B. Tinnin

Despite their own losses, the Israelis had succeeded in killing the majority of those on their wanted list. The surviving leaders had been frightened into hiding. For a few months the world could breathe more easily, because Arab terrorism had come to an almost complete standstill.

Even so, the Israelis had failed to get the man they wanted most—Ali Hassan Salameh. Now they had more reason than ever for wanting to kill him. The Israelis suspected that he had masterminded Alon's murder and that he might even have visited the United States personally to make the arrangements.

To the best of the Mossad's knowledge, Salameh did not risk using the telephone or shortwave radio for Black September communications. Instead, he relied on couriers to bring him information and carry orders to his agents.

In early July, his trackers suddenly flashed an alert. Ali Hassan Salameh had ventured beyond the Ulm-Stuttgart-Frankfurt triangle. He was headed toward France.

Mossad headquarters was exultant and ordered the hit team to track him down. Until then, the various kills had not been graced with operational names, but the taking of the thirteenth victim seemed to deserve a title. The Mossad called it "The Chase for the Red Prince."

After leaving his Ulm hideaway and a German girl friend, Salameh went to Paris. There he gave the Israeli trackers fits by moving about continually. He would stay one day in a luxury hotel and the next in a hovel in an Arab bidonville outside the city. While he was in a hotel on the Left Bank, the Israelis did manage to place a listening device in his room. They overheard bits and pieces of conversations that indicated he was planning a new operation involving a skyjacking.

"Red Prince" was too fast for the Israelis. Maybe he sensed he was being trailed, or maybe he was only obeying his survival technique of never remaining in one place for very long. In any event, while the hit team still was waiting for the kill-order from Tel Aviv, Salameh abruptly left Paris. The Mossad agents tried and failed to corner him in the northwest French city of Lille.

They picked up his tracks again in Hamburg, but he eluded them again. His direction was northward and that spelled trouble to Israeli intelligence. For more than a year, they had been collecting clues that Black September was planning an attack in Scandinavia, most likely against an Israeli embassy or ambassador's residence. On Christmas Eve 1972, for example, a twenty-four-year-old Palestinian named Mohammed Abdel Karin Fuheid was arrested at London airport as he attempted to pass through customs. His luggage was filled with weapons and explosives, which he confessed were intended for a strike against the Israeli embassy in Stockholm.

Hence, when the Mossad chiefs learned that Salameh was traveling toward Scandinavia, they decided to send an advance squad at once to Stockholm, which seemed Salameh's most obvious destination. At that time, Stockholm was a center of terrorist organizations and the European outpost of the Japanese Red Army, which along with Dr. Habash's PFLP specializes in skyjackings. The Japanese Red Army even had access to a secret radio used for terrorist broadcasts.

On the morning of July 8, the telephone rang in the Herzliyya home of a man named Dan Aerbel. On the line was a high-ranking Mossad officer.

"Can we get together tomorrow?" he inquired.

At the rendezvous the next day, Aerbel was asked if he would go to Sweden for three or four days, where he would act as a translator for other agents who were going to prevent a terrorist attack against Israeli property in Stockholm. Aerbel would not be paid for his services, but the Mossad would cover his expenses and make up for the loss of salary during the assignment.

A suave and successful businessman, Dan Aerbel had worked his way up through a series of sales jobs to become the export chief of OSEM, Israel's largest food company. His background was highly cosmopolitan and he could move with ease in many different societies. He had been born in Denmark of well-to-do Jewish parents in 1937, had escaped to Sweden during World War II, and attended high school and university in the United

States. He settled in Israel in 1963 and later changed his family name from Ert to Aerbel, since the latter was easier for Israelis to pronounce. He married a beautiful Sabra, who bore him three children, and was completing a modernistic home north of Tel Aviv.

Despite his ties to Israel, he retained Danish citizenship and had two Danish passports. Occasionally, the Mossad used Aerbel on special assignments, and his Danish identity was a good cover for a secret agent.

Aerbel managed to take a few days' leave from his job. On July 10, he boarded a Lufthansa jet for a flight to Frankfurt. His two companions were full-time Mossad agents, traveling under false identities. One was posing as an Austrian named Gustav Pistauer, and the other was supposedly Jean-Luc Sévenier, a Frenchman.

Eager to know more about the mission, Aerbel kept pressing Pistauer for information. But Pistauer, who was in charge of the trio, grew impatient.

"You don't need to know any more," he said tersely.

After a night's layover in Frankfurt, they continued toward Stockholm. During a change of planes in Copenhagen, Aerbel phoned his sister who lives there. He told her he was on his way to an international congress of vegetarians that was to meet in Sweden, a credible story since she knew he did not eat meat.

Upon arrival in Stockholm, the agents checked into the Grand Hotel, just opposite the royal palace. Then Pistauer gave Aerbel his first assignment. He was to rent a large, quiet apartment where a number of people could live at one time. He should have fifteen keys made for the front-door lock. Though Aerbel did not understand the significance of the number, the apartment was intended as a safe house for the hit team and each of the fifteen members was to have a separate key.

Nothing is known about what Pistauer and Sévenier (who was called François) did during the day. Presumably, they were trying to discover whether Ali Hassan Salameh had actually arrived in Stockholm. But their evening activities were remembered by several young ladies, who later recounted them to Swedish police investigators. On the evening of July 2, some girls who worked together in the same office had gone to a restaurant to have dinner together. Three men entered the dining room, and after a few minutes of exchanging glances, the new arrivals asked if they could join the girls at their table. The men introduced themselves as Gustav, Dan, and François. As the two younger men danced with the other girls, Anita chatted with Gustav, who evidently tried to be funny by saying he was from Vietnam.

Later that evening Dan and François offered to take the girls home, but first they said they wanted to ditch their older superior first. Whisking them away in a white rented Saab, Dan and François drove to the safe house in Solna to pick up a bottle. Gustav pursued them in a large black American car, drawing up next to the Saab while Dan was inside fetching the booze. But Pistauer finally must have sensed that he was not welcome, because he gave up the chase. The two couples drove to one of the girls' apartment where they finished off the bottle.

The next evening, Dan and François met two new acquaintances at the Monte Carlo restaurant in Stockholm. The girls were playing the slot machines. The two men came over and asked if they could buy them drinks. The four sat together for an hour or so before the girls went home. The following day, Dan telephoned and invited them to dinner. The girls were torn between the desire for a free meal and a lack of enchantment with their new friends. They were especially put off by the heavy scent of François's after-shave lotion. In any event, they accepted an invitation to meet in a cellar restaurant in Stockholm's old city, but they showed up about an hour late. Dan and François, who had probably become very impatient by then, escorted them to a table where Gustav was already seated.

It was Saturday evening and the girls found the place too noisy, smoky, and crowded for their liking. After a few minutes of strained conversation, they excused themselves.

"We are not feeling well," one of them explained. "We have to go to the toilet for a moment."

But instead, they walked from the restaurant, leaving the three men behind.

Dan, who surprisingly held no grudge against them, telephoned several times on Sunday morning to inquire if the two girls were all right. Dan said François would not leave Stockholm until he knew they were feeling better. After a few more calls, the girls agreed that François could visit them on Monday evening.

The Mossad agent arrived at the apartment at the appointed time only to find no one home. He waited for a while and then left.

When one of the girls returned later, she knew François had been there. The scent of his after-shave lotion still lingered in the stairwell.

Not surprisingly, the trio in Stockholm had failed to locate Ali Hassan Salameh, but a break came on another front.

On July 14, the Mossad station in Geneva flashed a highest-priority message to Tel Aviv. Israeli agents had observed an Arab named Kemal Benamane being driven to the airport in a car bearing a CD license plate. At the wheel was an official of the Saudi Arabian mission to the UN agencies.

Kemal Benamane was a man on whom the Israelis liked to keep close tabs. A good-looking, roguish Algerian in his mid-twenties, Benamane had just married into one of the city's finest families. He had suddenly appeared in Geneva in late 1972. His past was mysterious and uncheckable: he had been wandering for several years in the Near East and Eastern Europe, he said. Though he lived among hippies in Geneva, he managed to move easily among the Arab diplomatic set. He traveled on a new Algerian passport that had been issued in June 1973 by the consulate in Geneva. His behavior struck the Mossad as highly suspicious. After keeping him under surveillance for a while, the Institute concluded that he must be a Black September courier and probably ranked somewhere between twelfth and fifteenth in the organization's hierarchy.

The message from Geneva continued that Benamane had been seen boarding a plane for Copenhagen.

Well and good, thought the chiefs of the Mossad in

Tel Aviv, the second piece of the puzzle is falling into place. Benamane must be carrying messages from the Algerian consulate to Salameh. Therefore, his trail would lead to the "Red Prince." Tel Aviv instructed its agents in Scandinavia to be on the lookout for Benamane. On July 17, after word came that he had been spotted in Oslo, Tel Aviv ordered the three men in Stockholm to proceed at once to the Norwegian capital where they should start to track Kemal Benamane.

Even as the climactic hunt was beginning, the Mossad suddenly faced a highly ironic situation. For all these months while Israeli bullets cut down other targets, the hit team had been waiting for that moment when they could take the planner of the Munich massacre. Now Salameh had finally come into the open, but the hit team was in no condition to catch him. Ever since the war of kill and counterkill had started, the Israelis had been trying to do too much with too little. After more than eight months of unbroken and perilous combat duty in the silent war, the members of the first string were worn out, exhausted physically and mentally. True, Mossad headquarters had set up a system of rotation whereby members of the first string were to be spelled by replacements until they were rested and ready for action again. In practice, however, breaks had been far too short and infrequent. Anxiety and overwork had strained the first string to the breaking point. They had been living vulnerable and exposed for too long. They had spent too many nervous nights imagining each sound they heard was that of a Black September killer prying open a window or jimmying a door lock. They had calmed their frayed nerves for too long with sleeping pills and whiskey. They had worked nonstop for days on end, shadowing Arab terrorists throughout Europe, and never knowing when a bullet might cut them down. Now in an all-out attempt to corner Salameh, the first string had used up its last resources of will and energy. Its members were spread from Paris to Lille to Hamburg, and they lacked the resilience to regroup quickly and continue the chase. It would require several days, perhaps even a week, before the first string could be reassembled and once more put on Salameh's trail. In the meantime, the "Red Prince" would be free to plan more outrages against Israel.

Mossad headquarters was not alarmed by the state of its first string. Quite the contrary. The chiefs in Tel Aviv were delighted at the opportunity to take over the most important operation themselves. Until now, the agents in Europe had won all the glory while the actual architects of the hits had been forced to stand on the sidelines. Now the headquarters staff would get the chance to prove that they could execute missions as well as they could plan them.

The hit team in Europe was told to go on vacation. Tel Aviv would put together a new force made up of volunteers and the few experienced hit team members on leave in Israel. Mike's principal deputy, Abraham Gehmer, offered his services as number two in the team. Virtually the entire office—secretaries, desk clerks, and case officers—enthusiastically followed Gehmer's lead. Tamar, who liked adventurous assignments, told Mike she wanted to be counted in. Sylvia Rafael, on leave in Israel from the first-string team, agreed to help.

Since a hit team had never before gone into action in Scandinavia, Mike urgently needed to find two people for the Heth (cover) squad who could operate in a part of the world that the rest of the team would be unfamiliar with. One likely candidate was Dan Aerbel, who had already been dispatched to Stockholm.

Mike found the other Heth in a plump and sincere Swedish girl named Marianne Gladnikoff, twenty-five. She had immigrated to Israel two years earlier and worked in the firm doing data processing for Israeli intelligence. Hence, she had a security clearance. Better still, she had aspirations to become an agent. Marianne had just started the Mossad evening course that would qualify her in a year's time to apply for full-time intelligence training.

Gehmer was instructed to contact her. He phoned to inquire if she would meet him in a certain downtown restaurant in Tel Aviv.

The conversation lasted only a few minutes.

"Are you willing to perform a mission for the State of Israel?" asked Gehmer.

"Yes," replied Marianne.

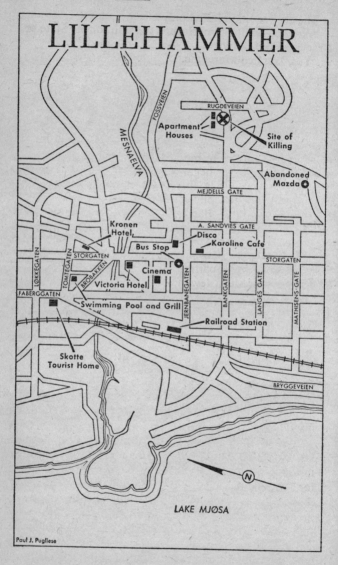

LILLEHAMMER

RUGDEVEIEN

FOSSVEIEN

MESNAELVA

Apartment
Houses

Site of
Killing

Abandoned
Mazda

MEJDELLS GATE

A. SANDVIES GATE

Kronen
Hotel

Disco

Bus Stop

Karoline Cafe

STORGATEN

LØKKEGATEN

TOMTEGATEN

STORGATEN

Cinema

BROBAKKEN

Victoria Hotel

FABERGGATEN

JERNBANEGATEN

BANKGATEN

LANGES GATE

MATHISENS GATE

Swimming Pool and Grill

Railroad Station

Skotte
Tourist Home

BRYGGEVEIEN

N

LAKE MJØSA

Paul J. Pugliese

FIVE

It was 5:30 on the morning of July 18 when the tan Mossad microbus began to collect agents in Tel Aviv. At a parking lot in the center of town, it picked up Marianne Gladnikoff, who had driven from her apartment in suburban Bat Yam. She left her car in the lot and gave the ignition keys to the bus driver for safekeeping.

Then the little bus made several turns before pulling up at a high-rise apartment building. The driver pressed a door bell and a few moments later a tall, strikingly attractive woman in her early thirties stepped aboard. She introduced herself to Marianne as Patricia Roxburgh, but in reality, of course, she was Sylvia Rafael.

The two women rode in silence as the bus swung north. Zipping past the Hilton Hotel on the seashore and the city's regional airport, it drove ten miles up the coast to Herzliyya, a lovely little town where many of Tel Aviv's leading businessmen and ranking government officials make their homes. Abraham Gehmer, a muscular and determined-looking man, was already waiting outside his apartment building. Both women knew who he was. But as he climbed on the bus, he introduced himself as Leslie Orbaum, his cover name for the mission. Like Sylvia, he was only in his early thirties, but already he held a senior position in Israeli intelligence, and he seemed destined for one of the very top posts. From 1966 to 1969 he operated under the cover of first secretary in the Israeli embassy in Paris, while actually playing a major role in the supervision of Mossad operations in Europe. In addition to his intelligence work, Gehmer took courses at Tel Aviv University, where he was studying for a master's degree in political science.

Finally the bus turned inland, speeding through flat citrus groves toward Ben-Gurion International Airport, better known by its geographical name Lod. At the terminal's main entrance, a Mossad contact man met the three agents and led them by a route that bypassed the security search and passport control to a large, pleasantly decorated room where seven people—two women and five men—were already gathered.

As a newcomer to the dark world of espionage, Marianne was impressed by the calm of the other members of the group. In her eyes, they seemed to be so relaxed and confident, while she was already feeling anxious and inadequate—"Like a little bird in a big-bird dance or a sparrow among cranes," as she later put it.

After the three new arrivals took seats, Mike began his short briefing. He said only that the Office (the term Mossad people use to refer to the organization) had learned that an Arab in whom they were interested was heading north. Mike had a picture of him and the agents would be told his name later. Marianne was surprised at the paucity of information, but Sylvia found Mike's brevity completely routine. She assumed that the people in the room were all rather unimportant and that they did not need to know more at that stage.

Mike told the team to proceed to Oslo in two groups. The first, composed of Marianne, Sylvia, Gehmer, and Jonathan Ingleby, would fly to Oslo via Zürich, where they would have to change planes. The second, made up of Mike and everybody else, would travel by way of Amsterdam. Each agent was given a large sum in cash—one thousand American dollars, one thousand French francs, and one thousand West German marks. (The Mossad is not stingy.) Marianne was the only person in the room using her own identity and traveling on her own Swedish passport. All the others were operating under assumed identities.

On the flight to Zürich, Marianne sat with Sylvia, while a few rows away Gehmer sat with Ingleby. In Zürich, the four passed through passport control as if

they were ordinary passengers debarking in Switzerland.
Mike had told them to split into couples in Zürich and
take separate planes to Oslo, but they found the schedule so inconvenient that they decided to travel together
anyway. They bought economy-class tickets on the
Scandinavian Airlines System flight SK 958, leaving
Zürich that afternoon at 5:20. Following Mike's instructions, Sylvia ordered a "big car" for pickup at the
Oslo airport.

They had more than six boring hours on their hands,
but Ingleby supplied a bit of distraction. His luggage,
which he had checked on the El Al flight in Tel Aviv,
had somehow failed to arrive in Zürich. Jonathan and
Marianne went by taxi to the city, where he used some
of his Mossad money to purchase new clothes, including
a gray suit, beige pants, two shirts, and pajamas. Sylvia
and Abraham passed the time by going into town for
lunch.

After changing planes in Copenhagen, the four
agents landed at Oslo's Fornebu airport at 9:20 that
evening. They quickly passed through the perfunctory
passport control and claimed their luggage in the baggage area. As they walked into the airport lobby, a
small nondescript man with a mousy mustache stepped
forward to meet them. It was Zwi Steinberg, who had
arrived earlier that day from the Netherlands, where he
was temporarily stationed in the Mossad office secreted
within the Israeli embassy in The Hague. Zwi had already spoken with Mike, whose flight had arrived earlier, and he was carrying instructions for the new group.

Even though Zwi was well acquainted with Sylvia,
Gehmer, and Ingleby, he betrayed no hint of recognition, and they, too, acted as if they were meeting a total
stranger. He introduced himself as Zwicka and said that
he had a message from Josi, which was the name Mike
used with him. Marianne and Jonathan should take a
cab to the Panorama Summer Hotel in Oslo, where single rooms had been reserved in their names. Sylvia and
Abraham were to pick up the auto she had previously
reserved and drive to the same hotel. Located on the
northern outskirts of Oslo, the Panorama Summer Ho-

tel is actually a dormitory of the University of Oslo, but in summer it is pressed into service as a tourist accommodation. Zwi also handed each of them a slip of paper on which he had written a telephone number—14 15 89. "If you get lost, dial that number," he said.

At the Panorama, Dan Aerbel was eagerly awaiting the new arrivals from Tel Aviv. A few minutes after Sylvia checked in, her telephone rang, and it was Dan, inviting her to come and have a drink in his room. She gladly accepted. They were old friends, who had operated as a pair on several Mossad missions in the past. Posing as European tourists, they had made a few trips together in Arab countries, spying on military activities and taking photographs of government buildings. According to Aerbel, they once even purchased a small yacht in Monaco, hired a crew, and sailed to the eastern Mediterranean. Acting like rich vacationers, they nosed into Turkish, Syrian, and Lebanese ports to check on Arab naval strength and the preparations of the terrorists, who were then building up fleets of small, fast boats to raid the Israeli coast.

At nine o'clock the next morning, Marianne Gladnikoff went to the Panorama's breakfast room where Jonathan joined her. "I need some help," he said. "I want to do some shopping." They took a taxi to central Oslo. Marianne felt ill at ease in Jonathan's presence, because he was so taciturn and purposeful. On their shopping expedition, he neither made small talk nor offered any explanation for his orders. "Find a toy shop," he told her. Marianne located one. Jonathan was interested in modeling clay and he examined several types before making a selection. Next he wanted to go to a hardware store. Marianne led him to one on the city's market square, where Jonathan chose a small file.

On the return taxi ride to the hotel, Jonathan warmed up a bit and confided to her that a certain Arab was also staying at the Panorama. Jonathan would use the clay and file to alter a key that would enable him to open the Arab's room. There, he hoped to find papers that would give some clue about Black September's plans in Scandinavia.

As Marianne and Jonathan stepped from the cab,

Abraham Gehmer met them with bad news. "He's
gone!" he said. Gehmer evidently had been trying to
find Benamane's room and had learned that he had
checked out. He reckoned, however, that the Arab was
probably still in Oslo and had only changed hotels. He
quickly drove Marianne and Jonathan to the main telephone and telegraph office in central Oslo. Marianne,
whose knowledge of Norwegian was proving to be invaluable, was told by Gehmer to ring up every hotel in
Oslo and inquire if they had a guest whose name was
Noman or Benamon, the variants the Israeli agents suspected he might be using in Oslo. Jonathan stayed with
her while she made the calls. Marianne went through a
list of forty-six hotels, but the Arab was registered at
none of them. By now, it was past noon and she and
Ingleby went to a nearby waterfront restaurant called
Guldfisken, where they were to meet Abraham Gehmer.

Actually, the new hit team was suffering already
from a serious communications gap. Kemal Benamane
had in fact left Oslo the day before and taken the train
one hundred and ten miles north to the small Norwegian resort town of Lillehammer. Gustav Pistauer apparently had shadowed him to the rail station and learned
his destination. While Gehmer was still trying to locate
Benamane in Oslo, Mike was already organizing other
members to drive north.

During the morning, Mike telephoned Sylvia in her
room at the Panorama and asked her to come to the
Theater-café in the Hotel Continental, where he and
Tamar were living. Befitting his rank, Mike had chosen
one of Oslo's best hotels, situated just downhill from the
royal palace. Gehmer drove Sylvia downtown and
dropped her off. The café—a delightful nineteenth-
century-style European coffeehouse—immediately reminded her of a German *Bierstube*.

She found Mike already seated at a table, talking
with three other agents—Dan Aerbel, Gustav Pistauer,
and a woman called Nora Heffner, who was traveling
on a forged West German passport. The conversation
concerned the Arab who had inexplicably left Oslo and
gone to Lillehammer. Mike said he wanted Sylvia and the

three others to drive there at once. When they had located the Arab, they should keep him under close surveillance to find out where he went and whom he met. After finishing their coffee, the four agents departed for Lillehammer in a rented Volvo. During the drive, Pistauer gave the two women a short description of the man they were hunting. He had black wavy hair, a beard, and his name was, as Sylvia remembered it, "Bena-something-or-other."

The carload of Mossad agents was already en route to Lillehammer when Marianne and Jonathan met Gehmer in the Guldfisken. He excused himself almost immediately, explaining he had a rendezvous with Mike. Shortly thereafter, Gehmer returned and told them that everything had changed. "Benamane has gone to Lillehammer," he said. "Marianne and I are to drive there now."

While Ingleby stayed behind at the Panorama, they collected a few of their belongings. Driving first to Oslo's red brick city hall, they picked up two Mossad agents, who introduced themselves to Marianne as Danny and François. Those names were false. So, too, were the French passports that identified Danny as Raoul Cousin and François as Jean Luc Sévenier. Marianne recognized Danny from the Lod briefing, but she had not seen François before. He was one of the Stockholm trio and dominated the conversation on the three-hour trip to Lillehammer with a highly fanciful account of his amorous exploits with Swedish girls. Marianne, not amused, found the heavy scent of François's aftershave lotion just as offensive as the girls in Stockholm did.

At Hamar, the last major town south of their destination, Gehmer stopped at a service station to make a telephone call. He was ringing the secret communications center manned by Zwicka, who told him to proceed to Lillehammer and meet Mike in the parking lot in front of the railroad station. Sure enough, as Gehmer pulled up his car at the station, a Mossad reception committee was waiting. There were Mike and Tamar, who had driven together in one car, and Sylvia, Nora, Pistauer, and Aerbel, who had arrived much earlier. In the course of a July afternoon, three autos and ten Mossad agents suddenly descended upon Lillehammer.

They could hardly have found a less likely scene of action. The hit team was accustomed to operating in a big-city environment where people take little or no interest in what is going on around them. The agents counted on being able to melt into the general urban hubbub in which a few extra cars parked on a street or a couple of men standing on a corner attract no special interest.

By contrast, Lillehammer is a small, quiet town of twenty thousand, deep in the Norwegian hinterland where a hit team could not hope to blend in. Though it has tourist attractions (Maihaugen, one of Norway's most famous historical museums, and cross-country skiing), Lillehammer remains a thoroughly provincial and self-contained community in which just about everybody knows everybody else. Because almost nothing ever happens in Lillehammer, the inhabitants take an intense interest in anything unusual. On Norwegian license plates, the two letters preceding the digits identify the auto's place of origin. For instance, DA and DB are Oslo, RE is Stravanger, HS is Lillehammer. Therefore, visitors are immediately spotted. Moreover, residents of Lillehammer are accustomed to light-skinned fellow Scandinavians as tourists. The men of Mike's hit team were predominantly swarthy in complexion, Semitic in feature. Sylvia and Tamar were so beautiful, they would have attracted attention anywhere. In Lillehammer, their Mediterranean coloring made them even more striking.

The field of action was ridiculously small and exposed. Lillehammer nestles on a hill beside Lake Mjøsa. It has one main shopping street, which stretches for about six blocks. There are no crowded streets, no congested back alleys, no dark stairwells. There are only straight, well-lighted streets, brightly painted clapboard houses, small shops, a few outdoor cafés, and, farther up the hillside, partly hidden behind tall fir trees, a cluster of modern apartments.

In such a small place, it was not difficult to trace

Benamane. Earlier that afternoon, Dan Aerbel and
Gustav Pistauer had inquired about him at the town's
tourist office, where an unsuspecting clerk had told
them that he had checked in at the Skotte (Scot) tourist
home, an inexpensive hostel located on the main highway, about two blocks north of the railroad station.
While Nora and Sylvia had gone window-shopping
along the main street, called Storgaten, the two men had
tried to find Benamane, but he had not been in his
room. (Unbeknown to the Mossad agents, their prey,
bored with Lillehammer's limited diversions, had gone
to the indoor swimming pool.) Nora and Pistauer had
taken turns with Sylvia and Dan Aerbel in keeping a
watch on the Skotte, but they had not spotted him.

Consequently, as the three carloads of Mossad
agents rendezvoused in the railroad station parking lot,
Mike told Marianne and Raoul ("Danny") Cousin to
check in at the Skotte. A double room had already been
booked in Marianne's name. Gehmer drove them to the
tourist home where they were assigned room 6 on the
second floor. Danny avoided filling out the registration
form required of alien hotel guests in Norway by telling
the lady clerk that he was entitled to control-free travel
throughout Scandinavia because Marianne, his wife,
was Swedish.

After putting their small suitcase in their room, the
two agents took seats in the Skotte's small ground-floor
television lounge, where they could see Benamane if he
came in or went out. They did not know where he was
at that moment. Actually, by then he had returned from
the pool and fallen asleep.

*For about three hours, Marianne and Danny sat in
the TV lounge, but there was no sign of Benamane.
Then at about ten, he came into the room and slumped
into an easy chair only a few feet from them. Marianne
and Danny could hardly contain the tension, but Kemal
took absolutely no notice of them. The television set
was on and for a few moments he looked at the program. But he quickly became bored. And no wonder.
The film playing on Norwegian TV that evening was
entitled Fishery East in the Mountains, and the plot was
as uninspiring as the title. It was the story of the trials*

and tribulations of fishermen in a small Baltic coastal town and the dialogue was in Swedish. Benamane tried to amuse himself by flipping through European magazines and Norwegian newspapers. As the film ended, the few other guests in the lounge went to their rooms, leaving the three of them alone.

For another fifteen minutes, Benamane paged idly through periodicals before he, too, went upstairs. Marianne and Danny waited a while to see if he would come down again. When it appeared that the Arab really had gone to bed, they walked to the rendezvous point in the rail station parking lot where Mike was waiting for their report. After learning the details of the strange interlude in the TV lounge, he told Danny to watch the departure of the 7:05 A.M. train to Oslo just in case Benamane might decide to try to elude his shadowers.

As instructed, Danny was on hand for the departure of that train the next morning, but the Arab was not among the passengers. Danny went back to the Skotte, and he and Marianne were eating breakfast in the tourist home's dining room when Kemal Benamane walked in. They dawdled over their food until he had finished his breakfast. As he left and went to the reception desk, Marianne and Danny lingered a few feet behind. They saw that he was asking a question, but all they could overhear of the lady receptionist's reply in English was "ten o'clock." They assumed that Benamane had inquired about the train schedule and had been given a departure time. Benamane thanked the receptionist and went upstairs.

Sensing an opportunity, Danny ordered Marianne into action. "Get a look at the guest book," he said. "Try to find out how Benamane signs his name and how long he said he would stay."

Marianne quickly improvised an excuse to have a look at the registry. "A girl friend of mine stayed recently at the Skotte and I would like to find out the exact dates," she told the receptionist, giving a fictitious name for her supposed friend.

The receptionist obligingly opened the book and Marianne had just caught a glimpse of Benamane's signature when he came downstairs and walked out the door. He was, however, not carrying luggage. Danny ordered Marianne to forget about the guest book and see in which direction he walked. He was headed toward the center of town. Danny quickly decided they should check out and go to the team's meeting place, which that day was the market square just below Storgaten.

According to Mike's orders, the rendezvous point would serve as command post for the team, which otherwise had no means of communication. Mike wanted the shadowers to spread out across town to pick up Benamane in relays. Hence, there was bound to be a problem of coordination. Agents who had information to report or who were not presently engaged in shadowing were to gather at the rendezvous point. At least one agent would always be on hand there to take messages and relay instructions. Mike would come to the command post when he needed agents for new assignments. The system meant a great deal of running back and forth for Mike and long, frustrating waiting periods for his agents.

On the way to the market square, Marianne and Danny saw Mike and Tamar on the other side of the street. Mike made a hand sign to them, but they failed to understand what he meant. Mike and Tamar were obviously on the hunt for Benamane. At the rendezvous point, Nora, seated in a white auto, was holding down the command post. Marianne and Danny asked her if she had seen Benamane and she replied no. They put their hand luggage into the car and walked to the railroad station to observe the departure of the 10:55 train, in the event the Arab might after all be taking it. They scanned the faces of all boarding passengers but, again, he was not among them.

Returning to the market square, Marianne and Danny sat down on a couple of large curbstones for want of anything better to do. A short time later, Mike rushed up.

"We have found him!" he said. Benamane was sitting in the outdoor café at the Hotel Kronen, about two hundred yards away. Marianne and Danny should go there and shadow him.

They were hurrying in that direction when Pistauer intercepted them.

"We lost him," he cried.

Disappointed, Marianne and Danny went back to the market square where they spent more than an hour sitting in the car with Nora.

At about noon, Mike once again dashed across the market square.

"We found him!" he exclaimed. Benamane was in another outdoor café, farther along the main street. And guess with whom he was talking? An Arab!

In the minds of the Mossad agents, this was the climactic moment. Benamane had made his contact! After a two-thousand-mile trip and six desultory days in Norway, he was now locked in conversation with a man of his own race.

The café in question was the Karoline. It is a collection of tables, chairs, and umbrellas that are placed during the summer in the northern half of a small plaza in front of the city hall, police station, and state liquor store. As Marianne and Danny approached the Karoline, they were met by Pistauer, who walked with them to the plaza. They took seats on a park bench directly opposite the outdoor café and less than five yards from the table where Benamane was sitting with the other Arab. A European-looking man was also at the table, but the Israeli agents paid no attention to him.

Fearful that Benamane might recognize her from the previous evening, Marianne tried to avert her face. Pistauer, though, had no such worries. He was staring intently at the Arab with Benamane. His job was to make the identification, and in his cupped hand, Pistauer held a small picture. His glance darted continually from the photo to Benamane's companion, and back to the photo again.

"Is that the same man?" he asked. Pistauer turned the picture so that Danny could see it but he tried to shield it from Marianne. She saw it anyhow. It was an enlargement of an amateur color snapshot, which showed a young Arab from his waist up. In the background was a white house.

The man in the photo was Ali Hassan Salameh.

Marianne pointed out that the man in the photo did not have a mustache like the Arab sitting with Benamane. But Pistauer shrugged off her objection. Since mustaches can wax and wane, they are not regarded as decisive elements in making an identification. Danny, also, was not convinced that the two men were the same. The uncertainty was understandable, because the picture was small and not especially sharp.

After ten or fifteen minutes, Pistauer came to a definite conclusion: it was the same person. The Mossad's original supposition had been correct—Benamane had led the Israelis to Ali Hassan Salameh. The behavior of the two Arabs only buttressed Pistauer's conclusion. As they sat together at the Karoline, they were absorbed in conversation and exchanging pieces of paper, which the Mossad agents believed were names of contacts and plans for a terrorist attack.

Soon thereafter, Benamane and his Arab friend shook hands and parted. The latter pedaled away on a bicycle, while Benamane walked north on Storgaten. He was accompanied by another young European man, who had joined the two Arabs at their table. Inexplicably, the Mossad agents did not follow their new target; perhaps he was too fast for them with his bicycle. However, six of them were on Benamane's trail, but they lost him near the Victoria Hotel.

Actually, he had entered the hotel by a rear door to have lunch and had invited the European to come along for company. Then Benamane collected his things at the Skotte and caught the 2:08 train for Oslo, climbing into the last car.

Either Mike knew in advance about Benamane's plans or he was a very astute predictor. In any event, he had sent Sylvia, Gehmer, and Dan Aerbel to Oslo earlier that day to await Benamane's return. They were standing on the platform when the Arab's train pulled in at 4:35 and they shadowed him as he asked at the tourist information office in the station about a hotel room. The Israelis followed his taxi to the Stefan Hotel, a modest establishment in central Oslo, and Aerbel stood watch outside.

After a few moments, Benamane, who had changed

Regular: 5 mg. "tar", 0.4 mg. nicotine av. per cigarette, FTC Report Dec. 1976.
Menthol: 5 mg. "tar", 0.4 mg. nicotine av. per cigarette, by FTC Method.
True slashes tar in half!
Only
5
MGS. TAR
TRUE
MENTHOL FILTER
5 MGS. TAR, 0.4 MGS. NICOTINE
TRUE
FILTER CIGARETTES
5 MGS. TAR, 0.4 MGS. NICOTINE
And a taste worth smoking.
Warning: The Surgeon General Has Determined That Cigarette Smoking Is Dangerous to Your Health.

*Alive
with pleasure!*
Newport

©Lorillard, U.S.A., 1976

18 mg. "tar", 1.2 mg. nicotine
av. per cigarette, FTC Report Dec. 1976.

Warning: The Surgeon General Has Determined
That Cigarette Smoking Is Dangerous to Your Health.

from dark clothes into a natty light suit, came down from his room. He chatted with the porter, as if inquiring about directions, and then walked out. In a leisurely manner, he strode five blocks across Oslo's main boulevard, Karl Johansgate, to the bookshop in the Hotel Continental where he bought a copy of *Le Monde*. With Dan Aerbel and Gehmer on his trail, Benamane walked up the boulevard to the shopping area behind the parliament building and went into a self-service restaurant where he spent half an hour eating dinner as he read the paper.

When the Arab returned to his hotel room, Gehmer went to make a phone call, leaving Sylvia and Dan Aerbel in a car parked across from the Stefan. Gehmer returned with an urgent message: Mike said that Benamane was no longer "interesting" and that the three agents should leave at once for Lillehammer. The other Mossad operatives reported they had discovered the hiding place of Ali Hassan Salameh.

Espionage is a devious business and sometimes the chief has to play tricks on his own agents. Mike's telephone message was intended to remove Gehmer and his two companions from the scene so he could speak unobserved with Benamane. Mike, who had driven down secretly from Lillehammer with Tamar, knew something the rest of the team was unaware of. The others believed that Benamane was a courier for Black September. Only Mike knew of the second role. According to one Israeli explanation, the Arab had been grabbed by the Mossad in Switzerland and given a simple choice: "A bullet or your cooperation!" In that manner, he was forced into the most anxiety-laden and perilous of occupations—double agent. A person holding that unenviable job realizes that the agency, which has "turned him around," does not trust him and is keeping him alive only so long as he continues to be valuable. He fears that his new masters will kill him or expose him to his original employers, who will do the dirty work for them.

A double agent's life depends on his contact, or control, in the agency for which he is doubling and he generally develops an obsessive attachment for the control officer, exceeding in intensity even that of a patient to his psychoanalyst. The double agent has one overriding desire—to get out of the espionage business while still alive.

By a combination of threats and promises, the control cajoles him into undertaking just one more operation, and then another and another. But some day, he vows, the double agent will be allowed to retire with rich rewards. The unhappy pawn thrives on those assurances and does not want the relationship with his control to change in even the minutest detail. Any alteration in routine or sign of lessening interest can plunge the double agent into paroxysms of fright.

On that evening, Benamane was confronted by one of the most dreaded eventualities: without warning or explanation, he was switched to a new officer. His own control had remained in Switzerland, and Mike had a code word or hand signal that identified him to Benamane as a person to whom he must talk. But the double agent knows that if a new control moves in, all promises are empty. The bonds are broken, the bets off. Most likely, the next development is either an Israeli bullet or one from the other side.

Mike wanted to grill Benamane about the Arab he had met in Lillehammer. When a double agent makes the identification of a target, the control officer wants to make certain he has not been misled. He quizzes the agent, usually in a most ungentle way, and reminds him that he can expose him to his own side at any time and that they are very unforgiving. As a final test, the control officer may thrust a pistol into the double agent's hand. "OK, if you are so certain, you go shoot him!"

No outsider knows exactly what transpired between Mike and Benamane that evening, or even if they met. There were no witnesses. Benamane, who professes utter ignorance of the entire affair, contends that he spent the evening trying to telephone his wife in Geneva.

An Israeli account is totally different. According to that story, Mike indeed met Benamane in Oslo and began to question him about Ali Hassan Salameh. Mike expressed his doubts, most likely in very direct language.

"Is this man really Ali Hassan Salameh?" he asked, in essence. "How can you be sure? He seems to know his way around Lillehammer. He does not attract attention. How can that be?"

Benamane was adamant, utterly rejecting the doubts raised in Mike's questions.

"That man is Ali Hassan Salameh," he supposedly insisted. "He is the one in Black September who gives me my orders."

SIX

Lillehammer, 8:00 A.M., July 21, 1973. There are conflicting accounts about what took place on Friday evening in Oslo. But there is no doubt about what happened the next day. Mike returned to Lillehammer where he had a meeting with Danny at about eight o'clock Saturday morning. His orders were concise and clear: find Ali Hassan Salameh and keep him under surveillance.

Then Mike and Tamar registered at the Victoria Hotel, using Mike's fake French identity of Edouard Laskier. The couple was checked in by Toril Matre, a long-haired Bergen University student who worked as a receptionist during the summer and liked to practice her French.

"Combien de temps comptez-vous rester à Lillehammer?" asked Toril.

"At least four days," replied Mike, who explained that he and his wife were tourists driving through Scandinavia. He exchanged generalities with Toril about Norway in the summer, but "Mme. Laskier" did not join in the conversation. Toril was intrigued by the unusually dark red hue to her hair. "She must be wearing a wig," she thought. Actually, Tamar often wore wigs as disguise, especially blond ones, but her auburn hair, color and all, was her own.

Following the meeting with Mike, Danny and Marianne drove around Lillehammer in search of Salameh. But they did not see him.

10:00 A.M. By prearrangement, the team met at the rendezvous point, which that Saturday was the railroad station parking lot, and Mike told them that the command post would be located in a café across the street.

The agents waited in the cars until François, who had been conducting a search on foot, came rushing up. He reported that he had spotted Salameh in the outdoor café at the Kronen; it was where Benamane had been seen drinking coffee the morning before. Nora Heffner and Dan Aerbel went there with François, who pointed out Salameh to them. Marianne and Danny were also summoned to shadow the Arab. By this time, Salameh had paid his bill and gotten to his feet. With Marianne and Danny trailing behind, he made his way south on Storgaten.

On a Saturday morning, the small main street is filled with country people who come into Lillehammer to shop, and the narrow sidewalks are crowded with shopping carts and baby buggies. Evidently, in the crush, Salameh got too far ahead, because Danny and Marianne lost his tracks.

To soothe their disappointment, they popped into a coffee shop on Storgaten for a snack. They had just sat down at a table when Danny suddenly caught a glimpse of Salameh outside. Bolting to his feet, he dashed off in pursuit, shouting back to Marianne to go tell Mike that the Arab had been located. Marianne hurried to the command post in the café. Mike listened to her report. "OK, you wait here," he said.

A short time later, Danny hurried in with the news: "He's in the swimming pool!"

"Block all exits," Mike ordered.

11:15 A.M. It was a dramatic moment. The Mossad agents believed that Ali Hassan Salameh would be meeting another courier in the pool. Yesterday, they observed him receiving messages and exchanging papers with the Black September courier. Today, they were certain that he would be sending instructions to a terrorist squad probably already hidden somewhere in Norway.

Mike commanded Marianne to get into the pool as quickly as possible to see with whom the Arab met, and try to overhear the conversation. As she rushed toward the pool building, one of the men ran into a clothing store on the main street and bought her a yellow bikini.

"Indecently small," objected the buxom Marianne.

She used up extra minutes at the swimming-pool office to rent a modest one-piece blue suit. As soon as she entered the pool area, she saw the Arab standing in the shallow water, talking with a bearded man who appeared to be about thirty and looked European.

Marianne dived into the water and began to swim back and forth across the pool, each time edging a bit nearer. She came so close that she almost splashed water on them. Since the pool was filled with noisy children, Marianne could only make out that they were speaking French, but she could not catch the gist of the conversation. The two men paid no attention to her and soon headed for the locker room, still talking intently.

Changing into her street clothes, Marianne went outside to report her findings. She confirmed that the Arab had had a meeting, that he spoke French (one of Ali Hassan Salameh's languages), and that the two men seemed very serious about whatever they were discussing. Soon the Arab came out, accompanied by the bearded man and a European-looking young woman, who actually was a Lillehammer girl. The trio was trailed down Storgaten by Danny, Dan Aerbel, and Sylvia. Marianne followed a few paces back, and saw the others peel off one by one and position themselves along the main street as if to await Salameh's return. Marianne, who knew next to nothing about shadowing techniques, decided to drop out. She went into a sporting-goods store and bought a pair of sunglasses. Since the weather was rather rainy and her feet were continually getting wet, she also purchased a pair of rubber boots. Then she went back to the Kronen Hotel, where she shared a double room with Danny, and fell asleep.

Meanwhile, the other agents kept Salameh under surveillance. They watched him go into a combination coffee shop and store, called Bergseng, near the southern end of Storgaten.

12:30 P.M. Ali Hassan Salameh left the café and boarded a bus. With him was a woman who had blond Norwegian looks and was visibly pregnant. A Mossad auto followed the bus and the agents saw Salameh and the woman get off at a stop in an attractive residential area, two-thirds up the hill. The couple crossed the road and walked toward two identical nine-story apartment buildings that sit side by side among tall fir trees. They entered the one farther downhill, Rugdeveien 2A. The Mossad had now cornered the number one man on the Israeli wanted list.

The agents were determined not to let him slip away. Under the direction of Abraham Gehmer, four Mossad cars were deployed in the area, called Nybu, meaning "new dwellings." Five lookout stations were established, which covered all possible exit routes. Station one, the closest post, was located in a driveway directly across the street from Salamch's apartment house. For communications, walkie-talkies were handed out, and each car was assigned a call number. On the hour, the autos were to rotate among the five posts. But the agents, who quickly became bored and restless, wanted to chat together. They switched from car to car and sometimes two cars were parked at station one, where passersby and neighbors noticed the out-of-town licenses. Some of the team members carelessly toyed with the walkie-talkies. A young boy, eyeing the strange autos, spotted an antenna jutting from a car window.

Oslo's Fornebu airport, 1:00 P.M. Kemal Benamane boarded an SAS flight for the trip home. He was met at Geneva airport by men from the Algerian consulate. He was so low on money, he explained later, that he could not afford the cab fare to his apartment. Hence, before leaving Oslo, he called his wife and asked her to arrange for some of his Algerian friends to pick him up.

Lillehammer, Oppland Tourist Hotel, 2:00 P.M. A dark green Mercedes sedan braked to a halt on the gravel drive. Jonathan Ingleby and two companions climbed out. They walked into the hotel and asked the receptionist for a room "for two or three nights." They were assigned a small suite. With a flourish, Ingleby, who was wearing sporty British tweeds, signed the registry with his customary studied signature. The others, writing in a more natural manner, listed their names as Rolf Baehr and Gérard-Emile Lafond. Those were assumed identities. Like Ingleby, Baehr and Lafond were real pros. They were the Beth squad members from the first-string "A" team.

Baehr, who wore blue jeans and a red T-shirt, was a highly skilled getaway driver. He was using the identity of a German Jew who was born in Cologne. The real Baehr had filed reparations claims against the West German government for damages done him by the Nazis. Most likely it was this action that brought his name to the attention of Israeli intelligence experts, who filed it away for future use. The last known address of the genuine Baehr was Via Catone 3, in Rome. But he was no longer there and no one knew where he was. His Mossad impersonator was traveling on a fake West German passport, number 408948L, which had a serious flaw. West German passports in that number series have seven, not six digits.

Baehr's fellow Beth squad member was also using the identity of a real person and a forged French passport, number 996262. The real Lafond had immigrated to Israel two years earlier and settled in a kibbutz. Without asking permission, the Mossad had appropriated his identity.

After putting their luggage in their rooms, the three men had lunch on the Oppland's terrace.

Meanwhile at Nybu, the agents were getting hungry. Leaving François and Nora Heffner on duty, the others drove down the hill. Dan Aerbel and Danny joined Mike and Tamar for lunch at the Bakkegrillen, located in the ground floor of the indoor swimming-pool building. During lunch, Mike showed Danny additional pictures of Ali Hassan Salameh, and Dan Aerbel also caught a glimpse of them.

After lunch, Danny fetched Marianne from the hotel. The agents had become curious about the building in which Salameh was hiding. The only people entering and leaving it were young women in white uniforms. Marianne was to check out the building and look for Arab names on the directory and doorplates.

A blue-checked kerchief tied on her head, Marianne went into Rugdeveien 2A, but she evidently became flustered. An Arab name was listed on the directory board and on an apartment door, but she missed it. She did notice, however, the large number of women's first names and told her teammates that the building must be a nurses' home.

Hamar, 3:00 P.M. Using the name of Tahl, General Zwi Zamir, accompanied by an aide who doubled as a bodyguard, checked in at the Esso Olrud Autorast. It is a motel on Route E-6, about forty miles south of Lillehammer. Since he had stood in the control tower at Fürstenfeldbruck and watched Israeli hostages die helplessly, the chief of the Mossad obviously had a personal reason for wanting to be present at the close of "The Chase for the Red Prince." He had also been told by Golda Meir to be on hand. Make sure everything goes smoothly, she had told him.

Nybu, 3:00–7:00 P.M. It was a thoroughly boring afternoon. The Mossad agents made no further effort to locate the apartment in which their quarry was hiding or to discover his cover name. They nervously shifted from car to car, and drove about continually in the quiet, homey neighborhood. A police car came by while the autos were parked on intersecting roads above and below the building. At the sight of the police car, Marianne became frightened, but Dan Aerbel thought the patrol indicated cooperation between Israeli and Norwegian authorities. Danny, driving a rented Mazda, nearly ran off the road. Otherwise nothing happened.

As the hit team members yawned and chatted in their autos under the fir trees of Nybu, they had no way of imagining the urgency and anxiety that was gripping military and intelligence leaders in Tel Aviv. Nor could they have anticipated how events elsewhere would influence and decide their own actions. Unbeknown to the team members, they were being drawn into a maelstrom of bizarre, almost incredible developments.

It all began the day before. Less than four hours after Pistauer made the positive identification of Ali Hassan Salameh in Lillehammer, the skyjacking that Salameh had been plotting actually went into action. At 3:42 that afternoon, a Japan Airlines 747 carrying one hundred and twenty-three passengers had lifted off from

Amsterdam, bound for Tokyo with a stopover in Anchorage. It had been airborne only seventeen minutes when it suddenly was seized by a band of Arab and Japanese terrorists. True to standard terrorist procedures, the skyjackers informed the ground controllers that they were changing the call signal of the flight. From now on, the plane would respond only to the name of "Operation Mount Carmel."

For Israeli intelligence, the new call sign conjured up the ultimate nightmare. Haifa is built at the foot of Mount Carmel, and for months the Mossad had been picking up indications that Black September was planning a new "spectacular" that would surpass even Munich in horror. The plan called for crashing a hijacked jetliner onto an Israeli city. As bizarre as the threat might seem, Israeli leaders regarded it as genuine and immediate. But Israeli intelligence chiefs chose not to share their alarm with the rest of the world. They were apprehensive that the disclosure of the plan might challenge Black September into putting it into action.

It was precisely the fear of such an attack that had led five months earlier to the tragedy over the Sinai. Blinded by a sandstorm, a French pilot of a Libyan 727 had overflown his destination of Cairo airport. He had then blundered into the electronic no-man's-land above the Suez Canal where the radars and listening devices of the opposing sides fill the air with static and confusing signals. Unable to find his bearings, the pilot unfortunately turned into Israeli airspace. Aware of the Black September plot, Israeli authorities were afraid that the plane would crash, kamikazelike, onto an Israeli city. Israeli interceptors signaled the pilot to land, but he refused. Hence, they were ordered to shoot it down, causing one hundred and six deaths. After realizing their error, the Israelis preferred to remain silent rather than offer an explanation for having taken such drastic action.

If the Libyan episode had been a mistake, the JAL skyjacking seemed like the real thing. The behavior and pronouncements of the terrorists only confirmed the Israelis' worst fears. As the big plane turned southward and flew toward the Middle East, the commandos of

"Operation Mount Carmel" sent a radio message demanding the release of Kozo Okamoto, the survivor of the trio of Japanese Red Army gunmen who committed the Lod massacre. Over Cyprus, the hijackers broadcast another message: "We are determined to fight imperialism unto death." Then "Operation Mount Carmel" winged east toward Israel.

By now, Israel was in a state of partial military alert. Antiaircraft missile batteries were manned; runways not being used by the air force were blocked by trucks and tanks to keep the plane from perhaps trying to land in Israel. Air-to-air missiles bristling beneath their wings, Israeli Phantoms streaked upward to intercept the 747. Their command was to shoot it down as soon as it reached Israeli airspace, and there is no doubt they would have done just that.

Mercifully, while the Phantoms orbited over Haifa, the 747 flew slightly to the north of the Israeli border. It sought to land at Beirut, but permission was refused. It was also unwelcome at Basra and Bahrein, but it finally was allowed to put down at the tiny Persian Gulf sheikhdom of Dubai. When the Dubai control tower inquired what the plane's intentions were, the terrorists replied: "We are waiting for instructions."

And what would they be? Senior Israeli officials reckoned that the skyjackers would free the passengers and cabin crew at Dubai. Then "Mount Carmel" would be given the signal to lift off again, this time bound for Israel. The Israelis assumed that among the terrorists was a pilot, recruited most likely by the Japanese Red Army. At the last moment, he would take over the 747's controls and place the huge craft in a power drive for Haifa.

No one outside the handful of terrorists aboard the aircraft could know what was really happening. The leader of the operation was a woman who gave her name as Katie George Thomas and was traveling on a forged Ecuadorian passport. Actually, most likely she was an Iraqi who had worked as a secretary in one of the terrorist headquarters. Exercising his customary secretiveness, Salameh had confided the goal of the operation only to her. And she had told none of the other skyjackers about the mission's ultimate aim. Moments after the plane was airborne, Katie went upstairs to the first-class lounge on the 747's upper deck, the ideal spot from which to start a skyjacking, since it is located directly behind the cockpit. She took a seat in a luxurious armchair and placed her purse on the floor beside her. As the JAL steward poured champagne, Katie inquired how she could swivel the chair and the steward, seeking to be helpful, depressed the lever that allowed it to turn. As the chair rotated, Katie realized she was leaving behind her purse in which she had secreted a hand grenade. Reaching back abruptly to retrieve the handbag, she inadvertently dislodged the grenade's pin. As she put the purse on her lap, the grenade exploded, shredding her body from breast to loins.

Her companions went ahead with the skyjacking, but Salameh's plan died with Katie. The Israelis did not know, of course, that the threat had been lifted from their country in such an improbable manner. They did not relax their alert until the plane, after having sat aimlessly for three days on the sweltering runway in Dubai, flew to Benghazi where the skyjackers blew it up.

Thus, the entire finale in Lillehammer was an interaction with events taking place in the Middle East. In fact, it was on the afternoon of the hijacking that Mike made three crucial calls from the telegraph office in Lillehammer to Zwi Steinberg at the team's secret communications central in Oslo. The first two calls, made at 2:50 and 3:00, must have dealt with the discovery of Ali Hassan Salameh in Lillehammer. Steinberg relayed the information to the Israeli embassy in Oslo where another Mossad agent, Michael Dorf, was temporarily stationed. He encoded the message and radioed it to The Hague, which in turn relayed it to Tel Aviv. The message was beamed to the big Mossad electronic receiving facility just north of Tel Aviv; it is a large cluster of antennae in various sizes and shapes that Mossad agents refer to as "Tel Aviv Is Always Listening."

Therefore, just as Israeli intelligence and military chiefs were tensing against the expected attack of "Mount Carmel," the top-secret flash arrived that Has-

san Salameh had been found by Mike's team in Lillehammer. At the height of this new threat to Israel, the
Arab terrorist had been delivered into the hands of the
hit team.

Lillehammer, 7:00–10:35 P.M. The agents on duty
outside the apartment building had become hungry
again. Marianne and Danny were told to remain on
watch duty in the white Mazda while the others went to
have dinner. Their departure was very poorly timed. A
few minutes later, Ali Hassan Salameh and the woman
came walking across the lawn from the apartment and
headed toward town. Since the weather was threatening
rain, she wore a bright yellow waterproof coat. He was
dressed in a green Levi's jacket, brown cable-knit
sweater, and faded jeans.

As soon as Danny spotted them, he drove the Mazda
a short way down the hill to get ahead of the couple and
stopped. "You drive to Mike and tell him the Arab is
on the move," Danny told Marianne. "I'll shadow him
on foot."

But Marianne protested that she did not know how to
drive the Mazda. Danny tried to reason with her, but
she still would not obey his order. Her refusal was too
much for him. Danny flew into a rage and began yelling
and shaking his fist at her. Marianne's face was flushed,
and she was on the verge of tears. As they argued violently, the Arab and the woman strolled past. They
were talking and laughing. They took no notice of the
quarreling couple in the white Mazda.

Finally, Danny bolted from the car, slammed the
door, and stalked off down the hill in pursuit of Salameh.

After several gear-grinding false starts, Marianne
managed to get the Mazda moving. She pulled alongside Danny and pleaded with him to get in. But he did
not break his stride and refused even to look in her direction. She then turned left into Martin Seips vei where
she happened to meet Mike and Tamar who were driving in a Volvo.

They had just come from the Oppland Hotel where
they had been talking with Ingleby, Lafond, and Baehr.

During the course of the afternoon, Mike had made three calls to Zwi Steinberg. He had placed the last one only moments before from the Oppland. Zwi had given him a surprising urgent message: the operation was to take place that very evening. None of the team members had expected the action to be moved up to that night. But Tel Aviv had decided to speed things up.

Mike told Marianne to get ready to leave. She drove to the Kronen where she met François, who had already checked Marianne out of the hotel and had placed her luggage in one of the autos. The other agents were also hurrying to check out of their respective hotels.

At the Oppland, Jonathan Ingleby approached the reception desk. "Please give me the bill," he said in his best put-on British accent.

"Are you leaving?" asked the woman clerk, surprised. "We thought you were going to be with us for a couple of days."

"No, we have to go," he replied evenly.

When the bill was handed to him, Ingleby barely bothered to look at the sum. Opening a large black case, which probably also contained his Beretta, Ingleby drew out a thick wad of money and pealed off several hundred crown notes.

At the Victoria "M. et Mme. Edouard Laskier" were collecting their belongings. As Mike stepped to the reception desk, Toril Matre, ever eager for a bit more language practice, came forward. It was she who had received the couple only some eleven hours earlier. Since Mike was posing as a Frenchman, he felt compelled to put on a Gallic performance to explain the abrupt departure.

"Oh, you know these Frenchwomen!" he complained. "They are impossible. I want to stay, but she is restless and wants to move on," he said, throwing up his hands in gestures of helplessness. "What can you do with these women?"

At that moment, Toril decided that she really detested M. Edouard Laskier for talking so rudely about his wife. "A typical Frenchman," she thought to herself.

Mike said he would pay the full rate for the room,

but Toril refused to give him that satisfaction. "No," she countered politely. "The hotel will accept only half of the full day's rate."

As he settled the bill, Laskier continued to shake his head. *"Ma femme! Ma femme!"* he sighed. During his protestations, Tamar, wearing a cap against the threat of rain, walked from the lobby and climbed into their car.

By eight o'clock the team gathered at the railroad station parking lot to await further instructions. Danny arrived shortly thereafter and said that he had just watched the Arab and the woman go into the movie theater. There is only one cinema in Lillehammer. It is a squat and ugly concrete building, located on the northern edge of the market square, between Storgaten and the rail station.

The feature that Saturday evening was *Where Eagles Dare,* a mission-ridiculous firm about the fictitious World War II exploits of Allied commandos who free a captured American general from a Nazi mountain-top castle and in the process commit all sorts of mayhem. In addition to being abundantly violent, the film was also exceedingly long—two hours and thirty-five minutes. But the Mossad agents did not know that. Also, they were nervous and restless. Hence, as soon as Danny reported the Arab's whereabouts, the Mossad surveillance squad began to deploy at once for action. Danny rode with Dan Aerbel, Marianne, and Gehmer to the market square, while Sylvia drove alone in the white Peugeot and parked next to the cinema. Later, François entrusted her with a thin pack of small photos; they were the ones of Ali Hassan Salameh that Mike had shown earlier in the day. She should keep them for Mike. Sylvia tucked them inside her brassiere. François also told her that the call number for her walkie-talkie was five.

Meanwhile, at precisely 8:15, Jonathan Ingleby parked the white Mazda nose first across from the Maihaugen Museum, which is situated about six hundred yards below Nybu. Two minutes later, Mike drove up with Tamar, and almost immediately Lafond and Baehr arrived in the green Mercedes, which they handed over to Nora Heffner, who drove off. Leaving Tamar with the three men, Mike also departed.

Lillehammer, central area, 10:35–10:37 P.M. As the film ended, the moviegoers rushed from the exits. Positioned in front of the cinema, Marianne, Dan Aerbel, and Abraham Gehmer had no problem picking out Salameh because of the yellow raincoat worn by his companion. He and the woman walked at a fast pace across the market square toward Storgaten, followed by the three agents. Danny drove one of the autos to the main street and parked directly in the space reserved for the bus stop in front of the Bergseng coffee shop and store. A walkie-talkie message directed Sylvia, who was wearing a white safari suit and black turtle-neck sweater, to drive to Storgaten. She halted facing southward directly across from the town's only discotheque, the Grenadier, which is one block north of the bus stop.

At 10:37, the bus, traveling south on Storgaten, arrived in front of Bergseng, where Salameh and the pregnant woman were waiting. As the bus swung wide to miss his parked car, Danny spoke into his walkie-talkie.

"He's on the bus," he said.

Nybu, 10:40 P.M. There were only a few other passengers on the bus, and it made the ascent quickly to the second stop, where Salameh and his companion were the only ones to get off on a road named Furubakken. Because of the steep grade, the bus was slow in starting up. Impatient, the couple walked downhill a few steps and began to cross the road below the bus. Their debarking was closely watched. Parked under a streetlight in a driveway one hundred and fifty yards farther up the road was a white Mazda, its engine idling. Rolf Baehr had heard the walkie-talkie message and was tensed for action. As the couple came into his view behind the bus, he put the car into gear and eased it slowly onto the narrow gravel road.

Salameh and the woman turned uphill. They were walking hand in hand on the left side of Furubakken, facing the oncoming car. There was no other traffic or activity in the area.

Baehr kept the car under tight control, so that it moved slowly and evenly downhill, its parking lights glowing in the twilight of a Norwegian summer evening.

The Arab and the woman continued to walk uphill. They were not talking. They took no notice of the approaching car.

Traveling no faster than ten or fifteen miles an hour, the Mazda was coming very close. The bus had now disappeared up Furubakken and the only sound was that of the auto's tires crunching on the damp gravel.

The couple still did not look up at the oncoming car or break their stride. They had taken about fourteen steps uphill when the Mazda reached their level. As it rolled past, the car's right front fender nearly brushed Salameh, who was walking on the outside. Even so, he did not react. The woman, however, threw one quick glance at the auto and then looked away.

Baehr let the car roll past them. Then he abruptly hit the brakes. The wheels locked and bit into the gravel. Two doors flew open and Tamar and Ingleby sprang out, the Berettas in their hands.

Startled by the braking sound, Salameh and the woman wheeled around just in time to see the two persons climbing out.

Tamar and Ingleby raised their automatics.

The Arab saw the weapons trained on him.

"No!" he cried in a loud voice.

Without saying a word, Tamar and Jonathan opened fire. They were aiming at the largest target: the abdomen. The modified Beretta shoots almost as rapidly as the finger can squeeze the trigger.

Before Salameh could react, six slugs tore into his belly. They were so closely grouped that they ate a hole in his thick sweater.

In times of great anguish and shock, the mind records strange things. As she stood within a yard of the victim, the pregnant woman was astonished that she heard so little noise. She could tell that the weapons were firing only by the tiny tongues of flame that danced from the barrels.

Salameh was standing facing his killers. Now he turned and tried to run. But he was already too gravely hurt. He began to fall, his body pointing uphill. As he went down, Tamar and Jonathan continued to fire. One slug struck his skull at an angle and ricocheted into the concrete foundation of the apartment house. Another bullet caught him below the ear and bored to the base of his brain.

On seeing her companion fall, the woman threw herself to the ground. She lay huddled on the roadside directly above the victim.

As Salameh sprawled face down on the gravel, Tamar moved closer. After she had jumped out of the left rear door, she been firing from beside the left back fender at a distance of about five yards from her target. Now she stepped nearer. From two yards away, she pumped bullets directly into the Arab's back.

Ingleby, meanwhile, remained standing by the open front passenger door where he was shooting from a distance of about six yards. The bullets of each killer tattooed distinctive patterns on Salameh's back. Tamar's slugs, fired from an almost vertical angle, made smaller round entry wounds in contrast to Jonathan's bullets, which left long oval marks, reflecting the slanting angle of fire. Despite the difference in distance, Jonathan's aim was far better; his shots, hitting higher in the back, penetrated the victim's kidney and liver. Three of Tamar's bullets missed vital areas—two struck the left forearm, which lay alongside the body, and one hit his buttock.

Even so, from a coldly professional standpoint, the shooting was pretty fair. Each of the Berettas carried seven bullets, and fourteen slugs riddled Salameh. The one that ricocheted off his skull left two holes. Six bullets remained lodged in his body. Seven others, in spite of the lighter powder loading in the modified cartridges, had completely ripped through his flesh, leaving both entry and exit wounds.

Torn by a total of twenty-two holes, Salameh was bleeding heavily from wounds in his chest, abdomen, and neck. Three large pools of blood quickly began to form on the gravel road.

Israeli assassins are taught to get their shots off fast. The execution took no more than ten or fifteen seconds.

During that brief period, Rolf Baehr kept the engine turning over strongly, and the car rolled forward a few feet. Gérard Lafond, meanwhile, watched from the right rear passenger seat to see if the killers needed help.

Then Tamar and Ingleby jumped into the Mazda. The sound of slamming doors blended with the howl of an over-strained motor. Jamming his foot hard on the gas pedal, Rolf Baehr hurled the Mazda down Furubakken, its wheels kicking up loose gravel. At the first intersection, he made a tire-screeching left turn.

The woman who lay beside the victim lifted her head as the car sped away. She caught a glimpse of the license plate. It looked Norwegian to her.

After the white auto turned off Furugakken, a dark green Volvo drove slowly up the hill from the opposite direction. It came to a stop beside the stricken form of Ali Hassan Salameh. Mike looked out of the window. He was making certain his killers had accomplished their mission. Satisfied, he pulled away.

Seconds later, Mike raised his walkie-talkie.

"They took him," he said. "All cars go home."

A few moments earlier, a twenty-three-year-old pediatric nurse named Dagny Bring had been seized by a desire to stand up and move about. She was sitting in the apartment of a girl friend in Rugdeveien 2A. They were knitting and watching a British criminal serial entitled *The Bank Robbers* that was running on Norwegian TV. The installment playing that evening was called "Haven't We Met Before?" For no particular reason, Dagny walked to the apartment's small balcony and looked down on Furubakken. At that very moment, Salameh yelled "No!" and the killers went to work.

"This is murder!" Dagny screamed. "He's been shot!"

"Hush now," replied her girl friend Åse Midtsveen. "You've been watching too many serials."

"This is murder!" Dagny insisted. "This is murder!"

10:50 P.M. The police station received a telephone call that a man had been shot on Furubakken. Two police cars arrived three or four minutes later at the scene of the shooting.

11:04 P.M. An ambulance came from the nearby hospital. By now, the victim had been turned on his back, and a doctor and a nurse, who lived in the neighborhood, were applying mouth-to-mouth resuscitation and heart compressions. A heartbeat was barely detectable. Salameh was placed in the ambulance and sped to the hospital emergency room where doctors tried unsuccessfully to revive him. After fifteen minutes, he was pronounced dead.

Meanwhile, at Maihaugen, the Aleph and Beth squads were switching cars. Rolf Baehr drove the Mazda to a parking place directly across from the Museum. He coolly backed the car into a space until the rear wheels were flush with the curb, and pulled on the handbrake. The agents wiped the auto completely clean of fingerprints. They locked it, pocketed the keys, and took the car's documents, only leaving behind one piece of paper—a parking violation ticket from Oslo. Then they climbed into the green Mercedes brought by Nora.

Within a couple of minutes, Mike arrived from checking on the state of the victim. He collected all the weapons; he did not want the killers and guards to carry such incriminating evidence on their trip south. Then he drove by a separate route back to Oslo.

Sylvia's job had been to fetch the shadowers with the white Peugeot. When she picked up Abraham Gehmer, she slid over to allow him to take the wheel. Marianne and Dan Aerbel climbed in the back. After they heard the message "All cars go home," they made one additional tour of the main street. They were worried that François might have been left behind. Failing to find him, they assumed he must be riding with Danny. Then, not wanting to waste further time, they drove south, away from Lillehammer.

Route E-6, 11:25 P.M. A few miles outside the town, Gehmer saw Danny's car parked on the side of the highway. François was with him. The green

Mercedes was also there. Gehmer pulled over the Peugeot, and several of the agents got out of the cars to chat.

"Jesus!" exclaimed one of them. "What a way to spend a Saturday night in Norway!"

Danny came to the white Peugeot and asked, "Have you got one of the walkie-talkies?"

Sylvia handed her set to him through the window.

Then Jonathan Ingleby strolled over.

"How did it go?" Sylvia asked.

"A job is a job," he replied.

SEVEN

There had not been a killing in Lillehammer for forty years and the police were understandably at a loss to know what to do. Also, their radio set, which had been out of operation for two weeks, still had not been repaired. Hence, they were unable to alert a patrol car on duty in the southern outskirts of town at the time the hit team autos were making hurried exits. They were also unable to flash an alert to neighboring police forces. It took the Lillehammer police a full hour before they telephoned the station in Hamar with a request to set up a roadblock on E-6, the logical escape route to Oslo.

A young deputy sheriff named Per Erik Rustad pulled up his Volkswagen police car at the Hamar headquarters just as the request was being made. He and a partner were on a routine patrol from their station in the village of Stange, south of Hamar, and they had stopped in only to say hello. The Hamar police were so short of men that evening that the duty officer asked Rustad to help.

Since the occupants of the Mazda might be armed and dangerous, Rustad, his partner, and a Hamar constable grabbed flack jackets and checked out pistols from the police armory (Norwegian police usually do not carry weapons). Meanwhile, the duty officer selected the optimum spot for a roadblock, the final stretch of a wide segment of E-6 before secondary roads branch out.

Ironically, the site chosen for the roadblock was almost directly in front of the motel where General Zwi Zamir and an aide had been staying. They had checked out about two hours earlier, saying they were going to

Trondheim, a central Norwegian city situated on a fjord leading to the Atlantic Ocean.

Per drove the six miles to the junction at E-6 as fast as the Bug could manage. He knew he was racing time. Since Hamar is only forty miles south of Lillehammer, the wanted car might be approaching at that very moment, if it had not already gone past.

As Rustad brought the Bug to a sudden stop, he and the others piled out and ran toward the highway. They were in such a rush that they did not have time to slip on the bulky flack jackets properly. One of the men even pulled his on backwards.

Taking up positions on E-6, they began to make arm motions to the oncoming cars, signaling them to slow down. Per stood on the shoulder of the southbound lanes. As he made his go-slow signals, the first three drivers flashed by without paying even the slightest attention. Obviously, they were law-abiding Norwegian burghers, secure in their righteousness.

But the driver of the fourth car hit the brakes, and a white Peugeot began to slow down. Per caught sight of a very lovely young woman sitting in the front passenger seat. "What a beautiful girl!" he thought to himself. She must have been favorably impressed, too. For a second, their eyes locked, and as the car passed, she turned her head to maintain the contact. Sylvia stared at the young sheriff a fraction too long. Rustad's curiosity had been aroused.

"Shouldn't we check that car?" he yelled to his companions.

At that instant, Abraham Gehmer caught himself and accelerated. But Rustad managed to note the auto's license number—DA 97943. A white Peugeot is not, of course, a white Mazda. Even so, Rustad knew that the Peugeot model 504 and the Mazda model 616 sedans are very similar in size and shape. Also, the Peugeot was filled with adults just as the police expected the Mazda would be.

Per did not have a two-way radio in the Volkswagen, so he could not report his information. A few hours later, when a patrol car from Hamar stopped by the roadblock, he asked the officers to relay the license number to the central police headquarters in Oslo. Per remained on duty all night at the roadblock, but he saw nothing else worth reporting.

During the drive south that night, the atmosphere in the Peugeot was highly strained. Unnerved, Marianne was whimpering softly. Dan Aerbel, trying to conceal his own nervousness, took her hand in his. Gehmer remained silent. Sylvia also did not speak. She chain-smoked Gitanes and took nips from a flask of Chivas Regal before shoving the empty bottle under her seat.

Marianne remembered passing at least two more police checkpoints, but no one tried to stop them. Without further incident, they reached their destination. It was a flat in the Oslo suburb of Baerum that Dan Aerbel had rented from a Norwegian army general a few days earlier and had partially furnished. Gehmer put the Peugeot in a roofed parking space, and the four went into the modern, comfortable apartment. Sylvia removed the pictures of Salameh from her brassiere and placed them on the floor next to her belongings in one of the bedrooms. Then the four agents went to sleep.

At about 8:30 the next morning, the telephone rang and Sylvia answered. It was Mike, who had made his own way to Oslo and had just had breakfast with Zwicka at the Hotel Continental.

"How is everyone?" he asked.

"Fine," replied Sylvia sleepily.

"Zwi is on his way," said Mike. "He has a message for you." Then, promising to call again later, Mike rang off.

Zwi soon arrived with the green Volvo, which Mike had used in Lillehammer. His message was hardly momentous. "Mike wants you to turn in this car," he said.

After Zwi returned to Oslo by taxi, Dan Aerbel volunteered to drive the Volvo to the Hertz office at Fornebu airport. Marianne should follow in the Peugeot to bring him back. The arrangement pleased Sylvia, who wanted to take a long soaking bath. As soon as Gehmer finished washing his socks and underclothes, Sylvia, exercising the prerogative of a beautiful woman, appropriated the bathroom and drew a hot tub.

* * *

Join up for the great battles that turned the tide for freedom.

5603. Mustang at War. Roger A. Freeman. Lavishly illustrated history of P-51 fighter and pilots. Pub. ed. $10.

2170. Guderian: Creator of the Blitzkrieg. Kenneth Macksey. Full-scale story of the maverick genius of mechanical war. Pub. ed. $12.50.

4879. The Raid. Benjamin F. Schemmer. U.S. Army's incredible raid on Son Tay POW camp, North Vietnam. Pub. ed. 10.95.

7583. Titans of the Seas. James H. and William M. Belote. Story of Japanese and American carrier task forces in WWII. Pub. ed. $12.95.

3020. The Longest Day. Cornelius Ryan. Dramatic story of the Normandy invasion. Pub. ed. $12.50.

3079. U.S. Fighters. Lloyd S. Jones. Every ''P'' and ''F'' series plane, 1925-present. Rare photos and 3-view drawings. Pub. ed. $14.95.

8136. Nimitz. E. B. Potter. Definitive biography of the U.S. admiral whose tactics destroyed the Japanese navy. Pub. ed. $16.95.

2162. The Evaders. Leo Heaps. The story of how 250 allied troops eluded two German divisions—most amazing mass escape of WWII. Pub. ed. $8.95.

1347. The Encyclopedia of Sea Warfare. From the first ironclads to the present day. Pub. ed. $17.95. Counts as 2 selections.

Start with any 4 books for only 98¢ when you join The Military Book Club.

TURN OVER FOR SPECIAL OFFER.

All that Sunday morning, Mike and the other Mossad agents were behaving as if they were totally oblivious to the fact that Norway had police forces, which would begin to search for the Lillehammer killers. Actually, by that time the elite Norwegian federal investigative squad, known as the I-Group, had already been at work for several hours in Lillehammer. By interviewing local people and checking Oslo car rental companies, the I-Group inspectors had pieced together one possibly significant clue. Two of the out-of-town cars observed in Lillehammer on the day of the killing had been rented by foreigners. The white Mazda, found abandoned near the murder scene, turned out to be an Avis car, rented on July 16 by Gustav Pistauer of Vienna. The white Peugeot, whose license plate had been noted by Sheriff Rustad, belonged to the Scandinavian Rent-A-Car, which had let it to a Canadian woman named Patricia Roxburgh.

The police station near Oslo's Fornebu airport is called Sandvika, and the duty officer on that Sunday morning was a bulky police sergeant named Bjørn Trøan. As he began his watch at 8 A.M., he checked the telex transmissions that had arrived overnight. Surprised to see unusually long messages from the I-Group, he made certain that one copy was delivered to the police substation at Fornebu.

When the copy reached the airport, Inspector Hans Lillejordet, the officer in charge of the Fornebu detachment, told the constables on duty in the passport booths to be on the lookout for suspicious departing foreigners. They should also pass the word to airport workers and ticket clerks to watch for a white Peugeot. At 9:15 A.M., Constable Sigmund Dyrdal walked over to the various airline counters and gave the ticket agents the Peugeot's license number.

About forty-five minutes later, Asbjørn Slørdahl, a ticket officer at the SAS counter on the departure level, happened to glance to the street outside. There, in the space reserved for unloading taxis, stood a white Peugeot. He looked at the license number—and looked again. "Things like this just don't happen," he said to himself. He briskly crossed the lobby to the booth where Dyrdal was examining passports.

"Tell me that number again, will you?" asked Slørdahl.

"DA 97943," replied the policeman.

"It's parked outside," declared the SAS man.

Rushing to the ramp, Dyrdal found Marianne Gladnikoff sitting at the wheel. "May I check your driver's license?" he asked.

Marianne complied—a bit too quickly.

"Why are you stopping here?" the constable asked. "This is a no parking zone."

"Oh, I didn't know," replied Marianne, feigning chagrin. "I am waiting for a Danish friend who has gone to turn in his car at a rental office."

"Would you please come along with me?" asked the constable.

Dyrdal escorted Marianne to the airport police office, where Inspector Lillejordet noticed that her hands were shaking uncontrollably. He telephoned the Hertz office and learned that a Dan Ert (the earlier version of Aerbel's family name) had just returned a car.

"Find him," the inspector told Dyrdal.

The constable located Aerbel as he was walking toward the Peugeot. His arms loaded with two large bags full of food, Aerbel had just spent one hundred crowns in the airport cafeteria buying a wide assortment of tea bags, cookies, sandwiches, and the like.

"What do you have in those bags?" asked Dyrdal in a friendly manner.

"Groceries," replied Dan Aerbel, smiling.

"You can't eat all that food alone," countered Dyrdal.

"Of course not," responded Aerbel. "I have friends who are waiting for me."

"Come on," said Dyrdal. "We'll drive you to them."

Even as Marianne and Dan Aerbel were being apprehended at Fornebu, a far more important Mossad agent was making his way through the airport. He was Gérard Lafond. On that Sunday morning, he was catching a

10:30 SAS flight to Amsterdam. He must have reached the airport at about ten o'clock, and his taxi would have halted in exactly the same area where the white Peugeot was standing. Conceivably, Lafond may have witnessed the scene as Constable Dyrdal approached Marianne. At the very least, he must have seen the white Peugeot, and the sight of the car at Fornebu probably filled him with curiosity.

Despite the Norwegian alert for suspicious foreigners, Lafond encountered no difficulties. He presented his fake French passport to the officer who had replaced Dyrdal in the passport booth and was let through to the departure lounge. Lafond boarded SAS flight 545, which left on schedule for Amsterdam. Later the same day, Rolf Baehr also made his getaway by flying from Oslo to Amsterdam.

As members of one of the two key squads, Lafond and Baehr were following special escape procedures that were standard for the killers and the guards. Amsterdam was the staging area for their quick return to Israel. When they stepped from the SAS plane in the Netherlands, they could count on very effective help. As they entered the arrivals area, someone would hand them a key. It would open a locker in the terminal. There, they would find a small piece of luggage identical to the one they were carrying. They would take the new bag and leave the old one behind. The new luggage would contain another passport, money, air tickets, and instructions for the trip home, most likely on the next El Al flight. They could either put the locker key in an envelope and leave it at the information desk, marked for pickup by Mr. Shalom or whoever; or they could simply hand the key to an El Al employee.

Meanwhile, Tamar and Ingleby used the Mercedes for their escape from Norway. Quite possibly, they took along Nora Heffner. They went via ferry to Copenhagen where they abandoned the auto in a lot near the Hotel Scandinavia. (It was not found until much later.) Within less than two days of the killing in Lillehammer, the members of the Aleph and Beth squads had safely returned to Israel.

* * *

Back at the airport in Oslo, Marianne and Dan Aerbel were not so fortunate. No one had prepared a getaway route for them. In fact, no one had even devised a cover story to explain their presence in Norway. Now, as they fell into the hands of the Norwegian police, they had no idea what they should do or say.

Actually, at that early stage, their fright and naïveté were their best disguises. At Fornebu, the police officers could never have imagined whom they had caught. As they looked at the shaking hands and perspiring palms of the two suspects, the policemen did not suppose for one moment that they had just captured agents of the world's toughest intelligence service.

In the first minutes of his arrest, Dan Aerbel made an attempt to clarify the situation a bit.

"Why have I been picked up?" he asked in English.

"It is something in connection with your car and the use of it," replied Inspector Lillejordet. "We have to check."

Marianne and Dan Aerbel were taken to the Sandvika police station. They were informed that a killing had taken place in Lillehammer and their car had been seen in the neighborhood on the day of the crime. Marianne and Dan Aerbel tried to impress the police with their innocence by being overly cooperative. In short, separate interrogations, they both readily confirmed the police report that the Peugeot had been rented by a Canadian lady named Patricia Roxburgh. Marianne even gave her address in Oslo as that of the supposed safe house, and Dan Aerbel told the police that Patricia Roxburgh was staying with him.

"She is asleep in the apartment right now," he said.

In fact, Sylvia was far from asleep. After her luxurious bath, she had become increasingly nervous about the long absence of Marianne and Dan. By now it was 11:30 A.M. and they should have been back an hour ago. Unable to contain her anxiety any longer, Sylvia dialed the Hertz office at Fornebu.

"I am calling to find out if my husband has returned an auto," she said. "He is a Dane named Dan Ert."

Aware of the police interest in the Ert car, the clerk played for time.

"I'll check and call you back," he said, hoping to get her home telephone number.

But Sylvia was too clever. "Sorry," she said. "I'm calling from a booth in Oslo." Then she hung up.

Meanwhile, Sergeant Trøan of the Sandvika station had been in contact with the I-Group unit in Lillehammer. At 10:45, Trøan reported that the Dane had said he and his woman companion were living in a flat in Baerum with Patricia Roxburgh. The I-Group inspectors instructed him to keep the line open and to go put one question to Ert. The sergeant went to the cell and asked: "Have you ever been in Lillehammer?"

"No," replied Dan Aerbel. The I-Group, however, discounted his denial. By then, they had collected more reports about the peculiar behavior of out-of-town cars in Lillehammer. They told Trøan that both the Peugeot and the Volvo had been seen by a number of witnesses and that he should go ahead and book Marianne and the Dane on suspicion of having participated in a premeditated murder.

After having been charged, Dan Aerbel was searched and taken back to a cell. Marianne presented a problem. There was no policewoman at Sandvika to conduct the prescribed body search. Therefore, Trøan and another police officer put her in a police Volkswagen and set off for the headquarters in Oslo, where she could be searched and jailed. On the way, they intended to check on the flat in Baerum to see if Patricia Roxburgh was really there. The police were frankly dubious. Marianne and Aerbel had volunteered information so readily that the officers doubted they were telling the truth.

Marianne said she was only too glad to stop by the flat because she wanted to pick up her toilet articles. But she did not get a chance. She was kept in the Bug with the other officer while Trøan rang the bell. Sylvia opened the door at once.

To her credit, she maintained complete composure. Trøan asked permission to enter the apartment, and she allowed him in. He explained in English to Sylvia and Gehmer that there had been a killing in Lillehammer and that all cars seen in the area were being checked. Would they please come along to help clear up the situation? The two agents both feigned utter ignorance.

"Well, I don't know what we could possibly do to help," said Sylvia. "But of course we will come along."

Gehmer, who spoke English in gutturally accented tones (he would have been more at home in German) also made no objection.

Outside in the VW, Marianne Gladnikoff was already suffering pangs of regret for having given away her comrades. As they crowded into the back seat with her, Marianne tried nervously to keep up a line of cheerful but patently contrived chatter. Sylvia and Abraham did not play along, making her task all the more difficult. But she bravely kept up her patter, talking about the weather and the sights.

During the ride to the central police station, Marianne managed to roll up and toss from the car the piece of paper bearing the telephone number that Zwi Steinberg had given her four days earlier at Fornebu. At the police station, the three agents were asked to take seats in a corridor. While they waited, Sergeant Trøan went to the nearby office of Superintendent Jahrmann, who had been consulting with his investigators in Lillehammer, the local police there, and court officials in Oslo. The consensus was that the suspects should immediately be taken to Lillehammer for questioning. Dan Aerbel was brought separately by the Sandvika police to the Oslo headquarters.

At 3:30 P.M., Aerbel and Gehmer left for Lillehammer in an Oslo police car. A few moments later, a police couple (he a federal highway patrol man, and she a sergeant with the Oslo criminal squad) escorted Sylvia and Marianne. To Sylvia's amusement, the sergeant caught a speeder on the trip, and gave him a ticket.

While the four suspects were being driven northward, two investigators from the Sandvika station were sent at once to the flat in Baerum. To a trained eye, personal belongings can provide insights into the identity and background of suspects. As the investigators sorted through the stacks of goods in the flat, they were astonished. The place looked like a hardware store. Dan Aerbel, who was building a new home in Herzliyya, had been on a shopping spree while in Scandinavia. Among other things, he had bought three complete sets of faucets and washbasin fixtures, one hand shower with attachments, two Ericson telephones (one green and one red), a reading lamp, three lampshades, a vacuum-cleaner nozzle, several sets of curtains with rods, an assortment of tablecloths, and a wide variety of electrical plugs and connectors.

The inspectors also found traces of Aerbel's sojourn in Stockholm, including three tickets to the Midnight Sun Club, and slips of paper with telephone numbers that turned out to be those of the girls whom Aerbel, François, and Pistauer had met in Sweden. For the two inspectors, the final shock came when they discovered a batch of receipts and used tickets. Trained agents and professional killers simply do not carry around telltale evidence of where they have been. But Dan Aerbel, a conscientious businessman, had kept close tab on his expenditures. He was getting no pay for the mission, and he obviously wanted to be able to submit a completely substantiated expense account so that he would be fully reimbursed. Aerbel had carefully tucked away no fewer than nineteen receipts. They included the bill from the Grand Hotel in Stockholm, the air ticket from Stockholm to Oslo on July 17, a taxi bill for the ride from Fornebu to the Panorama Hotel in Oslo, currency-exchange receipts in Oslo, the Lillehammer-to-Oslo train ticket on July 20, a bill for gasoline in Lillehammer, and the bill for one night's stay at the Victoria Hotel in Lillehammer. It was easy for the police to reconstruct the movements of Dan Aerbel.

Finally, the two inspectors turned up a batch of commonplace personal belongings and three books, whose titles tickled them—*Night and Silence—Who Is Here?*; *This Bed, Thy Center;* and *Mr. Right Is Dead.*

The contents of the Baerum flat were quickly catalogued, and the most interesting evidence—notably the receipts—was sent by police car to Lillehammer. A plainclothesman, armed with an automatic pistol and provided with a two-way radio, was stationed in the flat. He was to remain hidden in case anyone else came there. His call sign was 45. He was not to use the telephone or answer it when it rang. If for any reason the police decided to contact him by phone rather than radio, the call would be placed three times in rapid succession. Only then should he pick up the receiver.

The only visitor to the flat was an unsuspecting sheriff in civilian clothes whose arrival the next morning provided a bit of comic relief. He was coming to deliver some legal documents to the flat's owner. When the bell rang, the plainclothesman, excited to have some action at last, admitted the caller. Then he promptly told him to put up his hands. The sheriff thought it was a stickup and tried to arrest the culprit. The plainclothesman, thinking he was dealing with a really dangerous character, told the sheriff that he was the one under arrest. And so they went on arresting each other until they finally satisfied themselves that both were on the same side of the law. This was the only incident at the Baerum flat. The watch produced no new clues.

It was late on Sunday afternoon when the Oslo police cars wheeled to a stop in front of the police station in Lillehammer. During the ride, subtle psychological changes had begun to take place in the minds of the four Israeli agents. They had started out acting like nonplussed and innocent tourists. Now they were behaving more like shaken prisoners. As they were led inside, Marianne and Sylvia tried to hide their faces from the crowd.

The four suspects were searched and their belongings confiscated. From Sylvia, the police took a Canadian passport, an international driving license from the Canadian Automobile Association, an international vaccination certificate, a Zurich-Copenhagen air ticket, a neck chain, pearls, earrings, two room-rental receipts from the Panorama, two car rental contracts, a notebook containing a number of addresses, and a container of contraceptive pills. They also took a blue pack of Gitane cigarettes similar to the one found under the front seat of the white Peugeot, and about one thousand dollars in cash in six currencies.

There was far less to confiscate from the three others. Aside from their passports and cash, they carried almost nothing. The police snipped hair samples to determine if any of them were using a false color. They kept Gehmer's maroon slacks and tan jacket because they wanted to show them to some witnesses in order to establish his movements in Lillehammer. He was given a set of warm-up togs belonging to the sports team of the local newspaper.

Then the four suspects were handed over to the I-Group interrogators. The senior interrogator was a short and powerfully built young man named Leif A. Lier who had begun his career as a handler in the Oslo dog patrol. He had his choice of suspects and, after chatting with all of them, selected Marianne Gladnikoff. He believed he would get more from her. Inspector Steinar Ravlo took Dan Aerbel, while Abraham Gehmer went to Ulf Valstad and Sylvia Rafael to Harald Rønning. At about 6:30 P.M., the agents were invited into separate offices.

A battle of wits was about to begin. The Israeli operatives were totally in the dark as to how much had been discovered regarding the real reason for their presence in Norway. But one thing they knew for certain was that they had to talk their way out of a very peril-laden situation. Until now, no hit team member had ever been captured and their method of operation remained secret. The hit teams had taken thirteen victims but no one could prove that the State of Israel sent them on their missions of quiet murder.

The I-Group's interrogation tactics are deceptively lenient and leisurely. At the outset, in accordance with Norwegian law, the suspects are informed that they have the right to remain silent if they choose, and that any testimony they do give may be used as evidence against them in court. The interrogation usually begins with a general question, for instance, "Please tell me all you know about this case and what connection, if any, you have to it."

To which Sylvia coolly replied, in effect: "None whatsoever." Her story went roughly like this:

"I am a Canadian citizen and a free-lance photographer. I was on vacation, and by sheer coincidence I happened to run into Leslie Orbaum in the Zurich airport. I've known him for several years; on the spur of the moment we decided to go to Norway together. We spent three days driving around sightseeing and met some other people with whom we moved in."

As Sylvia continued her story, speaking in what she terms her "North American accent," Abraham Gehmer was telling pretty much the same tale. During the tense hours that morning when Dan Aerbel and Marianne had failed to return from the airport, they had concocted a joint cover story that would explain their whereabouts for the past four days. But under questioning, they would have to do a lot of fast improvising. Gehmer's version ran about like this:

"I was born on March 12, 1944, in Leeds, England. I am a teacher and bookkeeper at the Queens Hill School in that city. I am on vacation and this year I decided to do things differently. I would travel on impulse. I would make no prior plans or reservations but would go wherever my desires of the moment led me. On the morning of Wednesday, the eighteenth of July, I went to Heathrow airport and bought an economy-class ticket to Zurich.

"No, I don't remember the exact time, but it was during the morning. In Zurich airport, by chance I met a woman whom I knew from years back. Her name is Patricia Roxburgh. She is a Canadian citizen, although she now lives in Paris. In Zurich we decided to travel together and selected Norway as our destination."

"Why Norway?" asked Inspector Valstad.

"To have some fun," replied Gehmer evenly.

His story continued: "We bought tickets on the first plane and arrived in Oslo at nine-thirty that evening. At the airport, while Patricia went to rent a car, I telephoned the Panorama Hotel and reserved a single room for myself. I got up around nine or ten Thursday morning, and then drove with Patricia around Oslo and visited villages within one hour of the city. On Friday we met Dan Ert, who was also staying at the Panorama. On that same day, I had a quarrel with Patricia."

"Why?"

"Well, there was something about her personality that annoyed me," explained Gehmer. "I thought Dan was aware of the problem because he suggested that I move to his apartment."

"Did it not strike you as very odd that Dan Ert would be living in a hotel if he had an apartment?" asked Valstad.

"Not at all," replied Abraham Gehmer, unruffled. "Dan gave me the address of his apartment and I went there by cab. On the way, I picked up a suitcase I had left in baggage storage at Oslo-East railroad station. When I reached Dan's apartment, it was locked. I rang the bell, but no one answered. I waited outside for about half an hour until Dan came walking down the street, accompanied by Patricia and a girl named Marianne. I soon got the picture that all four of us were to live in the apartment. I don't know if Dan had known Marianne previously. Within half an hour, I went to bed in a single room. At about nine the next morning, Dan and Marianne decided to return an auto to a car-rental agency. Patricia and I remained in the apartment until the police came."

"Have you ever been in Lillehammer before?" asked the interrogator.

"No, not until the police brought me here," he responded.

To be subject to an interrogation was a new experience for Gehmer, and he did not like it. He was a man accustomed to giving commands, to sitting on the side of the desk where the power lay, and to reading reports about the interrogations of others. A wave of anger was building up. Suddenly it swept over him.

"I refuse to answer any further questions," he abruptly told his interrogator. "I don't want to hear my statement read to me, and furthermore I refuse to sign it." Then Gehmer, his cold blue eyes glaring at Valstad, clamped shut his heavy jaw.

During the drive to Lillehammer, Gehmer evidently had succeeded in giving a few surreptitious hints to Dan Aerbel about the general plot of the cover story he and Sylvia had decided upon. A fanciful raconteur by nature, Aerbel began to spin his own colorful variation. But he was mixed up on a couple of key points, includ-

ing Gehmer's cover identity; Aerbel kept referring to
him as a Canadian.

"My name is Ert," he told Inspector Ravlo, as his
interrogation got underway. "I'm employed by a Danish
furniture company called Viking. For the past two
years, I've been living in Rome and traveling extensively for my company, which now is trying to sell our
products in Sweden and Norway. That's why I have a
rented apartment in Oslo. I came to Oslo by air and
went to the Panorama Hotel, where I became acquainted with Marianne and two Canadians, including
the lady named Patricia Roxburgh. I don't remember
the man's name, but the four of us spent the eveing together. I also rented a car for a man named Pistauer
whom I had met on the plane. He appeared to me to be
a businessman.

"What business?" asked Ravlo.

"I don't know," replied Aerbel. "But I did notice that
Pistauer seemed to have plenty of money.

"Yes, I found it a bit peculiar that Pistauer would
want someone else to rent a car for him, but I helped
him anyway.

"I spent Thursday, the nineteenth, looking at apartments in Oslo. In the evening, I returned to the Panorama and tried to contact my new friends, but I couldn't
locate them. At ten o'clock on Friday morning, I had an
appointment with a real estate agent to sign the contract
for the flat in Baerum. After that I rented a car and
drove to Ikea [a large discount department store on the
outskirts of Oslo], where I bought bedclothes, china,
and some furniture for a total of about three thousand
kroner.

"At about nine that evening, I returned to the Panorama to pick up my things and pay the bill. At the hotel, I met Patricia and she moved with me to the apartment. I didn't see Marianne or the Canadian that
evening. Patricia and I stayed in the apartment until the
next day. Then we agreed to go for a drive. First we
drove south from Oslo, but then we turned north and
came to Hamar. It is possible that we were also in Lillehammer. I saw a road sign with Lillehammer on it. But,
really, I'm simply not at all sure where we went. Patri-

cia is a type who likes to do the driving, and she made the decisions about where we went. We were only looking at the beautiful countryside and did not have any definite travel plans or schedule.

"It was perhaps at Hamar that we met Marianne and the Canadian, who came driving along in a Peugeot. It was some time in the afternoon between four and five. We drove together in the two cars, but I can't remember the names of the towns we passed through. About eight or nine, we returned to Oslo, and by that time I had invited Marianne and the Canadian to stay in the apartment until Monday, when they planned to travel onward. I didn't know where they were headed or whether they were planning to travel together."

"Could you give any more details about the drive on Saturday?" asked Ravlo.

"No," replied Aerbel. "I don't remember very much. I'd been sick that day with a fever and pains in my stomach. Patricia did most of the driving."

"Did you meet anyone else driving around in that area?" inquired Ravlo.

"I don't remember," answered Aerbel.

"Did you have a walkie-talkie or other means of communication in the car?"

"No," said Aerbel. "Definitely not."

Resuming his story, Aerbel stated that his three guests had spent Saturday night with him in the apartment.

"On Sunday morning," he went on, "Marianne and I drove to Fornebu—I was in the Volvo and she drove the Peugeot—to hand back the Volvo. At the same time, we planned to buy some food to take to the apartment. While we were at the airport, we were apprehended. I really have no knowledge of the background of the three people I have spent the past few days with. But I assume they are tourists. It seems to me we were all strangers when we met. I have not noticed anything peculiar about them."

"Do you have any knowledge whatsoever about the killing?" Ravlo asked.

"No," replied Aerbel. "I know nothing about it."

* * *

There were many conflicts between the statements of Gehmer and Dan Aerbel. One of the most glaring was that both had Patricia driving with them on that fateful Saturday. Still, for wholly unrehearsed and uncoordinated performances, they were not bad at all. It would take a while for the interrogators to sort out the discrepancies, and by that time—who knows?—the situation might be different. For the moment, the important thing was to maintain the deception and play for time.

In a nearby room where Marianne Gladnikoff faced Leif Lier, the dialogue was taking another direction. Marianne felt miserable and afraid. It was her first intelligence mission, and the pressure had been immense. The feeling of inadequacy that had gripped her during the briefing at Lod had only increased during the past four days. Marianne did not understand Hebrew very well, and she was seldom able to catch what the other team members were saying among themselves. She felt ill at ease with them. They were so quiet, so uncommunicative. Furthermore, she had been badly treated by some of the agents. She had been lied to, yelled at, overworked, and intimidated.

Back in Tel Aviv, she had been asked to do a service for Israel, and it had all seemed so noble. She had been reassured that she would not be asked to do anything illegal. Now she was caught, trapped, ruined. She was a respectable young woman from a fine Jewish family in Stockholm. She had never done anything wrong in her life and she had not intended to do anything wrong now. She had been misled to participate in a crime she did not even know was going to be committed. Her family would be mortified, her own life shattered.

In Marianne's eyes, Inspector Lier, who sat quietly biting on a briar pipe, did not appear to be an enemy. Quite the contrary, he seemed genuinely kind and understanding. He neither yelled at her nor ordered her about. He was a Scandinavian like herself. Despite her Jewishness, Marianne was discovering that she felt more at home among her Norwegian captors than she did with her Mossad comrades.

As she and Lier began to talk, she switched from English, in which Lier was not completely at ease, to their almost common language. She would speak Swedish and he Norwegian, but they both understood each other perfectly well. At first, Marianne spoke slowly and haltingly; then her story began to gush forth like a catharsis.

Though he maintained his calm exterior, Lier nearly bit his pipestem in two. He and the other interrogators had no idea that they were dealing with members of an Israeli liquidation team. Their only solid evidence was that cars rented by foreigners had been sighted in the area, and that these suspects had some connection with those cars. To Lier's utter astonishment, Marianne was relating a story that transformed a local killing into an event of highest international significance.

"I was asked if I were willing to perform a service for the State of Israel, and I felt obliged to do so, because I had not done military service," she explained. Then, step by step, Marianne told her involvement in the Lillehammer operation. She recounted details about the briefing at Lod, the air trip to Oslo, the stay at the Panorama Hotel, the shopping excursion with Ingleby, and the search for Benamane.

Masking his growing excitement, Lier asked to be excused. He went to confer with Magnhild Aanestad, a deputy chief of the I-Group who had come to Lillehammer to coordinate the interrogation. (During simultaneous questionings, the interrogators would periodically pop out and report what they were being told. Aanestad, in turn, would quickly brief the interrogators on what the others were learning. Thus, the interrogators knew what the other suspects were saying while the suspects themselves remained ignorant of what the others might be giving away.)

When Lier reported to Aanestad the gist of Marianne's confession, she advised him to be very wary. It all sounded too improbable and conflicted with the other statements.

"Watch out!" Aanestad said. "The young woman may be putting you on."

When Lier resumed the questions a few minutes later, Marianne's account became even more improbable. She told about the trip to Lillehammer and the further

pursuit of the mysterious Kemal Benamane. Because
she was a novice, Marianne did not understand everything about the operation and misinterpreted some of
the things she observed. Still, she had picked up quite a
lot. As she talked, she mentioned the names of the team
members—Mike, Tamar, Patricia, Danny, François,
and the others. In his own mind, Lier began to form an
impression of the size and complexity of the operation.
Marianne recounted the events of Thursday evening in
the Skotte, how she and Danny had sat almost side by
side with Benamane in the television lounge.

Lier interrupted to remind her of the significance of
her testimony. Her words, he warned, were indicting
her under a number of very serious paragraphs in the
Norwegian criminal law, including, at the very least,
paragraph 91a, which forbids persons to collect information for a foreign power on Norwegian soil. No matter. She wanted to keep on talking. Lier had a lawyer
called in as protection for her legal rights. But it was
already about 9 P.M. and after two hours, the lawyer
became weary and left.

Marianne still had much more to say.

"We saw Benamane sitting in an outdoor café and
talking with another Arab who had a mustache," she
continued. "Gustav Pistauer had a picture and was
comparing the man in the photograph with the one in
the café."

She recounted how the team's attention shifted to the
second Arab and described in great detail the search
and shadowing operation down to the moment he
stepped on the bus the night before in Lillehammer.

"I had no idea that a man was going to be murdered," she cried. "I didn't even know a killing had
taken place until the next day. Please don't punish
me!"

At 1:35 Monday morning, five hours and ten minutes after the interrogation had begun, a very exhausted
and vastly relieved Marianne Gladnikoff finally asked
to stop.

"I can't carry on any longer," she said.

An almost equally exhausted Leif Lier adjourned the
session. "We'll resume at nine," he said.

At nine o'clock, Lier was eager to continue the interrogation. After having talked with his colleagues, he knew that the three other suspects had related flimsy and contradictory accounts. He felt certain that Marianne was the only one telling the truth. But as she entered the interrogation room, Lier sensed that her mood had changed.

Marianne, who had enjoyed her first good rest in days, had regained her composure. "I absolutely refuse to make any further statement," she said. "I greatly regret having told you as much as I did."

Leif Lier bits his pipestem.

If Marianne Gladnikoff had spent a restorative night in the Lillehammer lockup, another member of the Mossad team most emphatically had not. For Dan Aerbel, the experience had been excruciating.

Dan Aerbel, the Mossad reserve officer, suffered from severe claustrophobia. His illness stemmed from a tragic childhood ordeal in German-occupied Denmark. In 1944, as the Nazis staged their last great roundup of Jews in Western Europe, Dan, then a boy of six, was hidden along with other Jewish children in the basement of a school. To conceal them from their German hunters, the children were bricked into a tiny space behind a new wall. In that small, dark, and airless sanctuary, Dan felt pangs of fright. But since safety lay in silence, he was given injections of a sedative to quiet him. After two weeks of hiding in the darkness, Dan, his older sister, and his parents managed to escape to Sweden.

But the little boy did not escape the consequences of the experience. For years, Dan was plagued by nightmares and would wake up screaming. Yet he had succeeded in hiding his weakness. On the surface, he grew into a polished and effective business executive. He liked expensive cars, elegant clothes, and living well. He married a beautiful Sabra. His intellectual interests included literature, languages, and, to a lesser degree, theology. He developed healthy habits—he neither smoked, drank, nor took any sort of medicine. But Aerbel was deathly afraid of riding in elevators. The bedroom in his new home in Herzliyya had no doors. Now he had been locked for hours in a small cell. He simply could not stand it. He feared he would lose his sanity.

As his second interrogation began at 2:20 on Monday afternoon after the night in the cell, Aerbel was very nervous. Still, he started out by bluffing. He said that the story he had told the night before was essentially correct. However, he wished to make a few elaborations. Then Dan Aerbel launched into a highly unlikely embroidered tale that was patently devised to cover more of his travels and account for the receipts, which he now suspected had been found.

But in the course of his explanations, he became increasingly entwined in contradictions and confusions. He insisted, for example, that he had passed through a city to the south of Oslo while on his way northward to Hamar.

As Inspector Ravlo pointed out the inconsistencies, Aerbel suddenly realized that his story would not stand up to intensive examination. "Why play games any longer?" he must have thought. He was absolutely convinced that if only the Norwegian authorities knew the truth about the operation, they would surely release him and his comrades. It stood to reason. They were not criminals. They were agents of Israel, soldiers in a secret war. They were the last guardians at the gate protecting the Western world against the invasion of the Arab terrorists. What was the big deal? The entire charade was only taking place because someone had failed to tell the Norwegians the truth. Well, it was high time they heard it, and he would tell them.

"What I have said is true in broad outline," declared Dan Aerbel. "But I do, however, have knowledge about the killing in Lillehammer.

"One of the reasons for my trip to Norway was to assist in that killing," he explained. "It is a political action carried out by the State of Israel against the movement Black September.

"Israeli intelligence," Aerbel continued, "had reason to believe that Black September was planning an attack against an Israeli embassy or property in Scandinavia. The request for the Mossad operation came from a high-ranking Israeli security officer, who for the time being is staying in Norway. I don't know his name, but I imagine that several Israeli diplomats are involved in this case. However, the only persons whom I know by name are those in the Mossad team, and with the sole exception of Marianne, those names are totally false."

If the Norwegian authorities did not believe him, he could furnish immediate proof that the killing was an official act, sanctioned at the highest levels of the Israeli government.

"My contact in the defense ministry is a man called Miko," Aerbel stated. "Telephone him! His number is Tel Aviv 25 62 30. He'll tell you the truth."

The Norwegian police did not need to do that. In Dan Aerbel's own papers they found the clue that linked the operation directly to the State of Israel. On the back page of Aerbel's Danish passport, the I-Group investigators noticed some figures—14 15 89. The digits looked suspiciously like an Oslo number, and the I-Group asked the telephone company if that were so. It was indeed an Oslo number, but an unlisted one. The subscriber had given his name as Zigal, and his profession as an employee for El Al.

That was very odd. El Al does not fly to Oslo. The I-Group investigators wanted to know more. They asked for a search to be conducted at the Zigal dwelling. Håkon Wiker, the tall, handsome state prosecutor who had been placed in charge of the case, applied for a search warrant, which was immediately granted.

On Tuesday evening, July 24, Rolf Jahrmann and Håkon Wiker relayed their joint request for a search to Oslo's police central. The senior inspector on night duty was Hans Holen, a stern and scrupulously correct police officer. Holen put out the calls that quickly assembled a group of eighteen men from four branches—the I-Group, counterintelligence, criminal police, and dog patrol. As he planned the operation, Holen had to contemplate dangers that almost never intrude upon the consciousness of an Oslo police inspector. He was to conduct a raid on a house that had been serving as a communications central for foreign agents who now were implicated in a killing. It was a potentially dangerous assignment. Prudently, Holen instructed the five uniformed officers in his party to wear flack jackets and carry weapons. He ordered the dog patrol to be in the first attack wave.

"A large dog has a calming effect," he said later.

The dwelling was located in row of town houses in a quiet and residential part of town. As the officers drove there in five cars, they maintained absolute radio silence. Otherwise, Oslo's eavesdropping journalists, who have police radios illegally installed in their own cars, would have rushed to the scene and spoiled the element of surprise.

With military precision, the raiding party went into action. Two uniformed officers took up positions in the yard. The others made their way inside. Two police, wearing flack jackets and armed with high-powered rifles, flattened themselves against the wall on either side of the front door.

"Go!" whispered one of them.

The other pressed the bell.

A woman opened the door. The two policemen brushed past her and charged inside. The German shepherd and his handler stormed in. Next came Hans Holen, dressed in civilian clothes, followed by agents from counterintelligence and criminal police.

It happened so fast that the occupants of the house were caught completely off guard. That was precisely what Holen had intended. There was no resistance.

"Up, up!" cried the officers as they burst into the living room. "Come on, up, and keep those hands high!"

Two men sitting on a couch looked at each other in a totally nonplussed manner. Then they rose obediently and put up their hands.

The police searched the chairs and sofas. One officer came up with a pistol, which was stuck between two seat cushions and covered by a pillow.

"Whose is this?" he demanded.

"Mine," replied a third man, who had jumped up at the instant the police rushed in. "Who is in charge here?" he cried angrily in English.

"I am," replied Holen.

"You have no right to do this," the man thundered at him. "I am an Israeli diplomat."

And so he was. His name was not Zigal as it had been listed in the telephone company records. It was Eyal—Yigal Eyal. He was not an employee of El Al. Zigal of El Al was a deception. Undoubtedly, he had misspelled his name to the phone company on purpose; it made him just that little bit more difficult to locate if and when Black September should decide to pay him a visit. Yigal Eyal was a high-ranking security officer and he produced his diplomatic credentials as well as an Oslo police permit to carry a weapon.

Meanwhile, other officers were searching the dwelling. In the guest room they found a packed suitcase. The two men were told to show their papers. They identified themselves as Michael Dorf and Zwi Steinberg; the packed bag belonged to the latter.

Eyal, who had been posted to Oslo from the Israeli embassy in Paris, was mindful of the consequences of their arrest. These men provided the direct link between the killing in Lillehammer and the State of Israel.

"Get out of my apartment at once," he told Holen. "It is Israeli diplomatic territory."

"Please keep your voices down," pleaded Mrs. Eyal. "The baby is asleep upstairs."

The German shepherd was sitting in the front room, definitely a calming influence.

Inspector Holen realized that he had been plunged into the midst of a serious diplomatic question. To this day, there is speculation in Oslo that higher police and intelligence authorities suspected that the "Zigal" apartment was in reality occupied by an Israeli diplomat but preferred to feign ignorance in order to test their hunch. Thus, they allowed the search to go on and failed to confide their suspicion to Holen. Until that evening, he had known nothing about the true ramifications of the Lillehammer case. Hence, he had to think fast.

"Yes, I will leave," Holen replied. "But those two men are coming with me."

"No, absolutely not," countered Eyal. "I won't allow them to be arrested. You are committing a grave offense against my diplomatic status."

In his own mind Holen thought, "Well, he may be correct." But the inspector was also weighing the power relationships. Backed by his squad of police, he could take the men by force now and no one would be able to stop him. If higher authorities decided later that he had acted incorrectly, the two men could be returned to the Israeli embassy or to Eyal's house and Norway could apologize to Israel. Holen was certain of one thing: it would be less complicated to hand them back than to get them at a later time. So he decided to take them with him.

Steinberg and Dorf started to protest, but realizing the helplessness of their situation, they went along quietly. Eyal reduced the volume of his objections so as not to wake the baby. Steinberg lugged his suitcase. Police found in his pocket a first-class rail ticket to Copenhagen for a train leaving at 10:20 that evening. In fact, Steinberg was preparing to say goodbye just as the raiding party had crashed into the house. Instead, he was taken in a police car to Lillehammer for questioning. Dorf was placed in a cell at the Oslo central police station.

Steinberg and Dorf told the interrogators very little. Steinberg, who pleaded he had a bad memory, said he had emigrated to Israel from Brazil in 1955, settled in Kibbutz Gan Shmuel, and served in the army as an infantry sergeant. In April, he decided "for personal reasons" to take a four-month vacation.

"I visited France and the Netherlands," he said. "On the eighteenth of July, I flew from Amsterdam to Oslo to visit a friend of mine, named Yigal Eyal, who is the security attaché in the Israeli embassy. We had been in the army together."

Dorf turned out to be a twenty-seven-year-old international telephone operator from Tel Aviv. Someone— he would not say who—asked him to go to Oslo and take a part-time job in the embassy. He maintained that he did only "clerical work," but he conceded that he was on duty all night from July 21 to 22.

If Steinberg and Dorf were closemouthed, their belongings spoke for them. In Steinberg's luggage police found two apartment keys attached to a blue nameplate. Those keys, it turned out, opened an apartment in Paris, which Zwi had rented the year before. In that dwelling were eleven other keys, eight of them labeled with names of Paris cinemas. They belonged to the hit team's apartments in Paris. Clues discovered in these flats linked several members of the Lillehammer operation to the earlier liquidations in Paris.

Among "Mikki" Dorf's belongings, the investigators turned up a notebook in which he had written the telex numbers of the Israeli embassies in The Hague and London. They also found an unlisted telephone number for The Hague embassy, and the name of an Israeli diplomat who evidently was his contact.

Most damaging of all, the Norwegian police found a note scribbled in Hebrew in one of his bags. The message, Mikki admitted, had been dictated to him the day before by his contact in the Israeli embassy in The Hague. The text, laboriously translated by scholars of the theological faculty at the University of Oslo, showed the intimate degree of supervision exercised by the Mossad's European Central over the operation in Norway.

The message contained six paragraphs, the first four directed to Steinberg, and the final two to Dorf. It said:

From the CNT [the abbreviation for Mossad's European office]:
1. Get away from Norway's capital by rail [he recommended going to Denmark's capital].
2. Depart as soon as you are in possession of an Israeli passport.
3. From Denmark's capital you are to proceed to Amsterdam and get in touch with CNT.
4. You must not bring along any controversial material or any document. Just the mentioned documentation.
5. Mikki is to stay behind in the embassy in Norway's capital, in hiding for the time being, to establish with KHT to track traffic until KHT lifts the contact.

6. Mikki is to report to base special news of the topic.

Norwegian intelligence officers easily deduced that "base" was the Mossad central in The Hague, "KHT" the Mossad's political intelligence division, and "topic" obviously Lillehammer.

During the months when Golda Meir had resisted the setting up of Israeli liquidation squads, she had always objected, "Some day our people will get caught, and tell me, what will we do then?"

Her fear had become a reality. Six Mossad agents were imprisoned in Norwegian jails, and two of them were talking.

EIGHT

In reality, the situation was worse than that which Golda Meir had feared. Not only were six Mossad agents under arrest, but something else drastic had also happened. Mike's hit team had made a terrible and irreversible mistake. They had killed the wrong man. The thirteenth victim was not Ali Hassan Salameh, the architect of the Munich massacre. The man who had been stitched by the Berettas was a waiter in a Lillehammer health resort. His name was Ahmed Bouchiki, and he was Moroccan by nationality. The woman who lay beside him while he was being shot was his Norwegian wife, Torill, pregnant with their child.

It took the Israelis a while to realize their mistake. On the day after the killing in Lillehammer, everything had seemed all right. There are no Sunday newspapers in Norway, and therefore Mike could not learn about the true identity of the victim. He was also unaware of the arrest of the four agents. During the hours in which his operation was being exposed as a full-fledged disaster, Mike continued to live under the impression that he had just scored the greatest triumph of his career. On that Sunday, he seemed in no hurry to leave Oslo himself or to send the remaining agents home. Apparently, he intended to leave the Baerum foursome behind to report on the aftermath of the operation.

Mike had a leisurely lunch with Zwi Steinberg. Then he met with General Zwi Zamir. The chief of the Mossad had not, of course, driven to Trondheim as he had told the receptionist at the Hamar motel, but had returned to Oslo instead.

Mike and Zwi Zamir must have been feeling exceptionally happy and self-content that afternoon. They had removed Israel's most dangerous surviving enemy—scratch the Red Prince. It was the perfect climax of Operation Hit Team. In little more than one year, the Israeli killers had eliminated thirteen Arabs and spread panic among the terrorist organizations. Never had a hit team written the Israeli threat more plainly than in Lillehammer: nowhere on this earth, not even in a remote Norwegian village, can a terrorist hide from retribution. There are no "safe houses," no sanctuaries for the enemies of Israel.

On Monday morning, the Norwegian newspapers flooded onto the newsstands carrying banner headlines about the Lillehammer killing. No outsider knows for certain when Mike and Zamir left Norway. Later, after a thorough search through more than four thousand air tickets, Norwegian police found the ones belonging to Rolf Baehr and Gérard Lafond. But Zamir and Mike evidently managed to depart without leaving a trace. In any event, the two intelligence chiefs, wherever they were, quickly learned the details of the Norwegian press reports. To their dismay, they read that Patricia Roxburgh, Leslie Orbaum, Marianne Gladnikoff, and Dan Ert had been arraigned in a Lillehammer court on suspicion of participation in a premeditated murder and were being held for further questioning. They also learned that the victim was a local waiter.

At that stage, the press reports were mixed about the motive for the crime. The Norwegian police had withheld all information about the four suspects except their names. Therefore, newsmen were uncertain as to what role they might have played in Bouchiki's death. In those days, Lillehammer was a transit point for narcotics trafficking in Norway, because of its close proximity to the Swedish border. Some newsmen speculated that the murder was somehow connected to drug smuggling. Other journalists hazarded guesses that political factors were behind Bouchiki's death. Reflecting the confusion, *Verdens Gang,* Oslo's largest tabloid, ran a question as its headline: HOT DRUGS OR COLD POLITICS?

If the motive for the killing was unclear, the identity of the victim most assuredly was not. The dead man was a familiar figure in Lillehammer. And what is more, he had been acquainted with a journalist on the local newspaper, the *Lillehammer Tilskuer* (Observer). He was a reporter-photographer named Erik Hagen, and he happened to be visiting in the neighborhood at the time the shooting occurred. He reached the scene of the killing only seconds after the ambulance had picked up the riddled body of Ahmed Bouchiki. Sensing a big story, Hagen immediately began interviewing witnesses and taking pictures. By the next day, he had put together the definitive two-page article about the life and death of Ahmed Bouchiki. Hagen's piece was quoted in many Norwegian newspapers and extracts were published throughout the world.

The Israelis had assumed, of course, that Salameh would be operating under an alias, most likely an Arab one. And they had not been surprised when he was spotted in the company of a woman in Lillehammer. They knew that the Black September chieftain was a womanizer anyhow and the fact that the latest girl friend was heavy with child did not evoke any special curiosity on their part.

But Hagen's story exploded their assumptions. The Lillehammer journalist's report was so laden with biographical facts about the past several years of Bouchiki's life that the Israelis began to have profound second thoughts about whether they had gotten the right man. On Monday afternoon and evening, Israeli embassy officials in Oslo made inquiries on their own. By Tuesday morning, the political and intelligence leaders of Israel were convinced that a horrendous error had been committed.

While Mossad headquarters went into a temporary state of shock, the Israeli foreign ministry began a frantic cover-up effort. Tuesday afternoon, the Israeli government issued an official statement denying any connection whatsoever to the incident in Lillehammer. But the official pronouncements fooled no one. A few days later, an Israeli magazine carried on its cover side-by-side pictures of Bouchiki and Salameh. SORRY, WRONG MAN! read the cover slash.

For the four agents who fell into the hands of the Norwegian police, the disclosure came much more quickly. As soon as they were taken to police headquarters in Lillehammer, they realized that the wrong man had been killed. As Sylvia recalled later: "Everyone in the police station was saying: 'Oh, poor man, and his poor wife who is about to have a child!' "

And what about the "right" man?

Ali Hassan Salameh was, in fact, in Scandinavia at the time the Israelis were hunting for him. He went to Stockholm first and had secret meetings with European and Arab terrorists. Then he traveled to Oslo where he also met with Arabs.

On Thursday, July 19, only two days before the Lillehammer killing, there was a full-scale hijacking alert at Oslo's international airport. Norwegian police had been tipped off that an Air France flight would be hijacked, and took massive countermeasures. The police action may have frightened off the would-be hijackers. Three passengers who were booked on the flight and had Arab names failed to pick up their tickets at the airport. Salameh may have been planning that hijacking. He was in Norway on the Friday the JAL jumbo was seized after takeoff from Amsterdam.

After hearing about Bouchiki's death, Ali Hassan Salameh evidently deduced that he had been the real target. At that time, in press reports there still had been no mention of his name in connection with the Lillehammer killing, but Salameh understood the implications. Quickly departing from Oslo, he made his way through Europe and returned safely to Beirut.

NINE

Then was the palm of the hand sent before him and this was the writing that was transcribed: God hath numbered thy kingdom and brought it to an end. Thou art weighed in the balance and found wanting.

—FROM THE BOOK OF DANIEL

As soon as the raiding party returned to Oslo police headquarters from Eyal's apartment, Inspector Hans Holen telephoned the duty officer at the Norwegian foreign ministry.

"You can expect a visit from the Israeli ambassador in the morning," he said.

The duty officer, in turn, immediately rang up the home of Kjell Eliassen, the chief counsel of the foreign ministry, and told him the news. Eliassen spent the first moments the next morning checking the sections of the Vienna Convention that deal with violation of diplomatic immunity. He had just formulated what he felt was a sound position when the Israeli ambassador arrived at the foreign ministry.

The Israeli diplomat made a very muted approach. Instead of lodging a formal protest, he merely referred to the sanctity conferred upon foreign diplomatic property by the Vienna Convention and stated that the two men must be released at once. Otherwise there would be "consequences."

Unmoved, Eliassen replied that the Norwegians were confident no real violation of Israeli diplomatic immunity had taken place. "At most, one might call it a technical violation," he stated. Citing several precedents, he contended that the Israelis had forfeited the right to diplomatic immunity in this incident. He went on to explain that diplomatic conventions and practice forbid embassies and residences from sheltering wanted persons except those seeking political asylum.

Eliassen's argument boiled down to this: if the Norwegians had presented warrants for the arrest of

Steinberg and Dorf to the embassy, the Israelis would have been obliged to surrender them. Otherwise, the Norwegians would have been justified in seizing the men by force. Hence, the events of Tuesday night were a violation only in so far as the Norwegians took the men before they were duly charged with a criminal act. Now, however, they were arraigned in accordance with Norwegian law, and it would make no sense at all to release them since they would be rearrested at once anyhow.

Faced with this uncompromising Norwegian position, the Israeli ambassador excused himself, saying he had to consult with his government.

Two days later, Eliassen had another visitor who suddenly arrived from Tel Aviv. He was Meir Rosenne, the chief legal counsel of the Israeli foreign ministry and therefore Eliassen's Israeli counterpart. Rosenne obviously hoped he would be able to persuade the Norwegians to adopt a more flexible attitude. But he was taken aback by the cool and distant behavior of his Norwegian colleague. As the Israeli dipomat began to speak, Eliassen fixed him with an even gaze. The first point on his agenda was the Israeli hope that the entire affair could be hushed up. But, as his words met only with disapproving silence, Rosenne went on to his next subjects.

Rephrasing the ambassador's words from two days earlier, he declared that Steinberg and Dorf had been seized under illegal conditions that required their immediate release to Israeli embassy officials.

In reply, Eliassen said that the Norwegians saw no reason to alter their standpoint.

Rosenne turned to his final major point—consular access to the six prisoners. He demanded that Israeli diplomats should be allowed to visit them and provide legal assistance.

Eliassen explained that the Norwegian judge in charge of the case had ruled that the prisoners were not to receive visitors or mail until the further investigations into the Lillehammer killing had been completed. However, if the Israeli government wished to present an argument to the court as to why it should be granted access to the prisoners, the foreign ministry would be willing to make the appropriate arrangements.

"But you should know," Eliassen cautioned his Israeli colleague, "that the state prosecutor will resist your efforts and you will have to be prepared to argue on your behalf in court."

Rosenne was faced with a dilemma. A few press reports had identified the six prisoners as Israeli agents on a liquidation mission, and *Time* would carry an accurate account of the murder-by-mistake that week. Even so, on July 27, the day this exchange took place, the direct and irrefutable links between the State of Israel and the Lillehammer affair had not been made public. The press reports were based primarily on leaks in Israel and speculation in Norway. They could be denied, and that, of course, was exactly what the Israeli government was doing. Therefore, Rosenne could not make an argument in a Norwegian court, claiming the right of access to the six defendants, while his government was maintaining the fiction that it had nothing to do with them. After a second meeting with Eliassen on August 7, Rosenne gave up and flew back to Tel Aviv.

The Israeli government arranged for the defendants to have counsel by pretending that their families at home were making the arrangements. Steinberg, for example, received a letter in English from the Israeli embassy in Oslo saying, in effect, your family has learned you have some legal problems and is making arrangements for you to be represented by a Scandinavian lawyer. Marianne Gladnikoff's family in Stockholm made separate legal arrangements for her defense.

Meanwhile, the investigation was continuing and expanding. Based on the disclosures by Marianne and Dan Aerbel, the state prosecutor issued warrants for the arrest of the other members of the hit team. The I-Group sent to Interpol detailed descriptions of both the wanted and already captured hit team members and soon replies began to arrive from Interpol contacts in Canada, South Africa, Europe, and the Middle East. The replies indicated that the wanted members of the team had been operating under fabricated or assumed identities. After an exchange of cables, the Canadian police stated definitively that the "Patricia Roxburgh" being held by Norwegian authorities was not the real Patricia Roxburgh. The Israeli version was carrying a false passport and gave autobiographical facts that did not jibe with the real person; the Israeli "Patricia's" parents were dead, for example, while the actual woman's mother and father were alive. Sylvia Rafael smilingly acknowledged that she was not the Canadian, but she refused to disclose her true identity. "My mother has a bad heart," she explained, "and it might kill her if she learned her daughter was in jail."

British police investigators quickly disclosed that there was no Leeds schoolmaster and accountant by the name of Leslie Orbaum, which was the flimsy cover that had been devised by the Mossad for Abraham Gehmer.

"You can't possibly be named Leslie Orbaum," a Norwegian interrogator told him. "He doesn't exist."

"Then I have no name," snapped Abraham Gehmer.

What went wrong with the Lillehammer operation? The answer, obviously, is just about everything.

It seems inconceivable that the intelligence agency regarded as one of the world's best, if not *the* best, could make such a series of blunders. Yet the riddled corpse of Ahmed Bouchiki and the six imprisoned agents were evidence of the mistakes. Though the Israeli government continued to deny involvement, the hand of Israel ultimately was fully exposed and, even before that took place, the hit team operation was disbanded as a result of the Norwegian fiasco.

The faults and failings of the Lillehammer operation fall roughly into the following categories:

The Fix Did Not Work

The Israelis evidently had the notion that Norwegian authorities would hush up the affair and free the captured agents. How did they arrive at such a mistaken idea?

No outsider knows for certain, and Norwegian Ministry of Justice officials deny that there were any prior agreements between the two intelligence services. But it can be speculated that Zwi Zamir and the chief of Norwegian counterintelligence had reached some vague understanding. They were acquainted and met twice a year at the secret sessions held by the chiefs of Western intelligence agencies, which the Israelis always attend. During their operations in Rome and Paris, Zamir and Mike had at least the tacit cooperation of special branches within the French and Italian intelligence agencies. It is reasonable to assume that they would have sought to make a similar arrangement in Norway.

General Zwi Zamir had visited Norway a couple of months before the Lillehammer operation as the guest of his Norwegian counterpart. For more than a year, the Israelis had been picking up clues that Black September was planning an operation against an Israeli embassy, residence, or El Al office in Scandinavia. It would have been odd if the two men did not talk about the possibility of Israeli countermeasures that could take the form of a hit team operating in Norway. Perhaps the Norwegian counterintelligence chief said something like this: "OK, but don't get caught."

It is also highly unlikely that Zamir would have come to Norway for the Salameh operation without informing his Norwegian colleague of his presence. Though he registered under the name of Tahl at the Hamar motel, Zamir was traveling with his own passport. Furthermore, Mike's relaxed behavior on Sunday, combined with the fact that he and Zamir had a meeting that day, indicates that they felt no fear of arrest or revealment.

However, the Israelis probably overestimated both the ability and willingness of Norwegian counterintelligence to come to their rescue if they did get caught. In Israel, the Mossad is far more a law unto itself than counterintelligence is in Norway. Once the Mossad agents were captured by police and charged with criminal offenses, the orderly process of the law took over—and no one, neither counterintelligence nor the foreign ministry, could or would try to interfere.

Norwegian counterintelligence refused to make any comment or response whatsoever to the speculation that it had knowledge of the Mossad operation. In fact, the agency's closemouthed conduct increased suspicions about its role. It refused to cooperate with the Norwegian police in the investigation of the case, and it refrained from advising State Prosecutor Håkon Wiker on the intelligence aspects of the affair.

It Was the Wrong Team

The idea of recruiting a new hit team mainly from the headquarters staff of the special branch was stupid and ill-conceived. From the start, the operation to liquidate Salameh should have been recognized as the most difficult one of all; he was an exceptionally crafty person, who was constantly on the move. It is far easier to identify and corner a relatively stationary target. When the first-string hit team exhausted itself in the chase after the Black September planner, the Mossad chiefs should have realized the difficulty of the mission and regrouped their best forces before resuming the operation.

The hastily recruited team sallied forth from Tel Aviv as if it were going on a company picnic. At best, the new members had been trained only as reservists. Yet they naturally felt as if they were bearing the prestige of their department and wanted to show the other sections within Mossad headquarters that they could perform in the field as well as push pencils and sit behind desks.

They seemed to think that political assassination was a simple matter. As chairborne warriors in Tel Aviv, they had marveled at how easy it looked, but failed to appreciate the skill and training the first-string team brought to its missions. They also had undoubtedly suffered from the jealousy that headquarters staff often feel toward front-line combatants. Most of all, the new hit team was afflicted by a disease widespread in Israel in those days—overconfidence. The members were supremely certain that they could do the job, but lacked the experience and knowledge to understand just how difficult the job would be.

There Was a Failure of Leadership

From start to finish, Mike bungled the operation. As a highly skilled intelligence expert with nearly thirty years of experience, he should have known better than to recruit and lead the headquarters team on such a challenging mission. Mike himself had established the rules and operational methods that brought success in the earlier operations. He had taught a whole generation of Israeli agents their skills. Yet, on "The Chase for the Red Prince," he allowed the cardinal rules to be broken and, what is more, broke them himself. He encouraged a mingling between the Aleph-Beth squads and the rest of the team that enabled the Norwegian police to easily deduce the makeup of the killer and guard units. His own relationship with Tamar was extremely unprofessional and not conducive to maintaining the discipline of the team.

Mike let the team behave as if it were a social group or a dining club. From an operational standpoint, it was prudent for the team to travel in couples, because a man and a woman attract less attention than two men or two women together. Yet, the hit team seems to have been overzealous about cultivating their heterosexual camouflage. Though Norwegian food is excellent, the agents' preoccupation with never missing a meal was ridiculous. Search and surveillance operations were suspended each time the hit team members got hungry. For example, the afternoon Sylvia, Nora, Dan Aerbel, and Pistauer first reached Lillehammer, supposedly hot on the trail of Benamane, they retired to the Victoria for a long lunch before carrying on with the search.

On the morning after the hit, Mike behaved as if there were no urgency to get the remainder of the team out of the country. His preoccupation with wanting to save a day's rental on an auto was absolutely mindless and led to the fateful arrest of Marianne and Dan Aerbel. He totally misjudged the Norwegian situation and the efficiency of the law-enforcement authorities.

Mike's lack of awareness literally delivered his agents into the hands of the Norwegian police.

Lillehammer Was the Wrong Place

The hit team should never have attempted to operate in Lillehammer. On the first moment they reached the town, they should have realized that it was not the proper setting for a political assassination. But after Mike blithely went ahead with the operation, the team should have made an effort to keep a lower profile. Instead, they behaved as if they were totally oblivious to local conditions. The high point of their insensitivity came during the Saturday afternoon watch on Nybu when they parked cars directly across from the Bouchikis' apartment building, switched from one to the other to chat among themselves, and even had a walkie-talkie antenna sticking out of a car window. Marianne saw a man staring down at the cars from a balcony and became frightened. But the other team members seemed unconcerned about whether anyone saw them. In fact, their blatant behavior attracted attention all over Lillehammer and caused some people to jot down the license numbers of their cars.

Lillehammer was also far too remote a place to carry out an execution. The lines of retreat are long and arduous. Though the Oslo-Lillehammer highway is graced with the designation E-6 (for European highway number 6), it is for the greater part only a winding two-lane road that is poorly marked with directional signs. It is not the sort of route a fifteen-member team should be dependent on for escape.

Tel Aviv Was Overly Anxious

The fact that the mistaken identification of Bouchiki as Salameh came within hours of the JAL jumbo hijacking is an ironic and tragic coincidence. It introduced an element of urgency that caused an already sloppy hit team operation to become even more disorganized and unprofessional.

The leaders of Israeli intelligence had developed a phobia about Ali Hassan Salameh. When they were hit, almost simultaneously, with two sensational pieces of news—the hijacking and his "discovery" in Lillehammer—they reacted emotionally.

The JAL incident exposed a serious weakness in the chain of command. The Israelis have a tradition of "leading from the front," whereby the intelligence chief or army general engages directly in operations. From an inspirational point of view, such action is commendable, but the disadvantage is great because the leader gets out of touch with the overall situation and command decisions must be made by his subordinates.

On the day of the hit, Zamir was holed up in the motel near Hamar, cut off from both the operational scene and the headquarters. On Saturday evening, he may have had a premonition of impending disaster, since he became highly nervous. He attracted the attention of the motel staff by behaving in an agitated manner and standing in the lobby staring out the window at E-6. He was looking at the very spot where Sheriff Rustad and Sylvia later locked eyes.

There is no way of knowing for certain whether Zamir would have exercised a calming influence on the decision-making process if he had been in touch with the Tel Aviv headquarters. But he was known as a sensible and unflappable person. As it was, the home office put increasing pressure on the hit team to move up its schedule of operation. The compressed timetable left no further opportunity for the verification of Bouchiki's real identity. It is likely that if Mike and his agents had been given a few more days to observe Bouchiki, they would have realized that his way of life in no way conformed with that of a Black September chieftain on the run. Even the most elementary inquiry about Bouchiki would have disclosed that he was a genuine person, not the cover for Ali Hassan Salameh. They would also have had second thoughts about their assumption that Kemal Benamane had led them to the proper target.

Marianne Gladnikoff and Dan Aerbel Were Not Hit Team Material

Even after all the other blunders had been committed, the hit team might have been spared complete exposure if two of its members had not been amateurs and totally miscast as participants in a liquidation operation.

Marianne Gladnikoff had believed the assurances that she would not be required to do anything illegal. She also accepted the idea that the team's mission was to uncover information about Black September's plans in Scandinavia and to tip off the local police. This was a sensible impression since it was widely known at the time that the Mossad was performing precisely that function. To her shock, Marianne suddenly found herself involved in a liquidation operation, and she was neither emotionally nor professionally prepared to cope with the momentous strain. Once she was brought before an interrogator, she felt a compulsion to confess. Utterly without wile or guile, she spilled all she knew, and made none of the selective omissions or distortions that an experienced agent would have used to confuse the investigators. The Mossad had played upon her naïveté and goodwill, and she repaid their misuse by remaining naïve and goodwilled even in the hands of her captors.

For years, Dan Aerbel had delighted at playing on the fringes of intelligence work. It enhanced his feeling of self-importance to drop hints to friends and family that he was deeply involved in serious Mossad business. Actually, he was sent only on selected jobs where his genuine Danish passport and earlier connections with Scandinavian furniture-makers provided a good cover. He and Sylvia apparently made several trips to Arab countries together, but their spying missions were limited to observing naval preparations and taking pictures of government buildings. So far, Aerbel had found the dangers of espionage to be an exhilarating and fascinating experience.

Lillehammer was his undoing. The Mossad committed an extremely grave error in using a man who had claustrophobia. No outsider knows whether the Mossad was aware of his affliction, but he made no secret of it.

He was completely under the impression that the Mossad operation in Norway had been cleared with the local authorities. All he needed to do was to tell his interrogator the truth and everything would be fine. The Tel Aviv telephone number that Aerbel told Inspector Ravlo to call in order to verify his story about the team's mission was that of the Mossad duty officer, to be used only in grave emergencies.

Like Marianne, Dan Aerbel was psychologically incapable of participation in a premeditated murder, and the fact that he had become involved in a killing disturbed him greatly. After the failure of his efforts to spring the team by telling the truth, the once-boastful Mossad agent slumped into a state of anxious depression.

Who was Bouchiki?

As he awoke on the morning of his death, Ahmed Bouchiki had no inkling that he had been selected as the target of a highly effective killing machine. Nor did he have any notion of the tragic role his new friend, Kemal Benamane, was playing in his life.

Ahmed felt very far removed from the conflicts that pitted Arab against Jew. He was happy to have found a sheltered and pleasant corner of the world. Very few Arabs had ventured to small Nordic towns, so he was something of a rarity. He liked the younger Norwegians, whom he found friendly and open-minded, and the older ones, though often reserved and distant, were nevertheless correct and polite in their dealings with him. Jobs as dishwasher or waiter were easy to find. So, too, were girl friends, attracted by his dark looks.

Bouchiki was not a Palestinian. Yet, the conditions of his life in Norway were hauntingly echoed in verses, *Letter from an Exile,* by the Palestinian poet Mahmoud Darweesh.

I am grown now—over twenty
The burdens of life I shoulder like men

I work in a tavern as a dishwasher
And coffee maker
You should see me Ma
A smile on my face for the customer's sake!
I also smoke and stand at the corner
To speak with girls
Like other young men.
Life is unbearable without women.

Bouchiki had done far better than most Arab exiles. The letter writer in Darweesh's poem took comfort in the solitary fact that his clothes, though often mended, were not tattered. By contrast, Ahmed lived a relatively comfortable and secure life. He had a steady, if low-paying job as a waiter in a health resort. He was married to a local girl whose family was helping him get ahead. Her father managed the local community center, which contained the indoor swimming pool and the ground-floor Bakkegrillen where, most ironically, Mike and three Mossad agents had lunch on the day of Ahmed's murder. With his father-in-law's permission, Bouchiki was giving swimming lessons in the pool. He was also studying to pass the Norwegian lifeguard exam so that he could get a job there. His wife had a good position as lab technician in the nearby regional hospital, which provided them with a small, neat apartment at very low rent.

Bouchiki had been working on and off for the past four years in Lillehammer, and his main hobby was cultivating friendships and making acquaintances. He had brought to Lillehammer the Oriental love of sitting over cups of coffee and chatting endlessly about inconsequential topics. In summer, he delighted in meeting with friends in Lillehammer's handful of outdoor cafés where they innocently gossiped for hours about mutual friends, sports, and other common interests.

A good-looking, compact man, Ahmed stood five feet seven inches, and weighed about one hundred forty-five pounds. He had curly black hair, a thick mustache, which grew more bushy at the ends, and strong features. He kept in excellent physical condition and exuded an air of vitality. He smiled often, was irrepressibly friendly and engaging.

Ahmed Bouchiki had one experience in his past that made him especially intriguing to young Norwegians. He had served as a partisan during the Algerian war of independence. He had been born in Algeria on April 13, 1943, and at seventeen had become a member of the Algerian partisan movement. Bouchiki said he had been stationed in the desert on guard duty near the Moroccan border, and sometimes he would support his story by showing a picture of himself in the desert. He never disclosed whether he had actually participated in guerrilla fighting. In any event, the large-scale operations in Algeria had drawn to a close by the time Bouchiki joined the FLN. But his partisan past made him interesting and mysterious to young Nordic people who knew nothing of war. When pressed for more details about his guerrilla days, Bouchiki would become diffident. His reticence only heightened the curiosity of his Norwegian questioners.

"Yes," he would answer reluctantly. "I was a partisan for Algeria. I started as an idealist but moved more and more toward becoming a nationalist. In a war, patriotic feelings flare up to something nearing fanaticism. I was a partisan as long as the war lasted, but I was all too young to understand . . ."

Then he would let his voice trail off, as if he were pained by the memories of mayhem and conflict. Bouchiki frequently stressed his dedication to a peaceful way of life. "I am so absolutely against war and violence," he used to say.

He himself never brought up the subject of karate, which he had learned as part of his guerrilla training. But if questioned about it, he would emphasize the spiritual value of the sport.

"One thing that most people don't know," he would say, "is that karate is so much more than just a defense system. Part of the instruction is concentration and meditation. To me, karate is a very good way to live— almost like a religion. It gives mental calm, balance, and a clear view of the world. To train your body just to be able to beat down other people is meaningless. The spiritual training is the main thing."

He shunned controversial topics and took no interest whatsoever in politics. If he was questioned about his feelings as an Arab toward the Jews, his response was likely to be: "Many Jews are good friends of mine, and I see no reason why I should have anything against these people."

Aside from a few amorous adventures in Norway, Bouchiki seemed to have no vices. He did not drink, smoke, or use drugs. Though he earned low wages, he remained free of debts. "I'm careful to keep my record clean," he admitted. "The position of a foreigner in Norway is so sensitive that I can't afford to get mixed up in anything."

Bouchiki first came to Norway in 1965, and settled in the Atlantic coastal city of Bergen. He worked at odd jobs and taught karate to the police department. But he broke the law by failing to apply for a work permit. When he finally did get around to doing so eleven months too late, the alien office in Bergen ordered him to be deported, and he was promptly put on a ship bound for Rotterdam. But the Dutch refused to accept him and shipped him back to Bergen. The parents of one of his girl friends, evidently eager to be rid of the dark-eyed suitor, bought him a ship ticket, and he returned to his parents' home in France. The Bouchiki family had moved from Algeria in the early 1960s to the Rhone delta city of Arles.

No sooner had Ahmed been expelled from Norway, then he made arrangements to go back. Since his old Algerian passport was now stained by the deportation, he sought to acquire a new one. While his father was Algerian, his mother was Moroccan, so Ahmed persuaded the Moroccan consulate in Marseilles to issue him a passport and he became Moroccan. Then he wrote a letter in atrociously ungrammatical English to the alien authorities in Bergen, explaining that he had a new passport and would soon be coming back to Norway.

On September 9, 1966, he did just that, and this time duly registered with the Bergen alien office. He applied for, and was granted, a work permit. Whereupon Bouchiki began a long and undistinguished career among the pots and pans of Norwegian kitchens. His first job was as a dishwasher in the Hotel Norge in Bergen. Then he went to Oslo, where he plied the same trade in the Frascati Restaurant. Within a few months, he was back in the kitchens of Bergen.

It was a hard and lonely existence, and Bouchiki made one of his very few mistakes in Norway by becoming friends with dope traffickers in Bergen (though he was never suspected of being a dealer himself). On at least one occasion, he evidently did get into some trouble. One evening a taxi driver took him home for the night, because Bouchiki had been badly beaten up and was afraid to go back to his own flat.

Perhaps to get away from unsavory friends in Bergen, Bouchiki decided to go to sea. In the early spring of 1967, he signed on as a kitchen helper aboard the *M/S Havmøy,* a dry-cargo freighter sailing from Oslo. On Sundays he would spread out a canvas and, dressed in an exercise outfit, would give karate demonstrations for the crew. Ahmed was aboard the *Havmøy* during the Six Days' War and he persuaded the radioman to tune in Arab news broadcasts. The Norwegian crewmen laughed at him when he insisted that the Egyptians had invaded deep into Israel, since in reality the Arab armies were fleeing in defeat. Bouchiki liked to chat and visit with other crewmen too much to suit the *Havmøy*'s skipper. "Bouchiki did everything except what he was supposed to do," Captain Willy Augensen recalled later. When Ahmed signed off the ship in early summer, the captain marked his papers, "Not to be recommended."

Bouchiki went back to Bergen kitchens until the next spring when he moved to Kristiansand, a city on the southern tip of Norway, where he landed a better job as a trainee waiter. Later that year, he took a state-run vocational course and passed the tests to become a licensed waiter. The Norwegian employment office found him a job in a hillside hotel near Lillehammer. But Bouchiki felt ill at ease in the mountains and soon moved down to the valley where he became a waiter in the Lillehammer Tourist Hotel.

Shifting from job to job, Bouchiki was working by March 1969 at a hotel in Lillehammer. There he got to know an attractive fellow employee who was a breakfast cook, or "cold virgin," as they are known in Nordic slang. In Norway, breakfasts are served on smørgåsbords, and the "cold virgins" prepare the plates of smoked salmon, sausages, roast beef, and the like that are placed on the table.

She did not remain cold for long. Within one month Ahmed made her pregnant. Then he abruptly quit his job and took off for France to visit his family. Meanwhile, the girl moved to Denmark where she found a job in a vacation hotel maintained by British Petroleum for its employees. Bouchiki joined her in Denmark and worked as a waiter for two months in the same hotel. Then they went separate ways, he to the Sjusjøen Hotel near Lillehammer, and she to a hotel in the coastal town of Ålesund, about one hundred sixty miles away. On December 20, 1969, she gave birth to a son. Pleading poverty, Ahmed did not visit her until mid-March, and indeed he had lost his job when the hotel closed for the winter and was getting by on only sixteen kroner (about three dollars) per day in unemployment benefits.

Ahmed stayed with her for a few days before returning to Lillehammer. Then in the spring, he journeyed again to France. His friends, puzzled by the penniless Arab's ability to travel, often asked him how he could afford such trips. "Oh, I always go the cheapest way," he would reply, laughing off the question.

While on his trips, Ahmed sent numerous postcards. An inveterate address collector, he filled the pages of a notebook with no fewer than sixty-five names and addresses, mostly of girls he had met in the hotels where he worked. His messages were written in affectionate but poor English that showed little improvement over the years.

In the summer of 1970, Ahmed returned for the fourth time to Norway, but his girl friend and he were unable to come to terms about support for the child. Their argument ended in a paternity suit, which Ahmed lost. Nonetheless, he visited her twice in 1970; the second time he brought along his brother, and they stayed with her for about one week. Then both went back to France, and Ahmed worked for a time in Saint-Tropez before returning to Norway in June 1971. He went to work at the Nordseter Fjellstue Hotel, near Lillehammer, where he had been employed two years earlier. He explained to the management that he had had a child with a Norwegian woman and asked if she could get a job at the hotel too. His request was granted, and they lived together from July until December of 1971. But after another quarrel, Ahmed left her for good.

About this time, Bouchiki was injured in a serious auto accident that put him in the hospital for several weeks and kept him out of work for nearly three months. After his recovery, he finally found the job that suited him perfectly. Bouchiki was hired at Lillehammer's only discotheque, the Grenadier, as a jack-of-all-trades. He served variously as disc jockey, bartender, waiter, cook, and occasionally bouncer. "He could be very purposeful," remembers his employer at the Grenadier. In his new job, Ahmed could indulge to the fullest his love for chatting with friendly people. He met many girls at the discotheque, but he suddenly ceased his roaming. To friends Ahmed confided how happy he was to have finally found the woman with whom he wanted to spend the rest of his life.

She was Torill Larsen, a Lillehammer girl who worked in the regional hospital. The couple became acquainted at Easter and engaged on Christmas Eve. When they married on February 10, 1973, Torill was two months' pregnant. Now, in late July, the Bouchikis were looking forward to the birth in only two months. A slim girl, Torill already looked as if the baby were due at any moment. Because of the impending new arrival, Ahmed had taken a job at the Skogli Sanatorium, which paid a bit more than the Grenadier.

On the morning of July 21, Torill had gotten up early to work the Saturday shift from 7:30 until 10:30 in the hospital laboratory. Ahmed, who had never earned more than three thousand dollars in a single year, was eager to better his meager economic position and headed toward the swimming pool where he was preparing to pass the lifeguard exam. Typical of his easy-going nature, he was making his way there in leisurely stages when the Israeli agents spotted him having a coffee at the Hotel Kronen's outdoor café. Later, when Mike sent Marianne to the pool to spy on him, Ahmed undoubtedly did not notice her. The man with whom he was talking was one of his swimming pupils—a young Frenchman who worked as a dishwasher in Lillehammer.

As Bouchiki left the pool building, he was accompanied by the Frenchman and a Lillehammer girl who was a school friend of Torill's. They were going to meet Torill in Bergseng's café. Then the Bouchikis caught the bus for the short ride uphill to Nybu. It was at that time that the Mossad agents trailed "Ali Hassan Salameh" to his secret Norwegian hideaway.

Lillehammer shops close their doors at 1:30 on Saturday afternoon, and the little town becomes very quiet. Torill and Ahmed spent the entire afternoon in their flat, completely unmindful of the Israelis on stakeout duty outside. As the couple walked down Furubakken toward the cinema, they did not notice Marianne and Danny quarreling in the Mazda. Later, Torill's attention was drawn to the car parked in the bus stop space, and she felt something was strange when she saw a second car parked in an odd manner up the hill after they alighted from the bus. To the best of Torill's knowledge, Ahmed was unaware of anything out of the ordinary until he heard the car brake and saw the weapons point at him. "No!" was his last word.

Who was Benamane?

If Ahmed Bouchiki was a mere cipher in the world of political intrigue, Kemal Benamane remains a major question mark. In either case, if he were responsible, whether by accident or design, for misleading the Israelis, why did they not kill him? Kemal Benamane is alive. In some ways, that is a mystery itself.

In the most important aspects, the explanations of the Israelis and those of Benamane are diametrically opposed. It is completely clear from the testimony of the captured Mossad agents that they were following Bena-

mane and that his departure from Geneva triggered the
entire operation into motion. Furthermore, other Israelis state that a small handful of the Mossad chiefs
knew that Benamane was a double agent. Israeli operatives in Geneva, who saw Benamane being driven to the
airport, would not, by the way, have known that he was
a double agent. They were only keeping him under routine surveillance in case he left on a trip. But undoubtedly they believed, as did the members of the Lillehammer team, that he was a Black September courier.

For his part, Benamane denied that he ever was a
member of Black September. "I have never spoken in
favor of the Palestinian cause," he says.

So why did he go to Norway? It hardly seemed a pro-
pitious time to take a vacation alone. He had just gotten
married and was working as an unskilled laborer in a
factory near Geneva where he was paid fifteen hundred
Swiss francs per month (about six hundred and twenty-
five dollars) for inspecting finished jerry cans.

However, according to Kemal, he felt he needed to
get away for a while and, as will be seen later, in Norway he gave several different explanations for the trip.
Benamane had a strange way of selecting destinations
for his travels. When he got the urge to get away, he
never had any clear notion about where he wanted to
go. For help on settling upon a spot, he would turn to a
travel agency where he would ask an agent to make
suggestions about places that might interest him. Benamane would inquire for details and sometimes ask to
hear new names. Then suddenly a place would please
him—and that was it. He would buy a ticket and go.

In his own words, the choice of Oslo came about in
the following manner:

"Before I had a work permit, I had held a job for
three weeks at a Geneva travel agency called Voyages
pour l'Art, at seventeen rue de Lausanne. I went there
and talked with an elderly British woman who has a
Polish name. She mentioned a number of places she
thought I might like to visit. However, when she learned
that I had never been to the North, she said that was
the place I must go to. We talked about several cities,
among them was Copenhagen, but she urged that I go

to Oslo, and I accepted her suggestion. The next day I took money from the savings bank and went to the Swissair office to pay for my ticket, which had been ordered by the travel bureau. On July fourteenth, my wife and a friend drove me to the airport in Geneva. This is the friend who is a functionary in the Saudi Arabia diplomatic delegation accredited to the international agencies in Geneva. His name? I would prefer not to disclose it. He is an old friend of my wife's."

Upon arrival in Oslo, Benamane took a taxi to the Panorama Summer Hotel where a reservation had been made for him by the Geneva travel agency. When he checked in, the receptionist clerk was a Norwegian young woman. Benamane immediately struck up a conversation in French. Learning she was a student, he asked: "What is your specialty?"

"Sociology," she replied.

"What a coincidence!" he cried, feigning surprised delight. "I'm a sociologist myself, and I've been wanting to visit your country and study its social structures ever since I got to know a Norwegian friend of mine at the University of Geneva."

Benamane told her he would like to take her out, but he warned that they would have to go to a quiet place. He was very weary from his studies and could not stand noise. She thought the new guest acted very strangely. He seemed excessively nervous and said he could not bear to stay indoors. He showed her the two books he was carrying: one on alchemy and the other concerning a secret sect in Switzerland. Not finding Benamane amusing, she turned down his invitation for a date.

Alone and bored, Kemal decided to go out on the town anyway. He inquired about a night spot, and the hotel porter recommended the Club Seven. Overcoming his aversion to noise, Kemal went there. It happens to be just about the loudest night spot in Oslo. In the club, Kemal got to know a fellow Arab named Yusuf. Since Benamane spoke no Scandinavian language and only a little English, he was happy to meet someone with whom he could converse. Yusuf knew his way around Oslo where he had worked for more than a year in a bookstore, and he took Benamane on a tour of night spots. At one of them, the two Arabs picked up a couple of Norwegian girls. The foursome then repaired to a cabaret at the Metropol Restaurant, where Kemal bought champagne to impress his new friends.

The next morning, Benamane slept until nine o'clock, ate breakfast, and went back to bed again until noon. Then Yusuf came to the hotel and the two had lunch together. During the afternoon, they strolled in the hotel grounds. Then they took a taxi downtown. In a self-service restaurant, they met two girls, who came from the northern part of Norway. After dinner, Yusuf left with one girl, while the other remained with Kemal.

The next day—it was July 16—Benamane stayed in the Panorama until late afternoon. Then he took a subway to the downtown area where he had a rendezvous with the girl from the night before. That evening, Kemal telephoned his wife in Geneva. He had also sent her a postcard that day.

On the afternoon of July 17, he had another date with his new friend. They met at an outdoor café called King's Terrace, only a few hundred yards from the royal palace. "I am so very weary," he said. "I must get away from Oslo and go swimming somewhere."

She helped him find a bank where he changed some Swiss francs into Norwegian kroner. Then she took him to a tourist bureau where he launched into his routine.

The travel clerk was astonished to hear Benamane say that he was exhausted and needed to rest—the young Arab seemed so healthy. "I have just completed my doctoral exams at the University of Geneva," Benamane explained. "I must go some place where I can rest. I have seen the name of a town called Larvik. Would that be a good idea?"

As the dialogue progressed, the agent got the distinct impression that Benamane was trying to pull out of him names of Norwegian vacation towns. After reciting a long list of resorts, the agent finally said, "Well, what about Lillehammer?"

"Lillehammer!" exclaimed Benamane. "That sounds like a good place."

That evening, he telephoned his wife in Geneva to tell her that he was going to Lillehammer the next day.

He caught the ten o'clock train on Wednesday, July 18, for Lillehammer, and Pistauer apparently shadowed him to the rail station and learned his destination. Thus, he was already in Lillehammer when the two groups of agents arrived in Oslo from Tel Aviv.

Benamane found a room in Lillehammer by inquiring at the tourist office. He asked for something inexpensive and was advised to try the Skotte tourist home. After paying for three days in advance, he rested in his room most of the afternoon and then took a long walk. That evening he visited the Grenadier where he danced with a French woman.

On Thursday, July 19, as Jonathan Ingleby was preparing to break into Benamane's room at the Panorama, the Arab was strolling along the streets of Lillehammer in search of amusement. He found the town's diversions rather uninteresting and the girls not as friendly as in Oslo. He bought a copy of *Le Monde,* then popped into the tourist information office to ask if the indoor swimming pool was open. It was, and he walked back to the Skotte to fetch his swimming trunks.

Shortly after lunchtime, Benamane went to the pool. He took a leisurely shower, baked in the sauna, and plunged into the pool for a long swim. After that, he returned for another heat treatment. He had just stepped from the sauna and lit a cigarette when he saw an Arab-looking man approaching.

"Parlez-vous français?" the man asked.

"Yes, I speak French, but why don't we converse in our mother tongue?" Kemal responded.

In that manner, Kemal Benamane began talking with Ahmed Bouchiki, or at least that is the way Kemal tells it. For his part, Bouchiki told friends that an Arab approached him in the dressing room and spoke to him. Ahmed's father-in-law noticed that Ahmed was very excited at this time, as if "he had learned or been told something secret."

In any event, both men were delighted to be speaking Arabic and struck up an animated conversation.

"How did you get those welts on your side?" inquired Kemal, looking at the scars on his new friend's body.

"From an auto accident," replied Bouchiki.

The two men discovered they both were practitioners of karate, and talked excitedly about their skills and experiences. The subject shifted to Norwegian women and Benamane said that he had no trouble getting what he wanted. As Benamane recalled, both he and Bouchiki were trying to impress each other. According to Kemal, Bouchiki boasted that he had a really good life and was an important man in Lillehammer. He said that he was preparing to take an examination to qualify for a job as lifeguard in the pool and that he earned extra money by giving swimming lessons.

By then, it was about 4:20 P.M. Unbeknown to Benamane, Mossad agents already were sitting on benches outside the pool building to keep a watch on the Skotte. Bouchiki led Benamane back to the pool where a Frenchman was waiting for his swimming instruction. While Bouchiki gave the Frenchman his lesson, Kemal sat on the edge of the pool in a correct yoga position and talked loudly in French. He said that he traveled a great deal and told of trips to India, Pakistan, and Afghanistan. Then he spoke of his family. He was married to the daughter of a wealthy Geneva banker but was having quarrels with his father-in-law and had come to Norway to get a bit of rest. Actually, his father-in-law was already dead. During his brief stay in Norway, Benamane gave at least six different accounts of who he was. In addition to being a banker's son-in-law, he was a sociology student, a professor of sociology, a United Nations expert on narcotics, and a rich Arab who owned a home in Geneva. He had at least as many variations on the reason for his trip to Norway, but the underlying theme was always the same—to get some rest.

After the lesson, the Frenchman sat on the poolside with Kemal while Bouchiki swam alone.

"What is his name?" asked Kemal.

"Ahmed," the Frenchman replied.

From then on, Benamane used the name several times in conversation with Bouchiki.

It was drawing close to six o'clock, and Benamane was hungry. Ahmed suggested that he go to dinner at the Kronen Hotel.

"Can we meet later this evening?" Benamane asked.

"Yes, by all means," answered Bouchiki enthusiastically. "At nine o'clock at the Terrace Café [an outdoor restaurant next to the swimming pool]."

But Benamane did not go to the Kronen for dinner. Instead, he had a snack in the Bakkegrillen where at the time Sylvia and Dan Aerbel were sitting at a window table, keeping watch on the Skotte. They did not notice him until he left the Bakkegrillen and was halfway to the Skotte.

Weary from the swimming and sauna, Kemal fell asleep. With a start, he awoke at 10:30 and was terribly angry at himself for having missed the appointment with Bouchiki. Then, hearing rain fall outside, Benamane consoled himself with the thought that his new friend would not have come out in such weather anyhow.

(Actually, Bouchiki showed up at the Terrace Café at nine o'clock and waited for fifteen minutes.)

Unable to go back to sleep, Benamane went downstairs to the television lounge where a boring Swedish film was playing. He claims that he was completely unaware of the two Mossad agents who shared the lounge with him that evening.

The next morning, Benamane met Bouchiki by accident. Kemal had been sitting in the Kronen outdoor café. It was there that the Mossad spotted him, only to lose him a few minutes later as he wandered down Storgaten. He walked south on the narrow main street until he came to the Karoline, where he happened to see the Frenchman whom he had met in the pool the day before seated at a table with another Frenchman who was to be his replacement as dishwasher in a local hotel. As Benamane approached their table, they invited him to sit down. The Frenchman who was going home to France excused himself, explaining that he wanted to buy presents for his family. While they conversed in French, Kemal stuffed Dunhill tobacco in a well-used pipe. Then Ahmed Bouchiki came riding by on a bicycle and, seeing his friends, came to their table. Delighted to meet Benamane again, Bouchiki began to talk rapidly in Arabic.

After several minutes, the Frenchman, feeling left

out, interrupted. "What are you talking about?" he asked.

"Oh, just nonsense," Bouchiki replied.

Out of politeness, the two Arabs switched to French. Benamane wore elegant and flashy clothes during his visit to Norway, and Bouchiki evidently admired them.

"Will you buy me a leather jacket like yours when you go back to Switzerland?"

"Most assuredly, my friend, I want to make you a present of a jacket like this."

"No, no. I will give you the money to buy me one."

But Kemal refused and the topic turned to music.

Ahmed asked, "Tell me, are you able to buy records of Arab music in Geneva?"

Kemal replied, "Of course, my friend, and it would be a pleasure for me to send you some."

But again the conversation ran aground on the problem of the payment.

"Does anybody have a piece of paper?" Benamane asked. One of them produced a notebook and Benamane tore out a page on which he wrote his Geneva address. He handed the slip of paper to Bouchiki. Meanwhile, Bouchiki was writing his own address on another piece of paper taken from the other's notebook. He gave it to Benamane. Bouchiki placed the slip of paper in the pocket of his Levi's jacket where it was found after his death.

This was the exchange of papers that was observed so intently by Gustav Pistauer, Marianne, and Danny. The banal chatter about clothes and records was thought by the Mossad agents to concern the plans for a terrorist outrage.

After shopping for gifts, the Frenchman briefly rejoined the group and stayed for about twenty minutes. Then he said his good-byes. Benamane shook hands with him and delivered himself of a mysterious farewell. "If you see somebody that's black, that's me," he told the Frenchman.

The words puzzled both of the Frenchmen, who remembered the phrase when they were interrogated by Norwegian police. It seems likely that Benamane was toying with his new and uninitiated acquaintances by us-

ing the lines of a Black September recognition code.
Such passwords generally consist of four stanzas that require a response and affirmation by the two parties. It
would go something like this:

First speaker: *Do you see somebody black?*

Second speaker: *You mean a black month?*

First speaker: *The blackest month of all, my brother!*

Second speaker: *If you see somebody black, that's
me!*

After the shopper left, Bouchiki said he also had to
go. As they parted, he recommended the Victoria as a
good place for Benamane to have lunch. Then Bouchiki
climbed on his bicycle and pedaled away. Acting on his
advice, Benamane headed for the Victoria. To have
someone to talk with, he invited the Frenchman to be
his guest. Over lunch they chatted about a variety of
topics, including religion. Benamane spoke at length
about what his Islamic faith meant to him. To make
conversation, the Frenchman asked Kemal if he knew
France. "I'm not allowed to go to France," Kemal replied. Then he told him about his experiences in Bulgaria and Rumania.

The Arab paid the lunch tab, and his luncheon guest
tagged along while Kemal collected his belongings at the
Skotte. Kemal forgot to ask for reimbursement of the
third night's room rent, which he had paid in advance.
Benamane caught the 2:08 train back to Oslo.

When he stepped from the train at the Oslo-East station, he did not notice the Mossad shadowing squad
waiting for him. He went to the tourist information office in the station and asked for advice about an inexpensive place to stay. He was sent to the Stefan Hotel, a
modest establishment run by a missionary organization.
Then Kemal changed clothes and strolled out to buy *Le
Monde* and eat dinner before returning to his room.

All this time, he was closely watched by Sylvia, Dan
Aerbel, and Abraham Gehmer. It was after he came
back from dinner that Gehmer telephoned the communication post and received the message that Benamane
was no longer "interesting" and that he and his companions should rejoin the other agents in Lillehammer.

This was the ruse that gave Mike the chance to meet

Benamane in secret. Kemal, of course, denies that he ever saw Mike or had any contact whatsoever with the Mossad. According to his version, Kemal went to the Club Seven where he met Yusuf again, but he was so nervous and restless that evening that Benamane wanted to go to his hotel and Yusuf accompanied him there. Kemal told the night porter to put through a call to Geneva as quickly as possible and gave his wife's number. He said he was in such a rush for the call that he would wait and take it at the reception desk.

Unable to contain his restlessness, Benamane abruptly said good-bye to Yusuf, bolted into the elevator, and went to his room. In ten or fifteen minutes, the call came through. He scolded his wife for not having been home earlier. Then he asked her to have some friends in the Algerian consulate pick him up the next afternoon at Geneva airport, since he did not have enough money to take a cab to their apartment. Benamane returned to Geneva on Saturday as planned. He was traveling on an excursion ticket valid only on weekends.

On Monday evening, July 23, after putting in a day's work as a laborer in the J. Gallay factory, Benamane was drinking a beer and reading the Geneva newspaper *La Suisse* in a small bar. Suddenly he saw a short item about the mysterious killing of a Moroccan citizen named Ahmed Bouchiki in Lillehammer. He rushed home to double check the name with the one on the piece of paper given him by Bouchiki. It was the same.

Benamane realized that the Swiss police would be looking for him soon. According to him, he quit his job at the factory, because he did not want to be embarrassed by having the police come for him there. He also informed the Algerian consulate that he had met Bouchiki and hence might be questioned in connection with the murder.

Three days later, two Swiss plainclothesmen called for Benamane at his apartment. He was held for three days and questioned extensively. The Norwegians sent to Geneva two I-Group inspectors, including Leif Lier. They stayed in a separate room and drafted questions, which their Swiss colleagues put to Benamane.

Throughout the interrogation, the Arab remained

very cool and composed. He stuck to the story that he had traveled to Norway on the advice of the Geneva travel agent and that his actions and meetings were completely spontaneous and innocent. "I had no goal during my stay in Norway," he insisted.

He had his line down pat, perhaps a bit too pat. He would sometimes make a slip of the tongue in French and unconsciously use jargon from the intelligence trade. At one point, for example, he referred to his visit to the Algerian consulate in Geneva after learning of Bouchiki's murder as *"Nous avons avisé le Central"*— "We informed the Central."

About his background, Benamane told the police the following:

"I was born on May 15, 1945, in Mascara, Morocco. My father's name was Khera Ben Boufia and I have six brothers and sisters. At age three, I moved with my parents to the town of Tindouf, where I grew up and went to elementary and high school. Then I enrolled in the University of Fez as a student of sociology. When I completed my studies in Morocco, I decided to go abroad. I have hitchhiked through much of Europe and the Middle East, and have even traveled to India. In many of these places, I lived among university students, but I was not actually matriculated in any university. I have traveled a great deal in Eastern Europe, especially Yugoslavia, Bulgaria, and Hungary.

"No, I don't remember the names of the places I visited and people I met, but I spent six months in Rumania, mostly in Bucharest, before arriving in Switzerland in November 1972. In Geneva I lived at first at the YMCA, but I was soon admitted to the Cantonal Hospital where I was treated for an infection of my left eye. In fact, I'm still undergoing treatment. I was the object of an investigation by Geneva police authorities, dated December 20, 1972, about what I was doing in the city and whether I would become a public ward. I appealed to the Algerian consulate for help, and they submitted a report of my background.

"After my release from the hospital, I went to live with a friend in Milan and then I returned to Geneva.

During this period I met my wife, and on April 4 of this year, we were married.

"Since June of this year, I have been employed as an unskilled worker at the J. Gallay factory in Collonge-Bellerive on the outskirts of Geneva. My father was a noncommissioned officer in the French army and had some money. I get funds sent from home. I have no debt, except the eight hundred francs I owe to the Cantonal Hospital for my treatment. I have no motor vehicle; I move about with a Solex [a motorized bicycle]."

Part of Benamane's biography were completely uncheckable. Communist police and intelligence agencies do not cooperate with the Western police in verifying statements made in interrogations. On one point Benamane later conceded: his pretensions about being a university student or graduate were without basis; he never completed any studies beyond elementary school.

Despite repeated questions by the police, Benamane refused to budge from his story that he went to Norway on the advice of a travel agent, and that he had nothing to hide. "If the Norwegian authorities deem it necessary," he said, "I am willing to meet with them in Norway to verify my explanation." He demanded, however, that the Norwegians pay his travel expenses.

The Norwegian inspectors confronted Benamane with the allegation made by Aerbel that he was a high-ranking member of Black September and that he had led the Mossad team to Bouchiki.

Benamane was indignant. "I understand nothing of these accusations," he declared. "I believe someone has misused my name." He added: "I am a little scared for me and my wife."

The Norwegian inspectors posed a final question: "Did you have the impression that you were followed during your stay in Norway?"

"No," responded Kemal Benamane. "Since I was on vacation, I had no reason to look behind me."

Benamane's account reduces certain Israeli operatives to fits of laughter. According to their version, he had been spotted in Switzerland as a Black September courier and grabbed. Faced with the choice between

death and duplicity, he opted to become a double agent
and, so they claim, was paid five hundred dollars per
month. He was assigned an Israeli control officer, who
returned to Israel the moment he learned something had
gone wrong in Norway.

This theory goes as follows: The Israelis activated
Benamane for the search because they were convinced
that he had served as a courier to Salameh on earlier
occasions and would be able to approach him. But Benamane panicked while in Norway and was desperately
seeking a way out. He had failed to locate Salameh in
Oslo, and obviously was not trying very hard to do so.
Then, deciding to lead the Israelis on a merry chase, he
took off for Lillehammer where he met Bouchiki by accident. Later, when he learned that the Israelis had observed his conversation at the Karoline with Bouchiki
and had drawn the totally wrong conclusion, he was too
frightened for his own life to clear up the confusion.

His anxiety could have been produced by the change
in procedures. He did not know Mike, who used a code
word or hand signal to identify himself as Benamane's
new control. As Benamane was gasping with fright at
having been suddenly switched to an unfamiliar control
officer, Mike began to grill him about the man with
whom he was talking in the café.

"How can you be sure he is Ali Hassan Salameh?"
demanded Mike.

A double agent must think fast to survive, and truth
simply does not exist in the world of espionage. Benamane was afraid he would be killed if he admitted that
he had not located Salameh. Hence, hoping to win a
few more hours or days of life, he played along with the
Mossad's wrong conclusion about the identity of Bouchiki.

A darker variation of this theory is that Benamane
knowingly led the Israelis to the wrong man after he
had been unable to find Salameh. Then he compounded
his treachery by convincing Mike that he had pointed out
the correct target.

Why is Benamane still alive? Throughout the international intelligence community and the underworld, the
Israelis are known as the most unforgiving of employ-

ers. It is extremely surprising that a double agent could have lured the Mossad into a horrendous blunder without suffering fatal consequences himself.

If this explanation is true, then the answer seems to be that publicity was Benamane's best protector. After his name was mentioned in press reports about Bouchiki's death, he handled himself extremely cleverly. He peppered the Israeli embassy in Bern with telephone calls. He insisted that he be allowed to talk to someone in Israeli intelligence and clear up the misunderstanding. Benamane engaged a well-known Geneva lawyer, who also made a number of calls to the Israeli embassy. He was seeking to arrange a meeting in his office between representatives of Israeli intelligence and his client. After a while, the lawyer says, he received an anonymous message from the Israeli embassy, saying that if Benamane remained quiet, nothing would happen. Obviously, the Israelis realized that the Arab's sudden demise would spell big headlines, reviving memories of the Lillehammer blunder.

If Benamane had been working for the Israelis, why didn't the Arab side do him in? Again, publicity was his shield. If Black September had murdered Benamane, the Israelis could have put out the word: "Look, that proves our point, the Arabs killed Benamane because he was working for us." Also, either by accident or intention, Benamane performed a highly important service for the Black September cause by leading the hit team into a monumental mistake. Furthermore, if Benamane were a double agent for Israel, he may have informed his Black September superiors about his supposed recruitment and have become a triple agent who betrayed his new masters to his original employers. It is possible that after he was activated by the Israelis for the search for Salameh, Black September instructed him to lead them astray. The reason for the sudden trip to Lillehammer could have been to lure the Israelis from Oslo, since Salameh was coming there that week.

There is another theory that cannot be discounted—that Benamane was innocent and that his version of the trip to Norway, as improbable as it might sound in light of the circumstances, was true. If the Israelis made such a terrible blunder about Bouchiki, it is not impossible that they made one about Benamane, too.

One explanation might be that the Mossad agents in Geneva overestimated Benamane's importance. He is a braggadocio who might well have pretended he had Black September connections that existed only in his imagination. In 1972–1973, most Arabs as well as many West European radicals regarded Black September terrorists as heroes, and Benamane might have enjoyed being regarded as one of them. The Israelis, who spotted him in Geneva, may not have double checked his story thoroughly enough. Furthermore, his relationship to the Algerian consulate would have buttressed Israeli suspicions, since the consulate was believed to be the control center for Black September operations in Europe. Then, when he left for Oslo, the Mossad station report from Geneva—which carried the tantilizing embellishment about his being driven to the airport in a Saudi Arabian diplomatic car—created an impression in Tel Aviv far out of proportion to its real significance. The Israelis placed their reliance on a person who was not what they thought him to be, and the one error resulted in an even worse one.

The autopsy of Ahmed Bouchiki showed that at the time of death he was in sound physical condition, and his body bore no signs of disease. There was no trace either of alcohol or drugs in his blood. The cause of death was bullet wounds in the brain, lung, liver, kidney, and abdomen.

Oddly, both the Arabs and the Israelis were frustrated by the pointlessness of Bouchiki's death, and sought to make more out of him. His brother claimed his body and took it by air to Morocco where Ahmed was buried with full military honors. A militant trade union newspaper in Morocco carried a long article glorifying Bouchiki as a former regional secretary "who did not lose contact" with the movement. The article went on to state that "because of his Arabic and Islamic orientation, he was one of the glowing defenders of the Arab cause abroad and that led to his liquidation by imperialist terrorists."

Some Palestinian activists also maintained that he had been a publicist and information officer for their organizations in Norway.

The Israelis were only too happy about the Arab statements and attempted to verify them. If they could have proved that Bouchiki was involved with Arab affairs, they could have at least partially explained away their blunder. They could have leaked their discovery to journalists, saying, in effect: "OK, we didn't get Salameh, but we didn't do that badly after all. The Arab we killed in Lillehammer turned out to be a member of this or that organization." Aided by other friendly agencies, the Mossad conducted an extremely thorough check into Bouchiki's past, but they found nothing.

The simplicity and banality of Bouchiki's life defied the efforts of intelligence agencies and Arab propagandists alike to make him into something he was not. He was only what he seemed to be—a simple waiter. And his death, if it served any purpose at all, was only to illustrate how an innocent can be caught in the jaws of organized terror.

TEN

Yom Kippur is the most sacred day in the Jewish calendar. It commemorates the covenant between God and man upon which both Judaism and Christianity are based. God is benevolent, desiring only man's well-being. But man, because of his sinful nature, fails to live in accord with God and disrupts the divine relationship. In his mercy, God grants man the opportunity to atone for his sins through prayer and sacrifice. It is on Yom Kippur that the Jew seeks the forgiveness of sin and the reestablishment of rapport with God.

On that day, even the less religious Jew goes to the synagogue for hours of prayer and ceremony. On Yom Kippur, all activities in Israel cease, and the people turn to God.

On the dawn of Yom Kippur in 1973, the Arab forces began a sudden unannounced attack. Sirens broke the silence of the Day of Atonement, summoning the people of Israel from the synagogues. Army reservists, rushing for the fronts, had to put special emergency signs on their buses and trucks to stop the Orthodox Jews from stoning them. There should be no travel on Yom Kippur.

The Arabs had taken Israel totally by surprise. In an impressively coordinated onslaught, Egyptian troops bridged the Suez Canal, trapping Israeli soldiers inside their undermanned Bar Lev Line forts, while in the north Syrian tanks and assault infantry overwhelmed equally weak Israeli outposts.

The outside world was stunned. The unexpected outbreak of war was astonishing enough. But even more dumbfounding was the fact that Israel had been caught unprepared. That had never happened before. In the last two major Middle East wars, in 1956 and 1967, Israel's uncannily detailed foreknowledge of enemy capabilities and intentions had led to quick victories—and ignominious Arab defeats.

Now, the world was turned upside down. It was the Israelis who had been caught asleep. It was the Israelis who were dying under the rifle and cannon of vastly superior forces, and who were being forced to surrender.

Why was Israel caught off guard?

The question remains crucial, nagging, and by no means fully answered. In large measure, the explanation rests in the shift of emphasis within Israeli intelligence. In response to the threat of Arab terrorism, the Mossad's special branch was concentrating its efforts to a very high degree on countermeasures in Europe, and was no longer paying as much attention to the Arab countries on Israel's very borders. The Mossad has only limited personnel and resources, and was unable to conduct major intelligence campaigns on two fronts. Hence, by distracting Israeli intelligence from its original mission, Black September rendered a vital service to the Arab cause.

Even so, the outcome of the Yom Kippur attack could have been radically different. On the evening of October 4, 1973, two days before the outbreak of the war, a Mossad secret agent stepped from a jetliner at Lod airport. Middle-aged and nondescript, he operated in Europe under the cover of a university philologist. In his attaché case he carried a set of photostats about as thick as a Manhattan telephone directory. They were a copy of the Egyptian-Syrian war plan that envisaged a surprise attack on Israel on the dawn of Yom Kippur. The agent had achieved one of the greatest intelligence coups of all time. It was as if the Americans had discovered in advance the plans for the secret Japanese attack on Pearl Harbor, or the Germans had learned the exact day and landing zones of the Allied armies in France in 1944. His achievement was all the greater because the plan was an extremely closely held secret. It was known to no more than perhaps twenty or twenty-five of the highest political and military leaders in the two countries. Even on the day of the attack, Egyptian and Syrian army officers had not realized they were entering war rather than another exercise.

The code name for the war plan was Operation Badr. The Arabs could not have chosen words that reflected more poignantly the antithetical religious and cultural nature of the coming conflict. Operation Badr was a historical reference to the battle of Badr in A.D. 624 when the prophet Mohammed and his followers scored the decisive victory over the Meccanites that enabled them to capture Mecca and establish Islam as the dominant faith of the Arab world.

Upon the arrival of the secret agent, Zwi Zamir requested a meeting with Golda Meir the same evening. The three of them met shortly before midnight in her home in a Tel Aviv suburb, but she was not convinced that the information was genuine. Since the blunder in Lillehammer, the Mossad no longer enjoyed the complete credibility it once commanded among Israel's leaders.

"Look, I'm not an expert," she told Zamir. "Take all this to Moshe."

Moshe Dayan, who was in a melancholic mood, suspected that the Arabs were feeding false information to gullible Mossad agents. He consulted army intelligence officers, who were jealous of the Mossad and supported his view.

Despite other indications of Arab mobilization, the Mossad's information was not acted upon, and Israeli forces were not put on full alert for a surprise attack. On the dawn of Yom Kippur, the blood of Israeli soldiers was spilled because of lack of preparedness. It was not until two weeks later, when the army had finally fought the Arabs to a standoff, that the leaders of Israel belatedly realized that the Arab attack unfolded exactly as the war plan had said it would.

After the debacle of the War of Atonement, as the conflict was called, a commission of eminent Israeli citizens was appointed to investigate, among other things, the reasons for the lack of preparedness. In its report, the committee made the statement that the Egyptian-Syrian war plan had been brought to Israel before the attack. But the report did not follow up that sensational disclosure with any details.

The Mossad agent who had delivered Operation Badr to Tel Aviv was inconsolable. Time and again, he repeated to himself the words: "Thou art weighed in the balance and found wanting."

ELEVEN

As a private citizen of Norway I can understand the motivation of these defendants who felt they were fighting for their country in a cruel and ceaseless war. But as the prosecutor of the Kingdom of Norway, I cannot condone their acts.

With those words, State Prosecutor Håkon Wiker expressed his own conflicting feelings. He was speaking to the court that had been assembled to try the six Mossad agents, and his sentiments were shared by most of his fellow citizens. As a small country, which had suffered severe oppression during World War II, Norway had a special sympathy for Israel. Like Håkon Wiker, the vast majority of Norwegians believed that the six defendants were only soldiers in a war that had been forced upon them. The Arab terrorist, and those who stood behind him, was the real villain. Many people might even have closed their eyes to the Mossad's secret means of retribution and regretted the tragic series of blunders that landed six Israeli agents in the Norwegian dock. But now it was too late. The Norwegians had no choice except to apply the law as impartially and impeccably as possible.

The Lillehammer incident propelled an unwilling Norway into the conflict between Arab and Jew, making it vulnerable to attack and criticism by both sides. Norway has one of the world's largest merchant fleets, which includes a number of supertankers, or VLCCs (Very Large Crude Carriers, as they are known in the oil business). Norway's VLCCs, which loaded their supplies mostly at Arab ports, would be easy targets for terrorists. The Norwegian tanker owners feared that Black September might hijack a VLCC and threaten to blow it up unless Norway delivered the six Mossad agents into their hands. There was also the grave worry that Black September might get the impression that the Norwegians were too lenient with the Israeli defendants and would decide to teach Norway a lesson by hiding a time bomb somewhere in the cavernous hull of a VLCC. Even the smallest explosion could turn a tanker into a roaring inferno. Another obvious pressure point was Scandinavian Airlines System, whose jets could become targets of Black September reprisal.

Though the main concern centered on Black September, the Norwegians also worried about possible Jewish attempts to free the defendants. It was extremely unlikely that the State of Israel would attempt any further operations in Norway. But Norwegian security authorities feared that some free-lance group, such as the Jewish Defense League, might undertake some wild-eyed scheme to free the prisoners.

As the date for the trial approached, Norway tightened its security at airports, border crossings, major railroad stations, and ferry harbors. At the southern Norwegian port of Kristiansand, a large band of young Jews trying to enter the country aroused the suspicion of the police. The youths said they had come to go skiing, but were carrying no skis. Then they said they were musicians, but could produce no instruments. Security authorities ordered them to be placed on the next ferry to Denmark.

As the trial began on January 7, 1974, the proceedings were surrounded by the most extensive security precautions in the history of Norway. They exceeded even those at the time of the trial of Vidkund Quisling, the World War II collaborator who was convicted of treason in 1945 and executed. Since no Oslo courtroom was regarded as secure enough for the trial, the judicial authorities leased the auditorium in a large study center, called Apollonia, which is located in Oslo just across the street from the joint headquarters of the major Norwegian security services. The auditorium was favored because it is situated in the very middle of a large stone building, and has no windows facing the street and only two exits, which coud be easily guarded. It also had simultaneous translation facilities. (The defendants would speak English, the court officials Norwegian, and the entire proceedings would be carried in French, Norwegian, and English. Hebrew was not used in the court.) The auditorium, which had been searched for concealed bombs, was sealed off to all outsiders and protected night and day by armed police. The streets around the center were heavily patrolled by policemen with dogs.

The defendants, who had been brought to Oslo prisons from jails scattered about the country, were driven back and forth to the Apollonia in big windowless police vans with one armed guard riding beside the driver and two in the prisoners' compartment. The guards wore steel helmets and flack jackets, and carried submachine guns or carbines. Each van was preceded by a motorcycle patrol and police car with dogs, and followed by a vehicle crammed with additional heavily armed police. Sirens whining and blue lights flashing, the convoys drove at such high speeds that the big vans seemed about to tip over on a few occasions. Traffic police at intersections stopped all cars, while side streets were covered by other police on the lookout for suspicious persons. As an extra precaution, the routes were altered each day.

Upon arrival at the Apollonia, the vans backed onto the sidewalk to enable the defendants to step from the rear door almost directly into the building. Even for that short passage, police officers formed a human shield around them. Meanwhile, the surrounding buildings were constantly searched for snipers.

Access to the courtroom was restricted to journalists and a few observers, mainly diplomats. Admission was by special permit only, and it had to be shown to police officers every time the bearer entered the courtroom. For the first two days the press and observers were frisked; after that, the check concentrated on briefcases and handbags.

The courtroom, rectangular in shape, was not large. At one end were wedged some sixty journalists who had come from all over the world to report on the trial. To their left, on the longer side of the room, were two benches; on the first sat the defense counsel, and behind them the defendants, separated from one another by police officers. Directly across from the defendants were the tables and chairs of the state prosecutor and his staff. At the other narrow end of the room sat the judges and jury. Since the case dealt with issues never before adjudicated in a Norwegian court, the judicial authorities had decided to form a special tribunal composed of three judges and a panel of private citizens. In that manner, the Norwegian justices hoped that the court could arrive at a verdict in accord with contemporary opinions and values.

At the opening session, Justice Erling Haugen, the presiding judge, asked the defendants to state their names. Until that time, Gehmer had refused to say who he was, although the Norwegian police had already established his identity. At the judge's command, he finally spoke his name.

Jail and interrogation had left imprints on the defendants, and their characters, as they sat in the heavily guarded Oslo courtroom, were more sharply etched than ever.

Marianne Gladnikoff was the first defendant called to the stand. She gave the impression of being very frightened and insecure; she continually diverted her face from the press section and wore her long blond hair combed in a way that shielded her profile. Her testimony was so laden with names of restaurants and references to snacks that the newsmen informally dubbed her "The Hungry Spy." She also emphasized that she was an innocent, deceived, and totally unwitting member of the team. "I never got any advance briefing on what was about to happen," she told the court.

The judge and prosecutor pressed for information on several key points.

QUESTION: Who decided Ahmed Bouchiki was the right man?

MARIANNE: In my opinion, we did not know who he was. I thought at the time we were still investigating this, and that is why I was surprised when we left Lillehammer so suddenly.

Q.: Did you have any idea about who Ahmed Bouchiki was?

MARIANNE: No.

Q.: Have you heard about Black September?

MARIANNE: No—oh pardon me, yes! I heard about it. I know the man we were looking for belonged to this organization.

Q.: Did you hear any talk about a high-ranking member of Black September?

MARIANNE: Yes, it was said he was high up in the organization.

Q.: What would you have done if you had realized that a man was going to be murdered?

MARIANNE: I would have returned to Israel as soon as possible.

Sylvia Rafael, the second defendant called to the stand, made a striking appearance. Witty, poised, and coquettish, she wore tight sweaters and well-cut slacks that complemented her good figure. The press immediately began referring to her as "Beautiful Sylvia," but, as her testimony demonstrated, she was also Clever Sylvia. Speaking quietly in what she calls her "North American" accent, she used her charm and mental agility to skirt questions she did not want to answer. At one point, she held the courtroom in suspense as she ran her fingers along the cord of the simultaneous-translation earphones and pretended she might bite it.

On several occasions, Judge Haugen intervened in Sylvia's testimony to ask questions himself.

QUESTION: Did you at any time have the impression that your mission could be dangerous to the welfare of someone or damage the State of Norway?

SYLVIA: To the contrary.

Q.: But a confrontation with Black September is always dangerous, isn't it?

SYLVIA: It is not intelligent or logical to think like that!

Q.: What is intelligent then?

SYLVIA: Actions of the sort you have in mind always smack of revenge. We never talked about anything like that. Our mission was to gather facts. When we had gotten the details together, we would have handed them over to the Norwegian authorities, so that they could prevent the operation from taking place. After all, the authorities are better equipped for such tasks than a group of only twelve to fifteen people.

Q.: Would it not have been better if you had alerted Norwegian authorities in the beginning?

SYLVIA *(emphatically):* I agree with you wholeheartedly, Your Honor.

The judge then quizzed Sylvia about the walkie-talkie messages immediately after Bouchiki's death.

Q.: While you were in the car, did you hear the phrase "they took him"?

SYLVIA: No, I cannot remember that.

Q.: I guess it would have been natural to remember the remark?

SYLVIA: No, I don't think so—did it have any special meaning?

Q.: Are you going to start to cross-examine me?

SYLVIA *(catching herself):* No, but if I had heard such a remark, it would have meant nothing to me. Therefore I would not have remembered it.

When Justice Haugen asked how the Israeli agents went about locating Benamane in Lillehammer, Sylvia readily admitted that she, too, had been puzzled about how they would find him. "I asked Pistauer," she explained, "how on earth we could find a man when we did not know his identity or his address. 'The best we can do is go have lunch,' he told me, and that is what we did.

"I am sorry that food keeps popping up all the time, Your Honor," said Sylvia, batting her long lashes.

At another juncture, Prosecutor Wiker asked Sylvia about her knowledge concerning the background of the operation.

Q.: Have you heard the name Ali Hassan Salameh?

SYLVIA: Possibly, but it does not mean anything to me.

Q.: But I guess you have been told he was suspected to be the brains behind the Munich massacre?

SYLVIA: No, I have not heard that. At home we do not delve into wild speculations about things like that.

Abraham Gehmer, summoned as the third defendant, spent very little time on the stand, because his answers were so brief and unresponsive. In court, he remained aloof and unbending. Only his eyes moved. Otherwise his face betrayed no expression, except one of determination.

Even though he had originally told the I-Group interrogators a highly implausible story to explain his presence in Norway, Gehmer stuck to the broad outline of his initial fiction. When questioned about details disclosed by the other defendants, he would preface his noncommittal replies with phrases such as "I cannot rule it out," and "as far as I know." When Gehmer did say something new, it was only to stress that he played a subordinate role. "I knew little or nothing about what was going on," he declared. "I received orders from others."

When Prosecutor Wiker tried to grill him on certain points, Gehmer would glare angrily. Wiker, for example, was interested in the Paris phone numbers in Gehmer's address book (these numbers, written in code, linked him to Sylvia, Ingleby, Mike, and others in the hit team). Asked about the numbers, Gehmer said that "somebody" in Israel had told him to note them down, and he was to be told their significance later.

Unsatisfied, Wiker rephrased the question slightly, but received the identical response. When Wiker asked another question on the subject, Gehmer exploded: "I tell you now for the third time. . . ." And he gave the identical reply.

Dan Aerbel, the fourth defendant in the stand, appeared smitten and anxious. His hands jerked nervously, his eyes had a deeply troubled and haunted look. He seemed to feel uncomfortable in the presence of his fellow defendants, especially Gehmer who stared at him contemptuously.

Wiker pointed out to the court that Aerbel had given at least fourteen variations of his confession during his interrogations. In reply, Aerbel explained that because he suffered from claustrophobia, he had sought to prolong his interrogations as much as possible in order to stay away from his small cell.

Justice Haugen and Prosecutor Wiker wanted to establish why a man like Aerbel, who now presented such a pitiful sight, would have gotten mixed up in the operation.

> QUESTION: Tell me, you are a successful businessman. Why would you accept an inferior position as translator and jack-of-all-trades?
>
> AERBEL *(earnestly):* I was interested in the Scandinavian assignment because my expenses would be paid and at the same time I could buy furniture for my new home in Israel.
>
> Q.: Who ordered you back to Lillehammer after you had gone to Oslo to shadow Benamane?
>
> AERBEL: I believe it was Leslie.
>
> Q.: Didn't you wonder what you were doing back in Lillehammer again?
>
> AERBEL: I have been wondering about what I was doing since the day I left Tel Aviv. Everything I learned about the operation was so illogical and stupid.
>
> Q.: Did you really believe that the State of Israel would intervene on behalf of an illegal group operating in Norway?
>
> AERBEL: Because of the good relations between Norway and Israel, I really thought that the case would be settled quietly between the two states. It was maybe my own naïveté that made me think like that, but the fact is, that was my reasoning.

Under further questioning, Dan Aerbel related he had told his interrogator to verify his story by calling Miko in Tel Aviv. Then he cited the telephone number: 25 62 30.

At that disclosure, Abraham Gehmer angrily slammed down his notebook on the table. He was furious that Aerbel was giving away intelligence secrets. Through his defense counsel, Gehmer demanded that the court be closed to press and observators. Meanwhile, the journalists were bolting from their chairs to place calls to the number in Tel Aviv. When they got the connection, a recording repeated to them in English: "This is no longer a working number."

Because of Gehmer's protest, the rest of the testimony was heard *in camera.* Therefore, the last two defendants, Zwi Steinberg and Michael Dorf, were questioned in secret and the press did not discover what transpired. Most likely, the two men said very, very little. Steinberg was a close-mouthed pro, and Dorf had only limited knowledge of the operation.

On February 1, 1974, twenty-six days after the beginning of the trial, Judge Haugen asked the six defendants to rise.

Sylvia Rafael, Abraham Gehmer, and Dan Aerbel were found guilty of participating with foreknowledge in a second-degree murder. Rafael and Gehmer were deprived of freedom for five and a half years and Aerbel for five. Even so, the sentences were less than the six-year minimum normally handed down for second-degree murder. The court found their roles minor compared to those of the assassins and organizer who got away. Marianne Gladnikoff was convicted of involvement in a manslaughter. The punishment: two and a half years in prison. Zwi Steinberg was found guilty of collecting intelligence information for a foreign power. His penalty: one year.

Michael Dorf, the communications man, was exonerated of wrongdoing. He was not to be punished, the judge said.

As the sentences were pronounced, Sylvia Rafael and Abraham Gehmer betrayed no trace of emotion. Dan Aerbel's face went white and he seemed on the verge of fainting. Marianne Gladnikoff kept her head turned away from the press section, so that no one could observe her reaction. Zwi Steinberg was smiling. Michael Dorf was nonplussed.

It had all happened so fast that Dorf did not immediately grasp the significance of the judge's words. But the congratulations of the other team members quickly convinced him that he was free to go home.

The five other agents, still heavily guarded against assassination or rescue attempts, were led away to begin their sentences.

TWELVE

A news story:

YASIR ARAFAT URGES
PALESTINIAN STATE; ISRAEL
SAYS PLAN WOULD DESTROY HER

United Nations, N.Y. Nov. 13, 1974—

While hundreds of Jews staged protest demonstrations outside, Yasir Arafat, the Chairman of the Palestinian Liberation Organization, made his first appearance before the United Nations General Assembly today. In a ninety-minute address, which was frequently interrupted by applause by African, Asian, and Arab delegates, the Palestinian leader called for the abolition of Israel and its replacement by a democratic, nonsecular state in which Moslems, Christians, and Jews could live together in peace as equal citizens.

If Israel failed to agree to the establishment of the new state that would absorb the 2.3 million Palestinians now in exile, Arafat warned that it could face suspension from the U.N. just as South Africa has now been barred from full participation because of the latter's racial policies. A pistol holster visible beneath his jacket, Arafat made veiled warnings that a failure to meet Palestinian demands could lead to heightened terrorism. "I have come bearing an olive branch and a freedom fighter's gun," said Arafat, who spoke in Arabic. "Do not let the olive branch fall from my hand."

At the end of his speech, Arafat received a two-minute ovation by most of the delegates. Virtually the only diplomats who did not participate in the enormous outpouring of enthusiasm were those of the U.S. and some West European nations. The Israeli delegation was absent from the General Assembly during Arafat's speech.

LIKE A HEAD OF STATE

At the direction of the Assembly President, Algerian Foreign Minister Abdelaziz Bouteflika, Arafat was accorded treatment almost equal to that of a head of state. Bouteflika introduced Arafat as "commander in chief of the Palestinian Revolution," and an armchair used only for visiting heads of state was placed on the right side of the rostrum. Aware of Western protests over the Assembly President's elaborate preparations for his visit, Arafat avoided a possible diplomatic crisis by not sitting in the chair, but he placed his arm over its back during the ovation at the close of his address.

Arafat's U.N. appearance was a dramatic demonstration of the growing power of the Palestinian Liberation Organization, which has been widely castigated throughout much of the world for its alleged association with terrorist organizations, most notably the Black September movement. The PLO spokesman vehemently denied reports that two of Arafat's bodyguards had participated in the attack on the Saudi Arabian Embassy in Khartoum in which Black September terrorists killed one Belgian and two American diplomats.

Wire service reports from the Middle East told of widespread jubilation in the Palestinian refugee camps in Lebanon because of the U.N. visit. Arafat's speech was relayed by satellite to Lebanese television stations so that tens of thousands of Palestinian refugees were able to see it live. At the close of his speech, many Palestinian guerrillas fired their weapons into the air in celebration.

TIGHTEST SECURITY

The visit of the PLO delegation to the U.N. headquarters caused the tightest security precautions in the world organization's history. Hundreds of New York City police, FBI agents, and other federal law enforcement officers threw a protective screen around Arafat and the PLO delegation after leaders of the Jewish Defense League and other extremist Jewish groups vowed that the Palestinian leader and his lieutenants would not leave New York City alive. The city is the home of the world's largest single Jewish community.

ARAB WALKOUT

During the afternoon session, when Israel's representative, Ambassador Yosef Tekoah, began his rebuttal to Arafat, all twenty Arab delegations rose from their chairs and walked from the Assembly chamber in a display of solidarity with the Palestinian position.

"I rise to speak in the name of a people which, having at long last regained its freedom and sovereignty, remains embattled by those who would deny to it the rights of all nations," the Israeli chief delegate began, speaking with obvious emotion.

In contrast to Arafat, who used only circumlocutions to refer to Israel, Ambassador Tekoah rejected such diplomatic devices. Instead, he bluntly denounced Arafat and the PLO visitors as "murderers" and sharply criticized the U.N. for "tearing asunder its own principles and precepts and paying homage to bloodshed and bestiality."

The Israeli delegate characterized Arafat's proposals for a non secular Arab-Jewish state as rhetorical tricks similar to those used by the Nazis. "The Nazis killed millions of Jews in death camps, the gates of which bore the sign, 'Work Brings Free-

222 Delete David B. Tinnin

dom,'" the Israeli representative declared. "Arafat kills Jewish children and seeks to strangle the Jewish state under the slogan of creating a democratic Palestine."

Ambassador Tekoah concluded: "The murderers of athletes in the Olympic games in Munich, the butchers of children in Maalot, the assassins of diplomats in Khartoum do not belong in the international community."

DIPLOMATIC RECEPTION

During the evening, the chief Egyptian delegate, Ambassador Ahmed Esmat Abdel Mequid, gave a reception for Arafat in the delegates' dining room on the fourth floor of the U.N. headquarters. Arafat remained in his place in the reception line for more than one hour and warmly greeted large numbers of diplomats. Behind Arafat stood several members of the Palestinian Liberation Organization whose names were not made available to the press. It is believed that some of them are traveling under assumed identities.

THIRTEEN

The man standing directly behind Arafat was Ali Hassan Salameh.

WHERE THEY ARE NOW?

Zwi Zamir retired after a normal tour of duty as chief of the Mossad and became the board chairman of a construction company that is owned by the Israeli confederation of trade unions.

Mike ——— retained his position as the Mossad's director of covert operations and even managed to serve on the Institute's committee that was set up to investigate what went wrong in Lillehammer.

Gustav Pistauer sprained his leg shortly after making the false identification and left Lillehammer before the killing. He was fired from the Mossad for his mistake and found a new job as a security officer in Israeli industry.

Tamar disappeared somewhere along the shores of the Mediterranean.

Ali Hassan Salameh lives very quietly in Beirut. He is aware that the Mossad has not given up. Using the civil fighting in Lebanon as a diversion, they sent a hit team by helicopter to Beirut in mid-1975 to kill him. One evening an Israeli assassin fired a sniper's rifle with telescopic lense at a silhouette in a window, thought to be Salameh. It wasn't. Later in 1976, as Salameh was crossing the ceasefire line in Beirut to negotiate with the Christian faction, the Israelis tried again. They missed him, but wounded his companion. Meanwhile, Salameh has risen in the PLO hierarchy to become chief of internal security. He is regarded as a possible successor to Yasir Arafat.

Kemal Benamane works as a waiter in the Italian part of Switzerland. He is being divorced by his wife on the grounds of incompatibility. He has a large scar in his left shoulder caused by a gunshot wound that has resulted in his being declared fifty percent disabled by Swiss health authorities. Benamane, who has become a member of a Swiss marksmanship club, says that his weapon went off accidentally while he was cleaning it.

Jonathan Ingleby retired from the Mossad and now runs a private detective agency in Tel Aviv.

Rolf Baehr also retired and started a detective agency in Herzliyya.

Zwi Steinberg was released after serving seven months in a Norwegian prison and disappeared once again into covert intelligence work.

Yigal Eyal returned to Israel after being declared *persona non grata* in Norway. He is an officer in the Shin Beth department that specializes in the protection of Israeli diplomatic and commercial offices abroad.

Marianne Gladnikoff was released after fifteen months in an Oslo woman's prison and returned to Israel where she held a press conference. The Mossad paid her for the period spent in prison and she left Israel to go home to Sweden.

Sylvia Rafael whiled away the days in her Oslo cell by playing the guitar, studying psychology, and learning Hebrew, which at the time of her arrest she had understood but had neither spoken nor written well. She kept a diary illustrated with her own drawings—excerpts were published in Israeli, Norwegian, and South African newspapers. She also sent cartoons to Inspector Leif Lier in which she sketched herself as Little Red Riding Hood being pursued by a ferocious German shepherd dog whose face resembled Lier's and whose teeth clenched a pipe. After she learned that State Prosecutor Håkon Wiker had slipped on ice and broken a leg, she sent him a get-well card signed "005½, The Spy Who Came in from the Cold." The 5½ was a reference to her sentence of five and a half years. She was released after twenty-two months and returned immediately to Israel. Her first visit was to the kibbutz Ramat-Hakovsh located northeast of Tel Aviv, which had adopted her while she was in prison. The members had sent her letters and Hebrew grammar books. The kibbutz put out flags and flowers, and held a big dance. A short while later, Sylvia, accompanied by a bodyguard, flew to South Africa for a visit to her mother and brother. Then she came back to Tel Aviv. She retired from the Mossad and married the Norwegian lawyer who defended her in the Oslo trial. She hoped to live in Norway. But Norwegian Justice Department officials expelled her from the country. Her husband, abandoning his law practice, left Norway with Sylvia. They will most likely make their home in South Africa or Israel.

Abraham Gehmer was released at the same time as Sylvia and also returned at once to Israel. He was given an extended leave by the Mossad to complete his studies for a Master of Arts degree from Tel Aviv University. He settled again with his family in Herzliyya and remains an officer in the Mossad though he has not been assigned a new job.

Dan Aerbel was released after seven months. He returned to Israel where he got his old job back as advertising director at the OSEM Food Industries. He has completed the home for which he was buying plumbing fixtures and furnishings during his mission to Sweden and Norway. On a windy summer day, bright Scandinavian-style curtains can be seen billowing from the house's oddly shaped half-moon windows.

Torill Bouchiki still works at the regional hospital in Lillehammer, but she moved from Furubakken and lives in a small drab apartment in another section of town. She has not fully recovered from the shock of seeing her husband shot down before her eyes.

Malika Bouchiki, born two months after Ahmed's death, is still too young to realize the tragedy that she has inherited. A pretty child, she has her father's handsome dark looks. As she toddles around her mother's apartment, Malika frequently looks at a color photo on the dresser. It shows Torill and Ahmed on their wedding day.

AFTERWORD

On the morning of the Munich massacre, I entered my office in the Time-Life building in Paris totally unaware of the drama already unfolding in Olympic Village. As soon as I read the bulletins cascading from the Reuters news ticker, I caught the next plane to Munich. I had written the *Time* 1970 Man of the Year cover on West German Chancellor Willy Brandt and I was acquainted with him and several members of his staff. During that incredibly hectic day, I reported on political and diplomatic aspects of the crisis for a *Time* cover story, and hence I was privy to some of the inside drama portrayed in Chapter One of this book. I had, however, no intention of doing a book on Munich and returned from the Olympics to my regular assignment as the European Correspondent of *Time*.

Later, in the spring and summer of 1973, I became intrigued by the fragmentary reports in the European press about the mysterious deaths of an Arab here and an Israeli there. During the times I was in Paris, I was especially aware that something was going on between the Israelis and the Arabs, and I worked on a *Time* story in summer 1973 that was one of the first published anywhere to suggest that the killings were a part of an unseen war of the spooks. Shortly after that story appeared, I was on a trip when reports came of the killing of an Arab in the remote Norwegian town of Lillehammer. A researcher in the Paris office telephoned me to get my reactions to a file about the killing by *Time*'s Norwegian stringer, Dag Christensen. He was already speculating that the murder could have been the handiwork of Israeli intelligence. After hearing the files read, I confidently asserted, "No, the Israelis would never be so stupid as to get caught!" It was several months before I learned the full degree of my error.

Early in 1974 one of the world's major news stories was the Soviet persecution of Alexander Solzhenitsyn who was then still in Moscow defying the entire power of the Soviet State. Week after week, I reported on the events as best I could through sources in Western Europe who had direct links to Solzhenitsyn and various elements within the Soviet dissident movements. In February 1974, when Solzhenitsyn was forcibly expelled by Soviet authorities to West Germany, I followed him in his subsequent odyssey from West Germany to Zurich to Norway.

While in Norway, Solzhenitsyn traveled northward to Lillehammer to view some property that was offered to him as a new home for his family. I was accompanied on the trip to Lillehammer by Dag Christensen and while we were in the village together, often parked in a car in the snow waiting for a chance to talk with Solzhenitsyn, Dag recounted the details of the incident, which I had dismissed as erroneous the summer before. I learned from Dag that a great deal of material was available, which had not appeared in the foreign press beyond Scandinavia. Most importantly, he told me that although an official transcript of the trial had not been made public, a long summary of the case had been released by the court, and was available to the public in Norwegian.

Dag Christensen produced a thorough outline of the events in Norway, based on the court summary, newspaper reports, and his own knowledge gained from confidential sources. Thus briefed, in summer 1974 he and I visited Israel as "vacationing newsmen." We did not inform either Israeli or Arab authorities about our intentions, and during the next several weeks, we succeeded in gathering a large amount of pertinent material.

During the next eighteen months, I spent my vacations, long weekends, and two substantial leaves of absence shuttling between Washington, Paris, Tel Aviv, and Oslo, with a number of stops and side trips in between. I was tracking down, checking, rechecking, and triangulating against different sources the factual material on which *The Hit Team* is built.

This book is composed essentially of three layers of information. The first layer of material, which provided the over all framework of the book, is the public record as found in newspaper and newsmagazine reports, learned journals, and the like. It would astonish most readers to know just how much seemingly confidential or secret material has actually found its way into public domain some place in the world. For example, many of the details of Black September's planning for the Munich raid were revealed a few months later by a Black September official who was apprehended by Jordanian police while on a spying mission in Amman. After he broke down and spilled the secrets to his interrogators, he was promptly placed before television cameras where he repeated the story to the viewing public.

Most of the trial of the six Israeli agents in Oslo was open to members of the press; therefore even though an official transcript was not made available, a number of industrious newsmen kept accurate notes of the testimony. To the best of my knowledge, the fullest record was kept by the Lillehammer journalist Erik Hagen, and Dag and I approached him for his help. We were impressed by the incredible thoroughness of his reports. Large parts of the book rest upon the testimony given by witnesses and the accused under oath in the Oslo courtroom and recorded faithfully though unofficially by Erik Hagen. Other parts are based on information filed by *Time* Correspondent David Halevy of the Jerusalem Bureau, whose insightful reporting provided the full and first account of the Lillehammer episode.

The second layer of information is largely a follow-up on names and clues disclosed in the public reports. In Norway, Dag Christensen and I tracked down and talked to a large number of the witnesses and best-informed observers of the Lillehammer tragedy. The many quotes and detailed descriptions in Chapters Five through Nine are based almost exclusively upon these interviews. Through my own sources in other countries, I managed to meet a number of "interested parties," who supplied or corroborated important information.

One of these was Kemal Benamane, with whom I spoke for about five hours one afternoon in Geneva. Christensen and I were also helped by several official and non-official experts in antiterrorists operations, who were intrigued by our project and volunteered their advice. Seeking to understand more about the Palestinian motivations, I managed to meet many Arab diplomats, businessmen, and private citizens. Among others, I interviewed the brother of the first victim of the Israeli campaign of assassination. Drawing mainly on interviews with these contacts, I wrote the chapter dealing with the origins and mentality of Black September. I am indebted to the authors of the poems quoted in that chapter and that quoted in Chapter Nine for the right to use their writings, which were published in an anthology, *Enemy of the Sun: Poetry of Palestinian Resistance,* edited by Naseer Aruri and Edmund Ghareet, published by Drum and Spear Press, 1970.

The reader will undoubtedly be aware that the third layer of information for this book derives from material far more confidential than simply off-the-record interviews with sources whose names have already been publicly disclosed in court records and press reports. Some of this material came from Dag Christensen, who developed it through his own sources. Christensen is a reporter for the outstanding Oslo newspaper *Aftenposten* and a journalist of unassailable repute in Norway. His good name opened many doors that otherwise would have remained closed, bolted, and blocked.

Other material came from sources that I have developed over the years through my interest in diplomacy and international politics. Some of this information was, at least at the time, extremely sensitive and I am grateful for the trust my sources put in me. During the course of this reporting, I also had access over extended periods to certain reports and documents that had been kept out of public reach by being classified as secret or top secret. The persons who enabled me to examine those files had no voice at all in the way in which this book was written or the conclusions that I drew. I do wish, however, to express my gratitude to these people for allowing me to have a view beyond the surface events.

There are several other persons whose contribution to this book were absolutely crucial. I regret that I am unable to name them, but I hope in the final product they will see at least a limited justification of their decision to cooperate with me. The book is dedicated to them.

Once these layers of material had been assembled, the great question became how do you use them? As an author, I have fallen back on the experience and judgment gained over more than two decades of reporting and writing major stories for one of the world's most influential magazines. Many of the decisions on how to use the material were easy. For example, the direct quote by an auto driver in Rome, who pulled his car forward at the behest of Mike and Tamar, came directly from the text of his interrogation by Italian police. It was shown to me by a Western security official who was neither Italian nor Norwegian nor French by nationality. The majority of the direct quotes stem from official records and an unofficial court transcript. In both instances, these words were recorded by skilled and experienced investigators who were aware that even the phraseology of their notes might later be challenged in court or by higher authorities. Therefore, even though I cannot cite my specific sources, I am fully confident that the material I have taken from them is accurate and is placed within the proper context. There are a few other points where I was not able to rely on such exact recordings of conversation. Obviously I was not present at the cabinet deliberations in Jerusalem and Tel Aviv. I have relied on word-of-mouth reports by sources who in other instances always proved to be reliable. Furthermore, the quotes attributed to various ministers and intelligence officials accord with the developments that later took place.

A number of persons who read the text of *The Hit Team* prior to publication wondered if Christensen and I had placed ourselves in jeopardy. I hope the reader finds this book educative and entertaining. But I should add that, even though the events recorded in this book

have helped shape right down to the present day the
world in which we live, the war of kill and counterkill
ended shortly after Lillehammer. That is not to say that
the Mossad has given up its aim of killing Ali Hassan
Salameh. As the "Where Are They Now" shows, the
Israelis are still after him. But the organized war of hit
teams versus Black September assassins is past and, at
the date of this writing, mercifully has not resumed.
Hence, this book gives away no secrets that could lead
to another killing or rekindle the campaign of revenge.

To no one do I owe a greater debt of gratitude than
to Catherine Held who typed and retyped the false
starts, new versions, redrafts, inserts and final text that
ultimately produced this book. In addition to her patience, she brought a sense of literary grace that led to
many stylistic improvements that I gladly incorporated
in this text.

D.B.T.

After the Norwegian blunder, the Hit Team was disbanded and, as the preceding pages indicate, its members mostly retired or scattered to new assignments. Israel's political and intelligence leaders obviously would have preferred to forget the entire episode and, of course, they disavowed any complicity in the Lillehammer killing and the subsequent trial of the six apprehended Mossad agents. But, sadly for Israel, though they demobilized their most effective weapon in the clandestine conflict of kill and counterkill, the war of terrorism did not cease. Then on June 27, 1976, the terrorists struck such a cruel and clever blow at Israel that the Hit Team once again was called into being. The event: the skyjacking of Air France flight 139, a widebodied Airbus carrying 256 passengers and a crew of twelve. As the big plane took off from Athens on its regular Tel Aviv-Paris route, four terrorists—a German man and woman and two Palestinians—seized command of the aircraft. They ordered the pilot to set a course for the Libyan city of Benghazi. That was only to be the first stop. While still flying over the Mediterranean, the terrorists handed the Air France pilot a previously prepared flight plan that clearly marked the route to the final destination: Entebbe, the international and military airport on the banks of Lake Victoria serving the Ugandan capital of Kampala.

Thus began the tensest of all skyjackings so far. Much has been written and filmed about the sensational Israeli rescue of the hostages from Entebbe. But many of the authentic details of the operation remain secret. One of the best kept is the role the Hit Team played in preparing the way for Operation Thunderbolt.

The Entebbe skyjacking was no amateur, spur-of-the-moment operation. It was a carefully planned strike in the war of attrition and strangulation that the terrorists are ceaselessly waging against Israel. Entebbe was, in reality, a revenge operation for the earlier failure of a terrorist attempt to shoot down an El Al 707. But the attack squad was apprehended by Kenyan police near a runway approach as they were assembling a Soviet-made SAM-7 shoulder-held missile launcher. The police, who had been acting on an Israeli tip, tossed the terrorists into prison. The Kenyans do not like terrorists operating on their turf.

This failure was a grave blow to the prestige of a man who is one of Israel's most dangerous enemies. He is Wadia el Haddad and, at this writing, he is still alive, well and active, even though the Israelis have put two teams of six or more persons each on his trail. For many years, Haddad was a close friend of George Habash, the chief of the Popular Front for the Liberation of Palestine, which has played a key role in the birth of international terrorism. Like Habash, Haddad is a Christian and a physician who was also trained at the American University in Beirut. For several years, Haddad and Habash worked together in the eye clinic in Amman.

Haddad, in his 40s, is sturdy (about 5' 7"), fair-skinned by Arab standards and, by all accounts, remarkably virile. He is clever and cautious. As he moves continually between Baghdad, South Yemen and Somalia, he is always accompanied by bodyguards, and his residences are heavily protected. Since the late Sixties, he has done the detailed planning that has led to the most sensational hijackings. He orchestrated the simultaneous four-plane skyjacking that terrified the world in September 1970. He likes to use beautiful women as the leaders of his operations, and he freely mixes sex with business. In 1971, when the Israelis first tried to kill him, he was in bed in his Beirut apartment with the beautiful Leila Khaled, who had won fame in the late Sixties by hijacking a TWA jet to Damascus and blowing it up. Later, in June 1973, Haddad used a mistress who traveled under the name Katie George

Thomas to direct the capture of a Japanese Air Lines 747 jumbo out of Amsterdam. As the reader will remember, she was killed on board when she accidentally dislodged in the pin in a grenade that she was carrying in her purse. Of course, it was precisely this skyjacking that jarred Israeli Intelligence and caused a speeding up of the Lillehammer operation, which, in turn, led to the tragic killing of the wrong man. The Hit Team, or at least what was left of it, had a score to settle with Haddad.

After the arrest of the terrorist squad in Nairobi, Haddad dispatched spies to help him select the scene for a reprisal. Reports reached him in Baghdad that security was lax in Athens and that Air France flight 139 would be an easy target. Haddad sent a message through PLO and Arab diplomatic channels to Carlos, the international terrorist leader, then in Algiers, to ship him some operatives. Other messages brought West European and Palestinian terrorists to Baghdad for briefings. Among the visitors was a man from Carlos' ring, left-wing German lawyer and publisher Ernst Wilfried Böse. Another was a German woman: either Gabriele Kröcher-Tiedemann, or Eleanore Honel-Hausman, the widow of a German terrorist whom Haddad had sent to Israel on a suicide mission only a few weeks earlier.

And so the operation began to unfold. Haddad moved his base to Mogadishu, the capital of Somalia, to be closer to Entebbe. He named the operation after the aborted rocket-launch incident at Nairobi airport: "Remember the Kenyan Treachery."

The four skyjackers flew to Athens. Someone slipped them their weapons, four pistols and seven hand grenades that had been stored at the Libyan embassy in Greece. Meanwhile, at Haddad's request, Yasir Arafat had established contact with the mercurial and maniacal ruler of Uganda, "Big Daddy" Idi Amin. Arafat needed a terrorist success to boost the waning spirits of the Palestinians, then taking a terrible beating from the Syrians and Phalangists in the Lebanese civil war.

The Uganda events were an ironic turnabout. For years, Amin had been a great admirer of the Israelis, who had wooed him with technical assistance and military advisors and had even made him the present of an executive jet. But he had broken with the Israelis in 1972, because they refused to give him a squadron of American-made Phantom fighter-bombers, which he wanted for an attack on neighboring Kenya.

Angered, Amin turned to the Arabs for hardware help. The Arab governments, however, were frightened by his unpredictable behavior. Only the Palestinians responded to his overtures. They moved into the political-military vacuum left by the departed Israelis and were soon piloting Amin's Mig fighters; battle-dressed Palestinian gunmen—an odd sight in the heart of black Africa—began serving as his personal body-guards. The PLO established a propaganda center in the Ugandan capital of Kampala. In a radio-telephone conversation, Arafat won Amin's approval to use Entebbe as the destination of the soon-to-be-hijacked Air France Airbus. Five members of the terrorist team gathered with Haddad in the Somalian capital. Among them was the Palestinian Fouad Jabri, an experienced assassin who had been on the Israeli wanted list since 1968; he would serve as Haddad's on-the-scene commander in Entebbe.

Everything went according to plan. As the plane made its approach to the Ugandan airport, the German woman peered from the window. "We're safe now!" she exclaimed happily. "We have reached our base." The plane was directed to its parking place near the old terminal building. As the four hijackers bounced triumphantly down the air steps, they were warmly embraced by the five other terrorists who had traveled by air from Mogadishu to welcome them.

The Israelis desperately needed information about what was happening to the hostages—where they were held, the number and efficiency of the guards, whether the building was actually mined with dynamite, as the terrorists claimed. In several rambling long-distance telephone conversations with former Israeli military advisors to Uganda, Big Daddy inadvertently disclosed a few details about the location of the hostages and size of the guard force. But the Israelis could not put faith in Big Daddy's confused, and perhaps deliberately misleading, observations. They needed exact on-the-spot intelligence. That assignment went to Mike, the director of Israeli clandestine operations, who led the Hit Team. Tamar, his beautiful mistress who had been assigned to another country, was recalled to Israel. Four other Hit Team members were also recruited. The six used their tested old methods that had brought success in every mission, except the last one; they were given fake identities and forged passports that identified them as West European tourists.

Then, within three days after the Airbus had landed at Entebbe, the Hit Team members slipped singly or in pairs into Uganda. Some apparently traveled overland from Kenya; others came in by air, landing at the new Entebbe Terminal a few hundred yards from the old terminal where the hostages were being held.

By Thursday, July 1, the outside world had been led to believe that the area around the hostages was mined with explosives and that the terrorists were serious in their offer to exchange their Jewish prisoners for some 200 Arabs and assorted terrorists held in Israeli prisons. Mike's team learned differently. By means that remain secret, he and other Israeli agents managed to infiltrate the Entebbe airport and gain access to the old terminal. They reported all the essential information that was needed for planning a rescue operation. For example, they found no evidence of explosives; they also observed that the terrorists, overconfident, were sloppy about standing guard. As a rule, only six of the nine terrorists were present. The three others, including Fouad Jabri, were continuously shuttling back and forth between the terminal and the PLO office in Kampala, twenty-one miles away, which they were using as a communications center for conferring with Haddad.

Perhaps most important of all, the Israeli agents in Uganda managed to listen in on the conversations between Jabri and Haddad, who was masterminding the operation from Mogadishu. Exactly how they did this also remains secret. But what the Israelis heard had a crucial and decisive effect on the tense deliberations of the Israeli cabinet back in Tel Aviv. In fact, seldom in history has timely intelligence played a more significant role in a government's decision-making. Some ministers were in favor of breaking with the nation's traditional no-swap policy and agreeing to an exchange of prisoners, to be conducted by the Red Cross at Entebbe. But when Mike and his team eavesdropped as Haddad gave Jabri final instructions for the exchange, they overheard a death sentence for the Jewish hostages. According to the Israelis, Haddad said, "Do not allow one Jew to escape alive. As soon as our people are safe, fire on the Jewish hostages, even if it means hitting Red Cross workers."

Haddad's conversation was flashed via Nairobi to Israel, where the cabinet now realized that the offer of a prisoner exchange was only a trap. Shimon Peres, the defense minister, made a short speech that conjured up memories of Auschwitz, where the infamous Nazi doctor Josef Mengele stood between the lines of arriving Jews and by a flick of his hand sent some to immediate death in the gas chambers and others to work in the camp. "The State of Israel was not created to allow another Dr. Mengele to decide over life and death for Jews," declared Peres. "The State of Israel was created to save Jewish lives." Peres' emotional appeal, combined with the chilling information from Uganda, forced the cabinet to decide in favor of a military solution. For all practical purposes, Operation Thunderbolt was now underway.

The military was ready. Earlier in the week, Israeli commandos and pilots had already begun practicing for a possible military soluton to the Entebbe impasse. A replica of the old Entebbe terminal was easily constructed at a military base somewhere in Israel. The combat team of 100 or so elite troopers under the command of Lieutenant Colonel Yehonathan Netanyahu began practicing assaults. Meanwhile, Israeli air-force pilots aided by technicians began experimenting with night-sight devices similar to those used on tanks that would enable the pilots to see well enough to land safely the huge four-engine C-130 transports at night on an unlit airstrip.

On July 3, at an air base in the Sinai, the Israelis assembled a small airborne armada: the three C-130s, a

Boeing 707 that would serve as an airborne communications command post, and a number of Phantom fighter-bombers that would fly protective cover. To avoid Arab radar, the C-130s skimmed only fifty feet above the Red Sea, then turned inland over southern Sudan. Flying virtually at treetop level, the big planes— "hippos" in Israeli air-force slang—slipped in under the Ugandan radar. Just before the planes landed, the pilots opened the rear cargo ramps; as soon as the planes' wheels touched down, the vehicles inside began to roar out. There were several U.S.-made Armored Personnel Carriers bearing dozens of commandos.

Also on board were a black Mercedes and a couple of Land-Rovers. The Israelis had prepared a clever ruse. The black Mercedes was similar to the one used by Amin, who paid frequent visits to the hostages. The Land-Rovers were similar to the ones used by his Palestinian bodyguards, who accompanied him everywhere (he no longer trusted his own troops). Contrary to some reports, there was no Israeli made up in blackface to pose as Amin. Instead, there was only a burly Israeli commando dressed in a Ugandan camouflage uniform in the back seat of the Mercedes.

As the small caravan approached, the Ugandan sentries guarding the terminal snapped to attention and saluted. It won the Israelis three seconds—a vital margin. The "bodyguards" leaped from the Land-Rovers and stormed into the terminal where the hostages where being held. They were followed by more troopers from the Armored Personnel Carriers. Between firing bursts from their submachine guns, the commandos yelled in Hebrew, "Get down, get down! We're Israelis and we've come to take you home!"

Moments before the attack of the Israeli commandos, the Hit Team had stepped silently from the shadows where they had been hidden in and around the old terminal. Firing their soft-spoken Berettas, they cut down several of the terrorists, thus opening the way for the charging commandos. Because of the confusion of the firefight, no one can say for certain how many terrorists died from Hit Team slugs and how many from commando bullets, but the toll was clear: seven were killed, including the two Germans and Jabri. (In addition, three hostages died as a result of the operation. The Israelis lost only one commando, Colonel Netanyahu, the mission leader. An estimated twenty to thirty Ugandan troops perished under Israeli fire.)

Before they could be caught in the fire of their countrymen, the Hit Team members quietly slipped from the old terminal and disappeared into the night. They did not attempt to join up with the Israeli airborne forces and thus secure a speedy and safe escape. Relying on their fake passports and incredibly steady nerves, they remained behind in Uganda. They had operated in such an unseen manner that the hostages and commandos were not even aware of their existence. However, Ugandan security forces, who suspected that Israeli secret agents might have been active at Entebbe, arrested one West European businessman and held him for two weeks.

Meanwhile, Mike, Tamar and the others uneventfully left Uganda and, by circuitous routes, made their way to Israel. Because they had succeeded so completely in their mission, they received no publicity. In the lonely trade of intelligence, only failures, such as the Lillehammer tragedy, become public knowledge. Success remains unheralded, unsung. But a few insiders knew about their achievements, and to balance the record, told this story.